The Shadow of the Palms

Books by Janice Law

The Shadow of the Palms

Janice Law

HOUGHTON MIFFLIN COMPANY BOSTON

1980

Library of Congress Cataloging in Publication Data
Law, Janice.
The shadow of the palms.
I. Title.
PZ4.L415Sh 1980 [PS3562.A86] 813'.5'4 79–17096
ISBN 0–395–28591–7

Printed in the United States of America
S 10 9 8 7 6 5 4 3 2 1

For *Mary Galloway Hall*

The Shadow of the Palms

Chapter 1

I WAS DRYING my hands in the washroom when a jingle of bracelets, earrings, necklaces, and amulets announced the arrival of our urban Bedouin. Baby was in her customary working gear, a neon purple blouse cut like a poncho, a long, sloppy skirt, and a pair of high-laced sandals. Her hay-colored hair rose like the fur on an angry cat, and when she saw me she switched her gum from one side of her mouth to the other, held up the electric coil, and asked, "Wanna cup of coffee?"

"If you're making it."

She snapped the gum in reply and filled the pot. "Baby" was a misnomer for June Quigley, a tough little kid with a blue vocabulary, too many memories, and a thick skin. Jan kept her away from the gallery's more pretentious customers, because both her syntax and her manners were uncertain, but she was popular enough with the artists to rate as one of the attractions of Helios Workshop — a fact neither Jan nor my friend Harry cared to acknowledge. Besides, she was a demon at the typewriter, her spelling was kosher, and nobody better was available for the salary. I had gotten used to her brassy personality and her uncomplicated pleasures. From my point of view, the only drawback to her presence at Helios was her personal philosophy: Baby was a woman who had accepted liberation without solidarity. In other words, she made too obvious a play for Harry, and, having lived very comfortably with him for the last few years, I didn't encourage her to stick around after hours. If she had to drape herself over someone's lithographic stones and inhale art and culture, let her select one of the transients.

Recently, however, Baby seemed to have changed her tactics. Now she lingered in my office to ask if I'd had any interesting cases. Sooner or later, I suspected, she would ask me for a job. I might hire her. If business stayed as profitable as it had been, I would need another assistant, and Baby might just do. She really would be a lot better working for an investigation service than vamping visiting artists and scandalizing Jan Gorgon's art-hungry customers. Much better.

I got my mug, Baby doled out the instant and poured the hot water. Then she sat cross-legged on the top of her desk and puffed up a great cloud of cigarette smoke. That habit would have to go if she worked for me. Baby and I were already colleagues of a sort, because I rented office space from Helios Workshop. When Harry and Jan had renovated the old factory for their graphics workshop and gallery, they had included a suite of offices, as well as a number of artists' studios and apartments on the upper floors. My business was the only non-art concern in the outfit, and, needing little more than desk and file space, it was squeezed next to the skimpy cubicle where Baby typed up letters and prospectuses, descriptions of new graphic series, bills to Jan's stable of VIP customers, and orders for supplies. In between times, she hung around the workshop or attempted to fathom the operations of Executive Security, Inc., by keeping a wary eye on the comings and goings of my office.

"I forgot to tell you," Baby said after a moment. "You had a call a little while ago. Long distance."

"Did you take the name?"

"It's here somewhere."

"How about getting it for me?"

She stretched her supple back to rummage through the papers. "Here you go. An old guy. He said it was personal. I told him you were out on a case."

"Yes. Thanks." The name on the memo brought a twinge of mingled pleasure and apprehension. "Did he say what he wanted?"

"Nope. Just that it was a 'personal matter' and would you call him back."

I nodded and turned to go.

"Don't you want your coffee?"

"Later, maybe." I went into my office, carefully shut the door, and dialed long distance.

Harry was repairing a broken silk screen frame in the workshop, and as I described the conversation I watched him fit a new piece of wood, his large, sensitive hands moving quickly and neatly. When he was ready to fasten the clamps, he motioned for me to hold the glue-smeared corners together. "What do you think?" I asked.

He fastened the screws carefully. "You said you'd go, didn't you?"

"I'm going to have to, of course. I owe him a lot, you know."

Harry held up the frame and squinted to check that it was true. "It'll do you good to get away. You've been busy. You said yourself you'd had enough paperwork for a while."

"What puzzles me is that he didn't want me to come right away. He has some golf date!"

"So much the better. It can't be very important. You know how older people are. Take a trip and relax for a few days."

I shrugged. Probably Harry was right. Brammin, my former employer, friend, and benefactor, was now both rich and elderly. Like most important executives, he was used to being coddled, and although eminently decent and sensible, his ego might not be immune to the joys of personal service. There is a certain pleasure in being able to dismiss a problem with the phrase, "I know someone who'll take care of this for me" — "this" being anything from a million-dollar suit to a lost dog. Was that the case? "No, no, Tuesday's no good," he'd said on the telephone. "Big golf date that day. Wednesday. Do you have friends you could stay with? Come down for a few days. Enjoy the beach. It'll be worth your while — "

"There's a friend of ours in Sarasota — "

"Ideal. Of course, all your time is professional. Put it on my bill. No, I insist. Explain everything when you arrive. Shall we say Wednesday at one? There's a restaurant called The Lagoon. I'll meet you there. Just take a table for one. I'll find you. I appreciate this, Anna."

I fiddled with one of the heavy levers on Harry's hand press. "I thought I might stop in to see Hillary and Theresa in Sarasota. I'd like to meet her."

"Good idea. He would like that, and she's probably worth meeting if she's straightened him out." Harry smiled; he liked John Hillary a lot, which was interesting for a number of reasons. "Don't forget to tell him how much we enjoyed that TV program of his. That was quite a project." Harry shook his head. "Usually it's the other way around. A guy does wild things when he's drinking and turns cautious when he's sober. John's really become an adventurer since Terry got him off the sauce."

Harry's partner appeared in the doorway, curious as usual. "Anyone I know?" he asked.

"John Hillary, the reporter. I don't think you ever met him. He moved south before we started this outfit."

"Years before. Did you see the documentary he did?" I asked. "The one on the trade in Guatemalan antiquities?"

"A couple of months ago? Yes. Very good."

"Pretty traumatic for him," Harry remarked. "The guards being murdered while they were down there filming."

"Increased his audience, though." Jan Gorgon's basic cynicism had not been eliminated by the luxury of his current success. A wartime childhood had left him with a certain emotional coldness.

"No, I'm serious," Harry protested. "He was upset. He'd met their families. It was a bad scene."

"They're new to it, of course," the art dealer said, running one well-manicured hand over his handsome Slavic face. "Now in Italy, parts of Turkey, Egypt, looting's a family business. They've been robbing tombs for generations."

"What a snob you are," I said. "Only deal with the old families of art crime."

"Listen, Anna, I wouldn't touch that Latin American stuff. There's too much going on down there. Too many crazy people. Mayan art gets some people the way Greek art took the Victorians. They'll do anything — go down with a big saw, hack off the front of a lintel or a stela and ship it home."

"Why's that?"

He shrugged. "Adventure. You're down there in the jungle. Wild man stuff. And then, really first rate art is just sitting out collecting forest growth, anyway. Most of the good European and Middle Eastern pieces have already been stolen. But it's cowboys and Indians down there." He made an expressive face. "Not my style."

"I'll convey your compliments anyway. Maybe I can persuade Hillary to write something on your 'Captive Nations' graphics."

Jan made a rude gesture and took his silk shirt, French pants, Italian shoes, and his general gorgeousness out of the workshop.

"You really think that's a good idea, then?"

"Why not? He'd love to see you."

"I was thinking more about her. A bit much, maybe, showing up so soon?" Translation: Do you think she knows John and I once lived together?

"You'll soon find out," Harry said cheerfully. Translation: Serves you right for spending an irregular youth. "Of course if you want to put her mind at rest, I could be persuaded to visit the J.P.'s."

"I've my heart set on orange blossoms. Besides, your mom's just about reconciled to the present arrangement."

"In that case," Harry said, "you'll have to take your chances."

"All right. I'll call them."

"And here. I'll give you one of our new prints as a peace offering."

"Ideal. One of yours, please. Maybe Hillary will trade us for some hot antiquities."

"He'd better not. This is to show his wife your time is fully occupied," Harry said, and, with a proprietary grin, he began to wrap a handsome woodcut in tissue paper.

The plane swept over the opalescent evening sea in a graceful silver curve, then dropped like a rock. The white condominiums and marinas and the green and buff keys of outer Sarasota disappeared with a stomach-settling lurch, and we rushed over scrubby pines and palmettos and across a wide sweep of yellowish Florida grass. Outside, the bright evening was hot but less humid than D.C., with a fresh, persistent breeze off the Gulf. I rented a puce-colored Ford with a balky transmission and a stifling interior and, consulting my directions, bore right at the greyhound track and began a lengthy meander through some of the less prestigious neighborhoods in search of Hillary's "quaint tropical bungalow." Finally, soliciting the aid of a laconic young sentry on a banana bike, I found a narrow dead-end street darkened by undisciplined masses of mango, pine, and live oak. Black and white children flashed in and out of the shadows like zebra schools of fish, while, in the leafy mystery of back yards, hounds barked and someone relentlessly pursued the rewards of a perfectly tuned motorcycle. The Hillarys' house was situated halfway down the road. It was old enough to have been wood-built, but the yard was neat and some tubs of brilliant flowers thrived in front. I pulled into the drive and parked behind a shiny orange Toyota and Hillary's much faded MG.

" . . . don't take better care of yourself," a woman's voice said from the house.

I recognized John's reassuring mumble.

"Not the first time, is it?" A strong, low voice, touched with anger.

"It'll be all right."

"You call the police or I'll talk to my cousin."

"I'll be seeing Sergeant Perez — "

The response came in Italian, loud and eloquent, then "And I had to marry an Englishman! As if there weren't nice Italian boys with good sense my momma had in mind. I'm going to ask Luccio. He'll know what you should do."

"Love, I'll take care of it."

"You have no sense. None. I didn't like that assignment in the first place."

I opened the car door and closed it with a good loud slam.

"It'll be all right," John said.

A few more phrases in Italian followed, but unintelligible, as if the speaker had moved farther back into the house. I looked for a doorbell, found none, and tapped on the screen.

"Hello? Hello! It's Anna at last! Come in. Good to see you, old girl."

John swung open the screen, tall and thin as ever, but properly brushed, washed, and fed like a man well looked after. Hillary's formerly sallow complexion, a product of long days in air-conditioned Washington suites and longer nights in air-conditioned bars, had been burned a healthy brick red. There were other, more subtle changes: he was immaculately and, indeed, quite expensively dressed in a white shirt and twill khaki pants. His voice had been anglicized, too. The faint drawl that alcohol and the South had attempted to insinuate was gone. He now spoke as precisely as a BBC announcer broadcasting a coronation, and he had acquired, or reacquired, a certain prim formality of manner. It was as if having gone native so far as to marry an American and buy a bungalow, he'd felt the need to reassert his original identity. When he wore the white pith helmet that hung by the door, he must have resembled a pukka colonial administrator or explorer, and I wondered what the neighborhood made of such an archaic apparition.

"Hi. I'm sorry if I'm late. I had a little trouble finding the house."

"Don't worry. It's hard to find," his wife said, stepping through the archway at the back of the living room, a kitchen towel over one arm.

"Dear, this is Anna. Anna, Theresa."

We shook hands. She was a bit shorter than I, but plumper and more impressively put together. Her thick, dark hair was straight and well cut, and she had fine eyes and a rather large, stubborn jaw. Preliminary reports had suggested a volcanic temperament, but her smile was warm and unaffected. Theresa Hillary looked me up and down and decided to like what she saw: I was in rumpled slacks, bearing the marks of the indignities of Atlanta airport and of tricky connections on top of a hard day's work. She had on a snappy black dress and looked like a lady who'd gotten home from the office in time to put her feet up and her makeup on, and, if the good smell from the kitchen were any indication, a casserole in. Theresa was a CPA and clearly one of those brisk, efficient people for whom domesticity poses no pitfalls.

"We're a little late with a wedding present," I said, offering the print, "but Harry's work gets better all the time. I think this is a vintage one."

"That's very good of him. Come on, Terry's had dinner on hold. We were afraid you'd have problems with the directions."

"Quite a maze back here, but it's surprisingly convenient once you know your way around."

"Such beautiful trees," I said. "You forget how lush everything grows."

"Damn jungle," Hillary remarked, "but if you have to live in a jungle, I like the real thing. It was this or a trailer park. Terry hadn't passed her exams yet when we were house-hunting, and free-lance writers — "

"Have you left Reuters for good then?"

"Pretty much. There were a lot of free-lance opportunities in Miami."

"None of them good," Theresa said very firmly, and I had the feeling that her remark was connected with the discussion I'd overheard.

"What Terry means is that my tastes ran to unsavory topics which attracted a devoted, but unstable, readership." He gave a sly and oddly satisfied smile. "I became unpopular in certain quarters."

"You got reprinted in the *Congressional Record,* though."

"Did you see that?"

"Yes. Jan Gorgon did, actually. Harry's business partner," I explained to Theresa. "He sells art to half the Congress so he never misses a thing. Crusading young representatives like to be noticed as much as anyone."

"And they have offices to show off, and Georgetown homes to decorate just like the older fat cats."

"Sure, and Jan offers graphics for every taste, price, and ideology. He does pretty well, and he's even making some money for Harry — which isn't easy. Harry's not very worldly."

Theresa made a face. "What man with talent is? Right?" She looked at me for confirmation.

"Most of the time."

"Female chauvinists!"

"All right, then: people of talent, artists and idealistic investigative reporters like you."

"What a disgusting designation. No doubt a reaction to years in Washington. But what about collectors?" Hillary asked after just enough of a pause to make me think he was really interested.

"What about them?"

"Are they worldly, do you think?"

"Jan's customers certainly are. At least, he has no hesitation about his prices."

"I was thinking more about obsessions. About the collectors who will do almost anything to add to their treasures."

"The history of Italy," Theresa suggested.

"Certainly, my dear, and Greece even more so. The great collectors were often extremely impractical in their desires however worldly their methods."

"I suppose you saw that in Guatemala."

"Oh yes, although the actual looters are just poor devils trying to live. The collectors — well, you have the speculators, of course."

"That's what I see around Jan's gallery. Most are people looking for a hedge against inflation."

"I have more sympathy for the others," Hillary remarked. "What's fascinating about the Mayas is that they fell so suddenly. Like Atlantis. Eighth century, they had fabulous cities, magnificent art, a large population. One hundred years later, all gone. There's a romance surrounding their work, and I'm not surprised it attracts people of a certain temperament."

"Some of that came through in your program," I said. "By the way, all my artist friends send congratulations. They were impressed."

John nodded as though the program had inspired mixed feelings, but Theresa beamed. She was proud of him and proud of steering him away from such dangerous topics as Miami racketeering to the safe and respected ground of art and artists. "It's given him quite a reputation," she said, "but he needn't go off to the jungle again, fortunately. Tell Anna about the new Sebastian Museum — her friend would be interested."

"The county's being gifted with another big museum."

"Like the Ringling?"

"Similar scale, but the collection is principally nineteenth and twentieth century. One of the big wheeler-dealers is making a stab for high society."

"Watch you don't write it up that way," his wife scolded. "It's a fabulous collection. John and I were invited to one of the parties at Sebastian's home. He even has antique cars. Really remarkable."

"Yes," Hillary said drily. "In many ways."

"And it will make an excellent story. The building design is very innovative — or so I'm told — I don't know the first thing about architecture."

"You're quite right, my dear. Terry has ambitions for me to become an art and society writer," he explained.

"A lot safer than what you'd been doing," she said quickly. "John got himself into a lot of danger in Miami. Those articles the congressmen admired so much just about got him killed. You don't write about Miami racketeering, and you don't get involved with the Cuban factions. I've lived in the area all my life, but try to tell him — "

"Was that why you left Miami?"

"Do you know what happened?" Theresa began, but John cut her off. "Anna isn't interested in ancient history. Terry doesn't always understand how journalism works. You're not doing any good unless you're stepping on somebody's toes."

"Anna would be very interested. You do something in investigative work, right?"

"At rather a low level — employee thefts, that sort of thing."

"John was threatened several times." She looked paler as she spoke. "It was a very scary business, and lately — "

"Lately, I've turned to art and culture. Nothing like a trip to Guatemala to distract attention from misdeeds at home." He gave the bright, sardonic smile I remembered, and launched into a lively account of the negotiations for the new museum and the hoopla planned for its opening. Hillary could be very amusing and he made us both laugh, but I was more interested in watching the two of them and in matching this new Hillary, sober, married, professionally celebrated, with the one I'd known half a dozen years before, a clever writer, but a bitter and demoralized man. I hadn't been good for him; his wife was. Why? She had a loud laugh and a loud voice, and she was a manager. I decided she was the one who organized and indeed dominated their life. She'd planned the move to Sarasota, bought the house, steered Hillary into this new, and apparently quite successful, free-lance work. Aside from his writing, she had managed to revamp his life, creating a respectable property owner out of a writer with a drinking problem. I sensed that Hillary was the idol of her life, but, like all idols, he was expected to toe the line, and, being a forceful personality, Theresa probably had no qualms about alternately bullying and cajoling him. She had him, it seemed, almost thoroughly domesticated, and he was thriving on it, not least in his work, which I suddenly realized must be his last area of independence.

We were drinking our coffee after dinner, when someone knocked on the door. Terry froze, still holding her cup to her lips, her eyes seeking her husband's. It was dark out and late, but not too late for a neighbor to stop by, and I was surprised by her alarm. Another knock. She jumped up to answer it, but John prevented her. "I'll go. That'll be Max with the cricket scores."

She nodded, but listened intently as his footsteps faded on the living room rug then sounded again on the bare hall floor. A low Caribbean voice spoke, and John greeted his friend. The two men stood talking on the porch, and we heard exclamations of distress over the MCC's latest fortunes.

"Max is Jamaican," Terry said. "He's just bought a shortwave radio. When the West Indies is ahead, he always stops by. When England's leading, John has to call." She smiled indulgently and sipped her coffee, tension vanishing like air from an old balloon.

"Has some of that Miami trouble followed him?" I asked.

"There've been some funny things," she began, then abruptly she changed her mind. I was a stranger, after all, and perhaps she knew, or guessed, that I had once been close to her husband. Or else she'd simply decided to defer to his wishes about discretion. "This neighborhood is changing," she said quickly. "There are some rough kids running around here at night. We're going to move fairly soon. John likes it here, oddly enough, but it would be easier for us both closer to the center of town. Would you like more coffee?" Her smile was artificial, not nearly so nice as her earlier greeting; Theresa Hillary was a determined woman and nobody's fool.

"No, thank you. It's getting late. I really should check into the motel. They're not always reliable when you come in late."

The deficiencies of motel keepers was a subject we both

agreed upon, and she didn't press me to stay. When Hillary returned, disconsolate over a second-day England batting collapse, I said good-by, tentatively inviting them to dinner sometime before I went home. "I'm sure this business is strictly routine," I remarked. "A day or two at the most."

"That'll be fine," Hillary said. "I'll have wrapped up some new articles by then."

"And we'll take you by the museum," Theresa offered. "It's really going to be one of Sarasota's landmarks."

The next morning, I drove the twenty miles of palms, traffic, fast food, and wayside furniture shops to Ibis, where Brammin had recently bought a new house. This was a smallish town, set between the intercoastal waterway and the Gulf. Low, white stucco buildings were dwarfed by rows of royal palms along the main street, and a wide, handsome boulevard led to the water. Toward Sarasota and the bay, condominiums made a canyon of the beach, but to the south, there were only houses and palmetto scrub, accented with the white flowers and dark green spikes of Spanish bayonet. I was curious enough about the town to make a circuit from the fishing pier as far as the highway's crowded business district. Then I parked at the public beach, put on my swimsuit, and sampled that promised relaxation.

It was a perfect day: the sky was a high, cloudless, saturated blue, and the Gulf spread alternating bands of green and azure like the lazily opening tendrils of a sea anemone. Only at the water line were the glassy tones broken by little transparent curls as stylized and clearly defined as waves in a Japanese print. Riding the thermals, pelicans glided off the tops of the condominiums, and egrets flapped across the sea, so white they seemed made of light. Up and down the shallows, bathers searched the water for sharks' teeth, and leather-skinned ancients crept along with their eyes on the sand or panned the crushed shells and stones at the tide line for fossils. Beyond the trucked-in white sand of the public beach, the natural shore was dark gray, the sand blackened by tiny fragments ground up from the great hecatombs of fish and beasts lying offshore.

Looking for their intact teeth was a pleasant pastime, and so was sitting on the sand watching the shore birds and the steady, hypnotic, rhythmic shifting of the water.

I took a swim, then walked far down the beach, which seemed to have suffered considerably from the winter storms. The washed-out dunes rose eight feet straight off the sand, and were anchored by a crown of tough, semitropical scrub. Fifty or sixty feet inland was the first band of low Florida houses with bright gravel roofs and glittering glass porches. Tall, bushy-topped pines provided the only height; everything else clustered near the ground, hot and lush under a sunlight so dazzling it even bleached their tropical colors.

I found the monotony of the sand and water soothing after a year spent establishing my investigation service. Executive Security specializes in cases of white collar crime that companies wish handled without publicity, and most of the time the work involves a maximum of paperwork and a minimum of excitement — or even imagination. I was tired of examining computer printouts and official forms, and the brilliant sea and the high, intense sky acted like an eraser, fading the memory of figures and faces and of dull hours working under the fluorescent lights in my office. The sound of the wind, the soft hiss of the surf disturbing the stones and sand, the high, frightened whistles of the sandpipers — otherwise silence. It was a place where one could spend a lot of time doing nothing, and, returning to the car, I was surprised to find that it was already afternoon. I changed hastily for the drive uptown to The Lagoon, which, despite connotations of tropical romance, was a family restaurant smack at the far end of the busy bay connecting the inland waterway with the Gulf. At ten to one, it was crowded with the vivid pastel hues worn by patrons of varying degrees of decrepitude, amongst whom I felt shockingly youthful. The hostess led me to a table by one of the large windows, where I drank a cocktail, watched the pleasure boats and water skiers, and absorbed a semilethal dose of Florida sunshine until Henry Brammin appeared in the back.

He was by this time in his early seventies and seemed smaller than I had remembered. His skin was burned to a light mahogany, except for his rather large nose, which was plain red, and he had conceded enough to Florida taste to outfit himself in a light blue blazer and blue and white plaid slacks. He stood with one leg a shade forward, as if for balance, and, finishing his consultation with the hostess, drew himself up stiff and proper, surveyed the room, and came briskly over to my table.

"Anna! What a surprise. What brings you here?"

"I'm visiting friends in Sarasota."

"Sit down, sit down. Can I join you?"

"Please."

"Isn't this a coincidence," he said to the hostess, a large, weary-looking woman with black hair and a lopsided purple mouth, who seemed used to cosseting her regular customers. "Just set another place for me here, Cheryl. This will be fine. It's been how long? Five, six years?"

"About that."

"We won't count them. Not at my age. Cheryl and I have stopped counting, haven't we?" he asked with a nod to his friend.

"Honey, you're so right." She pulled out his chair and settled him with a menu. "The usual for you, Mr. Brammin?"

"The usual, if you please. Have you ordered, Anna?"

"Not yet."

He proceeded to fuss with the menu, insisting I try the specialty of the house and put everything on his bill. When the orders had been taken and the waitress was gone, he ran his sharp eyes around the room and asked, "Did you have a good trip down?"

"Yes. Tried out the beach, too."

"Good. I had reasons for not inviting you directly to the house. I hope you don't mind."

"Not at all. Nor meeting here, either."

"This is a touch of intrigue for your professional benefit," he teased. "Also, their red snapper is excellent." He smiled, pleased with this mild joke, but the charming dither he had displayed for the hostess was the plainest affectation. I was relieved to see that he was as quick and logical as ever, and a little ashamed of myself too, because the peculiarity of his summons had made me think my old mentor had begun to fail. "How have things been going with you?" he asked.

I described Executive Security, and Harry's venture with Jan. Brammin was full of questions about the use of graphics as tax shelters, a new scheme he had recently encountered.

"That's Jan's department. Jan Gorgon. He's the art dealer who handles all the business arrangements. I've tried to stay completely out of that end of it."

"Wise girl. In marriage — or whatever — minding one's own business is very important. The tricky thing is knowing when to break that rule."

I nodded and studied him, sensing it was time to talk business.

He folded his napkin and straightened the crease with his thumbnail. "I'm about to break that rule," he said. "Here's the problem: my nephew has too much money."

Chapter 2

"I MADE about all the mistakes a man can make with his relatives," Brammin said. "My son, fortunately, was one of the exceptions. Dan's a good boy and he's done well. But I made up for it with the others."

I watched his deep blue patent leather shoes cross the dock. The water sparkled between the weathered boards, reflecting the all-pervading sun. The tops of my shoulders were beginning to feel sore.

"My brother," he continued, "had no talent for business. No sin in that. I did; he didn't. He had a lot of charm. He had the looks in our family. Wouldn't think there was too much by me, would you? And a very fine musician. He played the saxophone in a band for a while. Bill Something's Mellow Boys — they were good, but Martin was always trying to make money off some deal or other. He hadn't any more business sense than a sea gull. I finally set him up in a car dealership. I was doing all right by then, because I'd bought stock in New World Oil. It seemed the correct thing to do. Wasn't." He shook his head. "The only thing worse than doing much better than your kin-folks is helping them when they need it. I never helped him enough: there was no end to what he wanted and, on the other hand, it worried him to be in debt to me. He worried himself into a heart attack at age fifty. Then another one." Brammin lit his pipe and contemplated the shiny powerboats and the slim-waisted sailboats. "I made a lot of mistakes with Martin," he said.

"Some of them were probably inevitable."

"Yes, but someone has to be responsible."

The water lapped softly against the pilings.

"Martin left a small estate. Enough to pay the creditors. I put some money in trust for his wife and for my nephew's education. Perhaps a mistake there. It gave Rod a false sense of affluence. I had kind of a weakness for him, though. Reminded me of his dad. Good-looking boy, charming, and — " Brammin sighed, unable to put a name to his nephew's attractions. "Rod's clever, although he hasn't done much with his brains. He's one of the breed who'd rather study than work, and rather loaf than study. Oddly enough," he added, compressing his lips, "he has the one quality his dad lacked: he can turn anything to a dollar."

"Perhaps he's come by his sudden wealth honestly."

"I think that's unlikely. Although he's had one windfall. Ironic. He found some of his dad's old music — tunes, songs Martin had written, and sold them to a producer for background music for a movie about the forties. Martin should have stayed with the saxophone."

"What did he do with the money?"

"That's what I brought you here for. Look right over there." Brammin pointed to a large sailboat with a brilliant varnished deck and the ripple of the waves reflected on its silky white sides.

"Impressive."

"It is. That's a fifty-five-foot ketch with an auxiliary motor. You could go around the world in her."

"Beautiful boat."

"And expensive. Not just expensive to buy. Expensive to own. You're looking at marina and maintenance bills as long as your arm. A young man in my nephew's position can't afford her. I warned him him when he first came down. He was living on board then, and I occasionally stopped by to see him. I was a bit worried about Rod, because his marriage had just broken up. Carol was a sweet little girl, too. I don't know what happened, but I didn't think this was the right place for a young man." He looked at me, appraising my reaction. "I'll bet you think I have little to do if I'm so busy meddling in other people's business. Well, as a matter of fact, I didn't say anything to him, but a young man should be doing something constructive. Loafing around in the sun is demoralizing. There's something in the old idea that the tropics are unhealthy, but," he added drily, "it's easy to sound like a crank when you concern yourself with other people's affairs. To make a long story short, I expected him to sell the boat within a month or so. He'd had a nice cruise down here; he could have sold her and turned a profit. No. He's kept the boat and moved her to the fanciest marina in the country. He's opened a shop, rented a nice apartment, and, despite this cash outlay, he's been off cruising every other month or so. That means a crew and someone to take over the shop." Brammin gazed thoughtfully at the white ship resting on the water.

"Where does he go?"

"That's the sixty-four-dollar question. Rod doesn't confide in me, but she's a seagoing yacht."

"And these are long trips?"

"Yes. I've checked with the marina. He would have been able to make the crossing to Yucatán or down to Central America or to the Caribbean."

Brammin's concern was suddenly easy to understand. The coast of Florida, especially south Florida, is a smuggler's paradise, and the coke and marijuana trade is the state's largest growth industry. Profits are enormous, while the risks of arrest are minimal, but there are stolen boats and, once in a while, dead smugglers and murdered yachtsmen.

"Let's be clear about this," I said. "You're afraid your nephew is running pot or some other drug?"

"I have no proof, but I'm sure worried."

"Why not a powerboat, then? I thought all that was done from fast craft."

"It usually comes ashore that way, but remember there are

advantages to sail over a long trip. No refueling, for one thing. You can always be met for the run onto the beach. And then Rod is hardly a professional criminal — just a sailor tempted to make his hobby pay."

"Drugs aren't a beginner's pastime."

"That's why I asked you to come down. I had hired a detective; I've got his report here for you, but I didn't have much confidence in the man. He didn't seem to have the right finesse, and he would have stuck out like a sore thumb at some of the social gatherings Rod's begun to frequent. I called him off." He looked down at the dock for a few seconds before adding, "Frankly, it was too painful to discuss family business with a stranger. That was the real reason."

"I understand, but no one can guarantee there won't be unpleasantness from any investigation. They have a way of getting out of hand, and you don't dabble in the underworld very long before the undesirables show up. You must be prepared for that. If your nephew is involved in the drug traffic, his associates won't be the sort you'd like to meet."

Brammin watched the white sides of the *Melody* for a moment, then came to a decision. "I'll put it entirely in your hands, Anna. The only thing I'm going to ask is that you conceal the fact I hired you — at all cost. I don't want your presence here connected with me. That's very important."

"How shall I get in touch with you?"

He thought this over. "I'd like you to stay in Ibis, not in the city. There's a set of apartments — efficiency apartments — just a few blocks from the center of town. They're not the most modern, but they are comfortable enough and near the beach. You might as well enjoy your stay. I can call you there. Otherwise, leave a message at the golf club for me. I play almost every day. That will be the best plan."

"All right. However you want to do it, but I'll need Rod's address and the address of his shop. I'd like to have a look around."

"Surely. And this," he said, taking out a small Manila folder.

"You may read this, although there's nothing conclusive. The man thought I was checking a potential heir," he added with an attempt at humor, but I could see that this was no joking matter for Henry Brammin.

The nephew's shop was on St. Armand's Key on a fancy street off the boulevard that runs white and straight over the blue water of the bay and across the lush green keys where sleek cabin cruisers float before each dazzling house. My rented car wasn't fit for the neighborhood; the heat made it cough, and when we stopped half a block shy of a plate glass window bearing "Key Antiques" in an elegant script, it choked and rumbled and fouled the clear air with a belch of dark exhaust. I went for a stroll, noticed the antique shop was closed that day "except by appointment," and noticed, too, that the window display was meticulously arranged about a fine Chinese bowl and several elegant Sèvres cups. No dust, no clutter, no mystery — just money. Next door was a clothing store where I inspected a selection of patio dresses, although it's been a long time since I've felt disposed to put on something with a low neck, a print skirt, and ruffles to bask in the sun.

"That arrived this week," the saleswoman remarked. She'd utilized all the help Helena and Elizabeth can give without concealing a sharp, ferrety appearance that seemed promising for my purposes.

"We have some nice long skirts in, too," she continued, "and summer-weight slacks, of course," with a glance at mine that suggested the light poplin had picked up a smudge in the course of my visit to the dock.

"I really stopped to ask what time the antique store next door opens."

"Well, I can't be sure," she replied in a rather overrefined voice. "They don't keep the most regular hours."

"Perhaps I'd better call before I come out again."

"I would, although if he's going to be in at all, he'll appear around one."

"Bankers' hours."

"Golfers' hours, although he works quite a lot at night. I notice the lights on when I leave. He must do some of his own refinishing. We're not zoned for that here, but so far we haven't been bothered by fumes. If we are, there'll be changes made. I can't have a shop smelling like varnish and paint thinner. Not with our clientele. Oh, I'll be right with you," she trilled to a fortyish woman with teased straw hair, a skin like brown calf, and a bright pink mouth. The new arrival wore an expensive yellow linen suit and carried a small, panting terrier.

"I won't take any more of your time," I said, but I was already forgotten. The lady in yellow had an account large enough to send the saleswoman into ecstasies over the little dog, which vented its heat and ingratitude in snappish barks. I left the silk knits and designer labels to resume my stroll. At the cross street, the block was pierced by an alleyway wide enough for the storekeepers' cars and a couple of dumpsters. The deep shade of the buildings offered escape from the brilliant glare, and with relief I started down the passage. Brammin's shop was the fifth from the corner, with his name in brass script on a bright blue door, but I was more interested in the fragments of a large, flat packing crate stacked beside the dumpster. The crate had held screens, perhaps, or a knocked-down table. Whatever the contents, they had been packed in some kind of straw or dried grass, and, curious about this material, I looked for a shipping label, turning over the boards without success. Not so much as an address. That struck me as odd. A crate six or seven feet high, even empty, costs plenty to ship, and one hardly sends valuable antiques without identification marks. I flipped over the last slat with my foot and disturbed a creature with many black furry legs, which checked the surroundings before scurrying away under the weeds. Then a door opened farther down the row, and, abandoning my search, I, too, left the premises.

I spent the rest of the afternoon in negotiations with the manager of the efficiency apartments, and, after adding sizably

to the expense column of Brammin's account, I was installed on
the second floor of an old white stucco building with a gray tile
roof, an arched Spanish entry, and a flourishing banana plant
that dominated the ornamental planter behind the flagpole.
"ARMADA EFFICIENCY APARTMENTS — rentals by the week and
month" had served as a World War II nurses' dormitory, and
it retained a certain amount of Spartan period charm. The
paint was fading and the air conditioners rusty, but the loca-
tion was ideal and the lush tropical growth, atmospheric. "The
kitchenette," the proprietor said, waving his pallid hand toward a Formica table, metal chairs, a two burner-stove, and a
countertop refrigerator. There were glass plates in the cupboard, two coffee cups, and some juice glasses. "All very convenient," he breathed. He was a heavy man with puffy eyes and
a stone-colored complexion who seemed afflicted with terminal
boredom.

"I'll take it for the week."

"Pay in advance," the manager said. After pocketing the
money, he handed me a set of keys. "I lock the main door at
midnight. The larger key will get you in. I run a quiet place
here."

I looked as sober and decorous as possible. When he left to
wheeze down the stairs, I opened all the windows, switched on
the fan, poured myself a gin, and broke out the report on Brammin's nephew.

The detective had been employed for a little over a week, and
during that time he had faithfully logged Rod Brammin's activities, and, more to the point, had checked into his financial
obligations. Chief among these was the shop, rented from Lido
Bay Associates, which apparently owned the entire commercial
block. The figures quoted confirmed my opinion that the going
rates were steep, and Key Antiques, despite its tastefully arranged window, was no Parke-Bernet. Interestingly, Rod's
apartment, toward the center of the city, had also been obtained through Lido. Around the time he'd opened the shop,
Rod Brammin had floated a loan through the prestigious

Palmer Bank, probably using his boat as collateral. The detective could only report it was close to six figures, and I assumed that this had covered his initial stock in trade.

A couple of charge accounts in good condition and a Corvette half-paid-for completed Rod's indebtedness. Unless there were some hidden loans or assets, the main item in young Brammin's financial picture was Lido Bay Associates, and I was surprised that my predecessor had not bothered to list their names. I was even more surprised when I visited their Sarasota office the next morning. Lido Bay Associates was housed in a hunk of cement block, with soft beige rugs, muted Muzak, potted plants, and dance-floor-sized desks. The Associates handled an assortment of large apartment houses and commercial properties, and they listed their partners on an engraved brass plaque. The place oozed respectability and, unusual in booming Florida, permanency, while the staff was all eager efficiency. One of the junior sales agents assured me that I would be contacted immediately if a rental suitable for an art gallery was listed.

I thanked him and accepted a company brochure. Two of the names listed looked familiar. One I remembered from the detective's report as an official with the Palmer Bank; the other was Vladimir Sebastian. "Is this the same Sebastian who's building the new museum?" I asked.

"Mr. Sebastian? Yes, he was one of the original partners in the business. Semiretired now, of course. I'm afraid he won't be out looking for your gallery himself." The agent gave a wide grin that made the ends of his bushy mustache turn up. With his hair styled thick and low on his forehead, he looked as though he were being upholstered in brown Dynel.

I smiled politely.

"Once in a while he comes in, and I understand he still oversees some of the development projects. He had cancer a few years ago." My informant tapped his throat. "He used to speak occasionally at our annual meetings. A very inspiring speaker."

I expressed my regrets.

"He came up the hard way. That's what made him interesting, and a very modest, serious man. You'd never have known he was rich — unless you saw his house, that is. Anyway," he said, checking my card, "we'll follow up on your rental needs right away." The mustache twitched again like a signal, and, running his hand protectively over his lacquered hair, he vanished behind the glass doors that sealed Lido Bay Associates' expensive chill. I got my car and headed for their client on St. Armand's Key.

This time the shop was open and a glance down the alleyway revealed that the crate was gone, the dumpsters empty. I left my car at the head of the block and wandered back, window shopping. When I opened the door of Key Antiques, a bell rang softly, signaling the appearance of a lithe, muscular man in his late twenties. I had no doubt this was Rod Brammin: he had my friend's rather formidable nose and the same high, flattened cheekbones and low brows. But on the nephew, the effect was quite different. In spite of, or because of, his uncompromising features, Rod was a striking presence. His short black hair and wind-burned skin gave him a bluff, vigorous air, and his blue eyes were brilliant against his dark skin. He was simply, although expensively, dressed, rather in the style of a golf pro at an exclusive club, and he possessed an easy friendliness, combined, I was to discover, with an inner caution. His almond-shaped eyes were evasive, despite their depth — and the wattage of his smile. "Good morning," he said. "Just browsing or can I help you with something?"

"Just admiring at the moment, thank you." The shop was full of nicely displayed china and decorative objects. There were good prints on the walls and a few small desks and tables. The only things that would require a six-foot packing crate were the prices. "I'm decorating a new apartment."

"We have some handsome little accent pieces at the moment." He lifted a ceramic monkey from a high shelf. "Eighteenth-century Italian."

The sculpture was finely made, but the artist had caught the disagreeable side of primates only too accurately. "It looks as if it's after a flea."

"Probably was." He replaced the figure and contemplated the rest of his stock. "We've got a few instruments in." He pointed to a convoluted horn hanging on the wall.

"I don't think I'm at that stage yet. I am really looking for some larger things. I could do with a screen, carved or painted. There's an awful door I want to hide. And maybe I can use a table."

"Oh, for the screen you'll have to try Archer's in town. I specialize in porcelain, especially French, and in accent pieces. I work mainly with decorators."

"And where would I find furniture?"

He mentioned a few shops in Sarasota and what he described as an excellent one in Palm Beach. I thanked him, admired several attractive little bronzes with long price tags, and left for lunch in the restaurant across the way. I took a table at the window and observed that Key Antiques was not exactly overburdened with trade. Even considering the prices he charged, it would take Rod Brammin a good long time to pay off his rent, never mind turn a profit. "Things seem rather slow this time of year," I remarked to the waitress.

"All the snow birds are gone, now. Course we have our steady customers." She nodded with approval at the heavy-set businessmen, their copper-hued consorts, and the elderly shoppers.

"I imagine summer is hard for luxury shops — like the antique store."

"That one never does much. Must be a hobby with the owner."

"Expensive hobby."

"A lot of those down here," she said, wiping the table briskly.

I ordered another cup of coffee: I was beginning to sympathize with my old friend's concern. Barring the discovery of a second trunkful of his father's music, which although possible, did not seem likely, the nephew was either financing his shop and apartment illegally or giving someone a good reason for paying his bills. Conceivably both: he could be supplying something worth the several thousand dollars' rent a month. There were a number of things which might fit that requirement, and none was attractive.

The first order of business, I decided, was to eliminate the melodic windfall possibility, and I phoned my assistant in Washington to have her start checking applications for music copyrights in either Rod's or Martin Brammin's name. Then I called the Ibis Golf Course, and Old Brammin came on the line.

"Find out anything?"

"Not much yet. Could you tell me when Rod made his last few extended trips?"

"Yes, I could — at least to within a few days."

"Hold on. I want to write these down." I balanced a note pad on the ledge and scribbled the dates. The latest was only a couple of weeks before. "If I wanted the exact dates could I get them?"

"I doubt it. The marinas don't necessarily keep records. Last time, the fellow had just happened to see Rod's boat going out."

"Too bad."

"Anything else?" he asked.

"Not at the moment."

"I think you're on the right track with the boat. I think that's the main thing."

"It's certainly one of the contenders," I agreed, and said good-by.

Outside, I grilled for a moment in the Florida sun, while ladies with blue hair and brown faces swooped by in pairs, and elderly gents with Panama hats and flaming Bermudas leaned on their canes and exchanged ripe trifles over good cigars. There was a car parked in front of Brammin's Antiques, and, if that's what the clientele habitually drove, I was wrong about his finances. I was curious enough to wait a while, but the owner of the Lamborghini did not appear, and, declining to be conspicuous, I retrieved my Ford, coaxed it to a semblance of life, and headed across the causeway.

Like his shop, Rod Brammin's apartment had what's called a prestigious address, and my directions to it were appropriately complex. Getting there took twice as long as predicted, a stroke of good fortune I failed to appreciate at the time. Leaving the car on the street, I crossed the immaculate oblong of Bermuda grass to the main lobby, checked the boxes to make sure I was in the right place, and rang for the super. No answer. In the courtyard, a thin, round-shouldered man was pruning dark, particolored plants with leaves like semaphores. After I rang for the third time, he ambled over, pruning shears in hand.

"Looking for someone?"

"The superintendent. I understood there might be an apartment for rent."

A smile crossed the man's thin, sun-darkened face and vanished into the deep crevices around his mouth. "Wrong on both counts," he said. "Super's day off, and we're full up. No seasonal rents, anyway."

"I was interested in something permanent."

"What's permanent? Nothing's permanent." He cleaned some green mess off the blades of his shears and dropped it carelessly onto the carpet. He was clearly not the superintendent.

"For an extended period of time, then," I said.

"Huh. Our days are like grass; all of us. We can be cut down at any time." Again the smile; the idea seemed to please him. I wondered what fanatic fringe cult had proved mean-spirited enough to capture his imagination.

"Do you see a lot of that here?"

"Oh, they come and go. Plenty of money to do what they like."

I had the feeling he was going to spit on the rug for emphasis, but instead he flicked more stuff from the shears.

"You interested in a place here?"

"You said it was full."

He shrugged. "Why this one?"

"It seems convenient."

"Wouldn't recommend it."

"No?" Whether or not he would have elaborated this point remained uncertain, for a car roared into a parking lot at the back, and, an instant later, a high, cross voice called, "Arthur! Arthur!"

"Damn bitch," the gardener exclaimed, and left. I followed. Across the court, a young woman pointed to the tools and baskets blocking her parking space and elaborated on the situation in an acid voice. She looked a fair match for the gardener, but I was more interested in her car, the silver Lamborghini which had sat half an hour before in front of Brammin's shop.

"Didn't expect him home," Arthur drawled.

"You've got the whole court for that damn equipment. I backed into some cans last week."

"These are tenant's spaces. I can't keep track of casual visitors."

"You watch it," she said. "And see no one scrapes my car."

"It'll get scratched if you leave it there."

"That's your worry." She jerked open the rear door and lifted out a bundle. When she straightened up, I saw her face, a bony, well-shaped oval with large hazel eyes, an aquiline nose, and a wide, sensitive mouth with prominent lips. She had curly hair like a circle of fur around her head and an alert, almost arrogant expression, composed, I suspected, of equal parts nerves and money. This was erased an instant later, when a green Jaguar rolled in, disgorging a plump red-haired boy and two skinny blond girls.

"I thought you'd never come! Have you got everything? The wine, the chicken — "

"Yes, yes, Cheri."

"The cheesecake? I'll bet you've forgotten — "

"No, no."

"You'd think you were into catering," one of the girls

sneered, but Cheri dissolved her with a look. "It's got to be right," she said. "It's Rod's birthday, and after all the super parties he's given — " She broke off and began organizing them: Carry this, take that, the table was to be set out on the terrace, the barbecue lit. She whirled around with graceful, sweeping gestures sharpened a little by tension. The boy was enthralled. One of the girls was rebellious, but all three were under her sway. Cheri was one of those natural magnets who draw duller personalities to them like so many iron filings. Another car arrived, and there were more shrieks and giggles. The planning and execution of a surprise party without professional help seemed an amazing novelty, but soon the garden paraphernalia was moved, the Lamborghini parked, and the provisions carried upstairs. Sweetness radiated upon all, and the whole swarm fluttered about the large balcony like so many tropical birds. I strolled to where the gardener was standing, ostentatiously idle.

"Quite a crew."

He spit on the pavement.

"Birds of passage?" I asked.

"Kites and vultures."

He was of a curiously scriptural turn of mind.

"Would they be friends of Rod Brammin's?"

The lines around his mouth deepened, but his wet stone eyes glimmered with interest. "What's it to you?"

"He's a friend of a friend."

"That one doesn't have many friends."

"What about the girl? The sweetie with the Lamborghini. What's her name?"

"I've got work to do," he replied. He shook his wrist to adjust the flat, link bracelet he wore, then hefting the pruning shears, he resumed his assault on the greenery. I wandered around the lawn. "This is all private property," he added.

He was in the right there, and I was about to leave with the interesting question of why Mr. Malicious was so protective about Rod Brammin and his bratty friend, when one of the blond girls leaned over the terrace. "Arthur?" Her voice held a note of hesitancy that produced a contemptuous little smile from the gardener. "Arthur!"

"Right here."

"Miss Sebastian wants you to cut some of those — What are they again, Cheri? Those pink things."

"I'm not running a florist's," he said, but he gave a quick glance to see if I had been paying attention. "This here's private," he shouted at me, "and the security man comes on at four."

"That's definitely an asset. I'll contact the superintendent next week. Such a nice, friendly staff."

The gardener snapped the shears together and watched until I left the lobby. He didn't need to worry. I had gotten what I'd come for. If Cheri's father was the property tycoon who was building Sarasota's grand new museum, young Brammin's affluence might be honestly, if not exactly honorably, explained. Sebastian wouldn't be the first doting papa to set up a potential son-in-law. Pleased with this hopeful thought for my old friend, I drove to the Sarasota newspaper offices, where, posing as a visiting free-lance writer, I collected a file of clippings on Sebastian and his collection. The third cutting included a photograph of an angular old man accompanied by a striking girl with a long nose and a large, expressive mouth. The hair style was a bit different, but the expression was unmistakable. Cheri Sebastian had already acquired her air of alert irritability by age nineteen. There were a few more notices of social events, then the first trickle of what became a torrent of publicity about the new museum. Vladimir Sebastian was described in each as a developer and philanthropist, designations capable of covering a multitude of sins. The journalists never became more specific, and it appeared that their interest in the man was of recent vintage, since none of the clippings was more than three years old. This was odd, if Sebastian had been, as the real estate salesman claimed, one of the original partners in an old and distinguished land firm.

"Do you discard stories after a few years?" I asked the librarian.

"Discard?" He twitched his nose and slid his thick glasses farther up, the better to contemplate so subversive an idea. "No, of course not. Is something missing?" He stretched his hand imperiously for the folder.

"I don't know if there's anything missing, but I'd imagine a man as prominent as Mr. Sebastian would have appeared in the press before now."

The librarian adjusted his glasses again and ran an ink-stained finger down the face of each story. "There certainly are lots of stories on the museum. That's what you're interested in, aren't you?"

"I was hoping for some background on the man, too."

"I'm afraid this is the best we can do. Not everyone is publicity hungry."

"He's gotten enough over the past three years, though, and he's lived here a long time, hasn't he?"

"I wouldn't know," the librarian said, running his hand impatiently across the black corrugated waves of his hair. "From what I've read, he's lived very quietly. Is that all you need? I've some staff requests I'm busy on."

"Sure. Thanks," I said, as I made my exit.

On the surface, I now had all I needed to give Old Brammin an optimistic report about Rod, Cheri, and Cheri's rich papa, but after I had threaded Sarasota's hot, crowded highways back to my apartment, I sat outside for a few moments, tapping the steering wheel.

Fact: Vladimir Sebastian was solid money, real estate based.

Fact: He had an attractive, if clearly temperamental, daughter.

Fact: Daughter and Rod Brammin were good friends.

Fact: Rod had rented more property from Sebastian than he could afford.

Assessment: Rod's financial status rested on the sentiments of what looked like a spoiled and potentially skittish young woman.

There was not much an elderly uncle could do about the situation, a conclusion that was logical without being entirely satisfactory, and I got out of the car and walked to the pleasant cool of the rear yard, where big Florida pines and a cluster of straggly palms darkened the grass. I flopped into a lawn chair and put my feet up. Overhead wild parakeets flew in a rainbow cloud, and doves picked busily through the pine needles. These tropical beauties failed to remove the nagging doubts filed under "Curiosities." Such as: Why had Vladimir Sebastian kept his name out of the papers until three years ago, when, incidentally, his daughter Cheri turned nineteen? And what did Rod receive in large wooden crates at a shop specializing in bric-a-brac?

A daiquiri did not conjure coherent explanations for these irritating observations, and before I went off to supper I decided to call Harry and see how things were getting on in D.C. The phone in our house rang a long time before I hung up and called the workshop. Jan answered on the second ring. In the background, I could hear talking and laughing and the inimitable sound of Baby's transistor.

"Yeah, he's here. We're finishing up. Baby's cooking something on the hot plate."

"Watch your digestion."

"Naw. Kid's a natural. She's making curry. I think I'll promote her."

Lucky her. "Put Harry on, please, would you, Jan?"

He laughed. Harry said something in the background then came on the line. "What's happening down there?"

"Not a whole lot. I've even managed to get to the beach."

"What did I tell you? When are you coming home?"

"I'd hoped tomorrow."

"That's terrific. I miss you."

"But now I'm not so sure — "

"What? Hold on a minute. Turn it down, will you, Baby. Yeah?"

"I said I'm not sure I'll be home tomorrow. I want to do a good job for the old fellow, and at the moment it looks too simple."

There was a loud giggle in the background.

"What's going on back there? It sounds like a visiting rock group."

"It's just Baby making dinner. Whatever the stuff is, it smells delicious."

Hot-plate curry! No wonder Baby was a hit with the artistic colony. "I'll call you tomorrow afternoon and let you know for sure when I'll be back."

"After four, all right? I've got to drive to Annapolis — that exhibition I told you about — remember."

Jan began singing. He only sang in Polish and he only sang at parties. "Sounds like things are livening up."

"He made a good sale today."

Someone called Harry over the sound of the music. I was pretty sure it was Baby.

"Hurry up and come home," Harry said.

"Sure thing."

"Good night."

"Night, dear."

I hung up the phone feeling depressed and rather stupid. Stupid to be annoyed that Harry was enjoying a convivial dinner at the workshop instead of an egg at home, and even more stupid not to have told Old Brammin that he was wasting his money and my time. That's what comes of being in this line of work: everything becomes suspicious and everything looks significant — a mental attitude that ought to be resisted nine times out of ten. Deciding to be sensible, I changed into a decent dress and set out to allay both jealousy and professional unease with a plate of red snapper and a bottle of white wine.

Chapter 3

THAT NIGHT in Ibis, groundless irritation produced an unusually conscientious job. My initial impulse had been to settle with Brammin as soon as possible, return my balky car, and head for the airport. As a sop to my conscience before departing, I drove up the keys for dinner at a seafood place adjoining the marina where Rod Brammin docked the *Melody*. It was in the back of my mind, I think, that the antique store owner, Cheri, and her gaunt, enigmatic father would all appear with the innocence of their relationship apparent. I could then report to Old Brammin that, far from heading down the primrose path, Rod seemed set on making a very nice future for himself: I dislike giving bad news to friends as much as anybody.

Of course, Rod did not show up. Instead I ate a broiled snapper accompanied only by a little green lizard, which scuttled up and down the wall and periodically set its small dry feet on the white tablecloth as though testing the surface. Beyond the window, the ships of the marina rested on the tide, the *Melody* riding as lightly as a gull. Whatever its merits under sail, as a shape against the gold and blue of the Florida evening the ship was a lovely thing and a tempting possession regardless of utility. I wondered if my old friend understood that. Aside from the oriental rugs he'd kept in his office, he did not seem to take any interest in art or to have much aesthetic sense. That one might run to the edge of ruin for beautiful things was not a trait he would find either sympathetic or comprehensible.

His nephew, I thought, was a quite different story; and after loitering until the sudden tropical night shuttered up the colors in the West, I headed toward the city to discover what sort of furniture Rod Brammin refinished after hours. Over the causeway, the condominiums blazed with light, and the streets and bridges were reflected on the splendid velvet of the bay, but the avenue where the antique shop was located was already quiet. The cafe was closed, and only a few cars prowled, quiet and expensive, their interiors sealed against the night's warm breath. Only the windows of the dress shops and jewelry stores were lighted, their mannequins sun-tan brown, their furnishings bright in the black interiors. I drove to the end of the block, turned around in the side street, and parked near the alley. The area was deserted, and I felt momentarily foolish and a little vulnerable standing there in the dark dressed for dinner. Then I heard voices in the alley and walked quietly to the opening. A couple of the shops had spotlights mounted over their back doors, creating halos of white light, but Brammin's was dark, and I could barely make out a peculiar van with a rounded hood and old-fashioned headlights. The vehicle was empty, and when no one appeared I crossed the alley and walked rapidly through the shadows until my heels crunched on a bit of metal. I stopped. Overhead a bat squeaked before fluttering away like a scrap of blown paper. I moved more carefully, stopping behind the large dumpster where I had noticed the discarded crates on my first visit. Just then the door of the antique shop opened, banging against the wall as if someone had kicked it.

"Watch out."

"It's a heavy mother."

The door banged again.

"Why don't you sell tickets?" an angry voice exclaimed.

"All right, all right."

I looked around the edge. Rod Brammin and two other men were loading a square box into the rear of what I now saw was not a van, but an ancient wood-paneled station wagon. A fourth man waited by the open doorway with a tarpaulin to cover the load. "Is that it?" he asked.

"Just about. Not finished with the rest," Brammin replied.

The man made an unintelligible remark and Brammin shrugged. The rear door of the wagon was fastened shut, and its lights glared suddenly around the edge of the dumpster, projecting a wavering feminine shadow. I drew back, flattening myself against the stucco wall as the old station wagon started up with a roar that strongly suggested a modern souped-up engine. Another car door banged. The party appeared to be breaking up and, anxious to see where the antique-lovers might be heading, I edged along the wall, sliding hastily into a doorway as the wagon passed. When its brakes screeched and both doors sprang open, I thought they'd seen me and very nearly gave myself away with a sprint to the top of the alley, but they had only forgotten something. While a short, nondescript chap in a T-shirt returned to the shop, the other man strolled back, a cigar between his lips and his hands in his pockets. "Hey, hurry it up, will ya?" he called to his friend, but he seemed in no very great rush, for he walked toward where the second vehicle, Rod's sports car by the sound of it, was idling noisily. "Better fix that crate," he said.

I was impressed by the innocent noisiness of the group, but just the same I stayed close to the wall, hastily squeezed past the open wagon door, and left the alley. Once out of sight, I made a dash to my car, figuring the noise of the other engines would cover even its protesting start. Then I pulled around the corner onto the main street. Where to go? A single woman parked alone would definitely look suspicious, and I drove half a block to the phone outside the restaurant. Leaving my car running, I nipped into the booth, sticking my foot in the door to keep the light from going on. Almost immediately, the wagon and Rod's sleek Corvette appeared. I let them get a block or two ahead then followed over the causeway. There was a lot of traffic on the mainland, but not so much that I couldn't keep the heavy wood-and-metal body of the wagon in sight. Once or twice I closed the distance at the lights but, either by accident or design, a corner of the tarp had escaped from the back door, and the license plate was obscured. I was going to have to tail it to identify the owner, so when Rod Brammin turned off on a side road, I let him go and pursued the big wagon down US 41 past the billboards advertising Pelican Key and Sunset Cove and the restaurants, furniture stores, and malls that form a tacky neon strip across the palmetto scrub and swamp. A few miles south, the big car swung off at a trailer park and twisted through several blocks of cheap housing with cramped yards and barking dogs. Another bend and the neighborhood improved. The lights were fewer, but the acreage had expanded and the coarse lawns and spindly bushes gave way to lush thickets of mango and citrus and bamboo and ornamentals as the city water mains created a jungle from the parched scrub and wove remarkable arabesques of foliage in place of the monotony of pine, palm, and palmetto. Floodlights shot up from low beds to paint a cluster of date palms in reds and oranges or to stain the bulbous trunk of a pineapple palm electric green. Bay windows appeared like space ships in the gloom, and white gravel courts shone white in front of long houses of luxurious design. Now and then I saw the moon-washed water, first on one side, then on the other, for we were back on the keys, and, the road being virtually empty, I began dropping farther and farther back to keep from alerting the wagon's driver. The road became more winding, and at last I came around a corner and found the track ahead dead with no disappearing red lights. I stepped on the gas, but the wagon was gone. Exasperated by my caution, I reversed the car and began to search for a likely cut-off. There were half a dozen possibilities, dark lanes leading, one supposed, to identically opulent homes. I strained to pick out a few names and house numbers and was about to call it a night, when a pair of lights glowed in my mirror. Surprised by this sudden appearance, I picked up speed, but the black Chrysler had a lot more power than my rented Ford. I expected the driver to pass, but he did not, and I tried a quick turn at the first cross street. Not three blocks later, the Chrysler reappeared, its lights materializing out of the black Florida night. I took another side road, jogging sharply to avoid a dead end. The square hood stayed in my mirror, the driver remaining a dozen yards behind me.

This was a shade more excitement than I needed, and the two men in the dark car suggested new dimensions to Brammin's after-hours business. It was imperative that I get off the narrow key, and I tried several side roads, each of which wound toward the glitter of the inland waterway, before I blundered into a sprawling residential development. With the Chrysler in pursuit, I wove through blocks of neat stucco and cement houses, so similar I was afraid of getting lost in some quiet cul-de-sac where deserted vacation homes slumbered behind clouds of vegetation and where elderly ears were tuned to Lawrence Welk or the wrestling matches. I wanted to get back to the divided highway, where, if I couldn't lose the tail in the late evening traffic, I could abandon both car and pursuers at some crowded nightspot, but the base of the key led to a maze of small dark streets, down which the driver of the Chrysler seemed content to follow my aimless twists and turns. This puzzled me. The area was definitely busier than the isolated key road, and I was considering the possibility that I was being followed by kids out on a lark, when I spotted lights from the ugly band of condominiums along the shore.

Believing I had reached the Ibis harbor and the town beach, I accelerated toward lights and safety, but the big car pulled out sharply, forcing me to commit myself to the shore road, a flat straightaway that shot by rows of bungalows and then, without the slightest warning, passed over a small bridge into a dark, amorphous swampland, feathered above with the thin silhouettes of the pines. I glanced in my mirror. The Chrysler's lights exploded, big as searchlights, and the engine roared for the kill. I stamped on the gas pedal. My car did its best, but the pursuing lights only wavered a fraction before filling the entire mirror. Unless Rod Brammin's friends had a particularly vivid sense of humor, I was in trouble, and I let the Ford drift to the center of the road to prevent myself from being overtaken. This was futile. Neither fast nor maneuverable, my car was an eggshell compared to the heavy vehicle behind. I swerved back to avoid an oncoming motorcycle and, as soon as the biker flashed past, the Chrysler shot into the oncoming lane. My whole car shuddered as it was bumped on the side. I swerved slightly, struggling to keep the car on the road. Then there was a loud crash. The Chrysler crumpled my front fender, and the jolt sent the car spinning. I braked and tried to steer back onto the road, but one tire caught on the soft, sandy shoulder and, with a horrid jounce, the car thumped into the drainage ditch. I clutched the wheel, while the vines and palm fronds and the sharp palmetto fans rattled over the windows and along the sides like the angry hands of a mob. The undercarriage crunched, and I strained backward to avoid a certain collision with a jutting palm trunk, but the sandy soil slowed the car, and after several terrific lurches it splashed into a wet patch in the ditch and was stopped for good by a hefty branch that caught under the front fender and snapped with a loud crack. I was flung sideways, although the seat belt kept me from hitting the wheel or the windshield. Terrified that the car might explode, I wrestled with the door. It was jammed on an overhanging branch. I slid across, kicked open the passenger's door and struggled painfully up and out of the car, which was tilted crazily against the steep side of the ditch. Above me, enormous against the stars, was the square side of a large truck. A man jumped from the cab and scrambled down the ditch. "You all right?"

"Yes, I think so."

"Then, lady, get the hell away from the car. That gas tank's bust for sure."

I put on all the speed I could muster and only succeeded in floundering against the slope. There was a nasty slime underfoot, and the sharp-edged grasses on the bank were damp and slick. The truck driver grabbed one arm and hauled me onto the blacktop, which wove back and forth and up and down and sent my stomach into a flutter.

"You hurt?" In spite of his deep voice and effortless strength, the driver was young and alarmed.

"Nothing serious," I said, shivering. "Shock, that's all."

"Better sit down. I'll call the cops and an ambulance."

As I leaned against the side of his cab, the night came into focus. Red and blue lights winked ahead on an open meadow — an airstrip, perhaps, and through the trees on the right the pale horizon glow signaled the sea. "Forget the ambulance," I said. "Did you see what happened?"

The man fiddled with the knobs on his CB, producing a crackle of static. "All I saw was that big Chrysler — must have been hitting eighty — then I come round the bend and spotted you in the ditch — we've got a ten-thirty-three out on Airport Road about three miles south of Ibis. Sideswiped car. No, nobody badly hurt. Lucky that heap didn't blow up," he remarked as he put down his microphone.

"Lucky you came along. Thanks."

"Oh, there would have been someone this time of night."

"Maybe not in time," I said, thinking about the two men in the Chrysler.

"Can't do nothing if the gas catches. Saw one one time coming across from Lauderdale. Went up like a bomb. Whoo-eee. Tires and metal all over the road, but I don't suppose you care to hear about that." He wiped his face and took out a cigarette. "Want one?"

"No, thanks. I'll just let my stomach settle."

He reached into the cab and brought out a greasy windbreaker. "Better put this on. Shock makes you cold."

He was right. Even the tepid breeze off the Gulf felt frigid, and I realized I was shaking. The jacket smelled like fuel oil but felt heavenly. I hunched my shoulders and stuck my hands in the pockets. "Didn't notice the plates on that Chrysler, did you?"

"Shit, he went by like a rocket."

"He must have been loaded," I said.

"Kids, probably. Road's empty all the way to the next town. They roar up and down here all the time. Never think, you know."

I agreed. When the police arrived with their bicolored car and red lights and tape measures, one of them wrote that down. Drunken kids get blamed for a lot, and I wasn't in the mood for greater accuracy. So long as the truck driver could clear me of any reckless driving charge, I was content to set everything down as an unfortunate accident.

"We've put out a radio call on the car," the officer said, "but without the plate number we don't have much chance of getting him."

"I understand."

"We'll ask you to come in tomorrow and fill out the report. Better see a doctor, too, if there's to be any insurance claim."

I did not take this recommendation. I did accept their offer of a ride home, and, although I glanced around every so often to see what was behind us, the narrow roads with their margins of white sand all seemed empty. Only the blue glow of hidden television sets told us the houses were occupied, and no one seemed interested in the patrol car that deposited me in front of the apartments. The officer hoped the rest of my visit would be pleasant and said good night. I went upstairs, counted a variety of insects in the shower, and, unable to settle down after the evening's entertainments, put on a swimsuit and padded to the beach.

Without the smog and city lights, the stars were magnificent, large and brilliant, and on the dunes above the shore the white flowers of the Spanish bayonets stood out against the gray sand and the indigo sea. To the north, the condominiums twinkled, and, far south, the fishing pier was outlined with tiny points of light. I kicked off my shoes and wandered along the cool sand. A few birds called overhead, but otherwise the surf drowned all other sound, for the wind was coming in straight off the water, raising dark, heavy swells that caught on the shelf of the beach and exploded into white froth. I watched them for a while, and then, still restless, splashed into the surf. Underfoot were small stones with some larger, seaweed-covered rocks and, struggling for footing, I was almost knocked over by a wave that reared up, milky-topped, to hit my stomach like an express train. I slid into the turbulent water, floundered for a moment, then, catching the trough after a wave, struck out from the shore. The water felt much colder than it had in the blinding morning sun, and in the darkness the waves rippled like a roller coaster. Past the line of the breakers, however, it was quite pleasant to ride the smooth, powerful swells. The lines between sky, sea, and land seemed almost erased, with only the faint glow of the horizon and the foam at the edge of the shore for markers. The stars cast their iridescence onto the sea, and the lights and the white plumes of the dune flowers made one pattern of light against the blackness. I had never been swimming at night before, and the beauty and force of the water were exhilarating, an excitement on the edge of danger, like driving too fast or standing too near the line as an express whips past. There was the same sense of hovering above oblivion, and the night and the sea made me think again about Rod Brammin, cruising far out in the Gulf with the *Melody*. I wondered what it was like to sail in rough seas, what the danger felt like, and whether it was because the waves alone had ceased to provide that rapture on the verge of extinction that he had taken to porting some new cargo, financing the beautiful ship with yet another risk. Whatever that cargo was (and I was convinced there was one) it must be valuable. Drugs were the most likely prospect. Marijuana might be packed in large bales, but bales wouldn't be as heavy as whatever Brammin and company had been loading into the station wagon. Unless the drugs were stashed in something else. Some of the shop's wares? But there was nothing heavy. Just china and bric-a-brac. I remembered the men straining to lift the box. Something wrong there. You didn't hide drugs in an item that would draw attention to itself. Besides, the ship suggested something to me: its beauty on the water; the exhilaration of the sea, and the hypnotic power of the surf, curiously soothing as one grew tired and cold. I began to feel that I was losing control, that the surges of the tide were carrying me irresistibly into the current. I had gone far out, and I realized that like many competent swimmers I had overestimated my ability. Tired, I plowed on toward shore, but fatigue was not the only danger. More insidious was the lassitude induced by the roll of the waves, by the darkness, by the flashes of white foam that illuminated the sea. It seemed very pleasant to drift with the water, to ride up and down the curve of annihilation. The thirst for danger and mystery contains the wish for oblivion. I felt that and, realizing I was not immune to its temptations, I swam with all my strength. The crosscurrent was powerful, but soon the whole weight and force of the Gulf was thrusting the water toward shore. I was lifted high on a wave and thrown struggling into the surf. I tried to touch bottom, failed, and was propelled forward, swam a few more yards, then felt the stones underfoot. A wave arose from the blackness behind and broke over my head, forcing me down under tons of water. I fought to the surface, gasping for breath, and in my efforts to keep from being sucked down by the undertow I lost the germ of an idea, which vanished, like a piece of flotsam, to reappear much later, fully developed, in a frightening and surprising form.

Chapter 4

A YELLOW TROPICAL SUN filled the room, lighting up the fading stucco, the metal bedstead, the wooden chairs, and the lithograph of an ultramarine surf breaking against a golden beach. My watch read eleven, but I found that hard to believe. I wiggled one leg. It was stiff. The other likewise, and when I ventured to sit up I discovered my back was one great aching muscle. I lay down, but that was not the solution, either, for a myriad of little bumps and scratches had awakened with the sun, and as I gathered my forces to meet the day I ran over the previous night's activities. It was disagreeable to realize that I had done a number of foolish, reckless things, and it was only slightly more comfortable to consider the mysterious behavior of Rod Brammin, his associates, and the two demolition drivers in the Chrysler. Why had they bothered? There was nothing so unusual about an antique dealer making a late night delivery, and nothing suspicious about a heavy wooden box. The alley had been too dark to distinguish anyone's features. In fact, there had been only one remarkable thing, and, after a cup of coffee and the acquisition of another car, I stopped at the local library. Then I spent an hour telephoning antique car collectors within a one-hundred-mile radius, and by two o' clock when I phoned Old Brammin at his golf club, I had three names in my notebook. Waiting for him to come on the line, I scribbled a box around one and underlined it.

"Hello, Anna. How are you?"

"Fine, but I think I'd better see you this afternoon."

"Are you sure it can't wait? I was about to go off."

"Sorry, but I think we'd better talk — before this evening if possible."

He wasn't enthusiastic, but he agreed to meet me at the club. When I drove into its palm-shaded lot, he was waiting in front with an electric golf cart.

"Ideal, don't you think?"

"Reminds me of Richard Nixon."

"He should know about private conversations, shouldn't he? But no tapes in this contraption. I don't like carts for golf, myself, but I'll be coming to that one of these days. Soon, I'm afraid."

I smiled and got in. Brammin steered around the clubhouse to a hard earth path along the fairways. "Well?" he said.

"Why did you fire my predecessor?"

He raised his eyebrows. "I thought I'd told you: I didn't think he would work out. Nice fellow, but without much finesse."

"Yes, so you said. It's not like you to hire someone unsuitable."

"We all slip a little with age. And I'll tell you frankly, Anna, I don't like this whole business."

"So I gathered. That being the case, I think perhaps I ought to tell you what I've learned and drop the job."

This time it was his turn to feel awkward. "I have every confidence in you," he said.

"But I doubt I can give you any more information than your other investigator. He'd mentioned a girl named Cheri Sebastian, hadn't he?"

"A friend of Rod's?"

"A good friend by the looks of it and an important one. Her dad is a honcho in the realty company that owns both Rod's shop and his apartment. I'd say the old man is setting Rod up as a prospective son-in-law. Lucky him."

Brammin nodded noncommittally.

"You knew all that?"

"I'd heard."

"But you omitted it from the detective's report."

"That part was purely verbal."

The golf cart purred softly along a narrow stream overhung with vines and branches. Egrets and herons picked their way from bough to bough or stood motionless in the shallows, watching the water with expressionless yellow eyes. This was a difficult interview. Brammin was not only someone I liked, he was someone who had been important to my ethical development, and I feared disillusionment. "One thing I decided when I started my own business was not to do any personal work — no divorces or nonpayment of alimony actions — none of that sort of thing — strictly business work. Mostly, I handle cases of white collar crime that a company wants to keep within the family. Sometimes a little industrial espionage prevention — for smaller firms." A flicker set up an avian drum roll on one of the palms. "I also found it was unwise to work for friends. This sort of thing is never without human complications. The factors that make a person criminal are often complex, and so are the reasons other people want to find them out. Perhaps you have observed that yourself."

"And you broke this resolution for me."

"More or less."

"Now you regret it."

"Not yet, but I will if you aren't candid with me. Until last night, I thought that Rod was interested in a young woman whose father was prepared to smooth the path of true love."

"What happened last night?"

"Before I tell you, I want to ask you something. You can either answer me or take me off the job and accept the explanation I've just given you. That might be wiser."

"I see. Well, I didn't call you all the way down here for advice, did I? What do you want to know?"

"Do you know Vladimir Sebastian?"

"Cheri's father?"

"Yes, do you know him? Anything about him?"

Old Brammin steered the cart carefully over a small wooden bridge where jungle growth pressed in on both sides. "He's an important man in real estate around here."

"You don't know anything else about him?"

"No. I'm not social, Anna. Negotiating Florida high society is not my idea of a comfortable retirement."

He looked straight ahead and speeded up the cart a little as though he wanted to get by this patch of ground — or questions. To the best of my knowledge Henry Brammin had never lied to me, but at that moment I was sure he was concealing something. "Two guys in a Chrysler ran my car off the road last night," I began. He listened to my account with obvious distress.

"What did the police say? What are they going to do?"

"Very little, I hope."

"Now Anna, this is serious. When I asked you to come down I never imagined there would be any danger involved. This is another matter entirely."

"Agreed, but you were anxious to conceal any connection between us. If I had discussed everything with the police, they would certainly have wanted to know what I was doing in Ibis and how I'd provoked this trouble in the first place."

There was a pause, then he made up his mind. "That is of no matter," he said firmly. "I want you to contact the state police today, and of course you'll leave. There is no question about that."

"If you want to drop the case."

"You've told me what I wanted to know."

"Have I?"

"About Rod."

"Yes, but it's not just Rod, is it? It never was just Rod who made you nervous."

Brammin let the machine slow as we reached the rough for the ninth fairway. "Why do you say that?"

"It's not important — if you really are going to drop the matter."

"No — go on."

"Well — these elaborate precautions. Meeting at the golf club, never calling you at home, even that pleasant but somewhat antiquated apartment. What would they suggest to you?"

"My concern must have been obvious."

"Worse than that. If I hadn't been working for you, I'd have assumed I was being set up in some way. As it was, I figured you were afraid of someone."

Brammin didn't reply.

"Rod was my first thought, but he clearly doesn't have anything to gain by harming you. He's not your heir, and from what you've indicated he's not apt to be in your will for very much. Am I right?"

"It's not Rod," he said.

"No, so I'll ask you again: What do you know about Vlad Sebastian?"

Brammin leaned back in the cart and let the machine idle to a stop. I examined the lagoon with the islands of dead trees crammed with egrets, cormorants, and pelicans. A continuous hoarse croaking, vibrant and alien, issued from the rookery, and the snake birds on the top branches stretched their black wings like shamans' capes while the egrets shuffled their feet in a ritual dance.

"Did I ever tell you how I got into the petroleum business?" he asked.

"I don't think so."

"Started out in Chicago, you know. My dad had been a grocer, and by the time I was in my early twenties we had a fairly good wholesale produce business. Then my brother sold his share, and eventually we were taken over by one of the big chains. I went to work for them in administration. Funny thing, it was arranging shipments of provisions to one of the Texas oil operations that began my interest in petroleum. That was a long time ago." He paused and nodded. "Chicago was full of interesting characters in those days. Prohibition and its aftermath were to crime what the Texas oil rush was to petroleum. We had a lot of dealings with the trucking industry and the Teamsters in our business. You met everyone there. The Teamsters are the mother lode." His face took on an expression of disgust. On other, more pleasant occasions, Old Brammin had regaled his friends with tales of some of the colorful bootleggers and the even more vivid Chicago eccentrics and touts. This was the other side of the story. "Even a small firm like my family's — especially one that size — was vulnerable to pressure, usually in the form of labor troubles. You know, wildcat strikes; truckers refusing to handle your cargo for no apparent reason. This would continue for a while and then a fixer would appear. 'Deal with us and you won't have any problems.' I knew quite a few of them and dealt with a couple. There was no other way. Ancient history now. I learned a lot, believe me. But the point of this is that I met a young man, an apprentice thug — or so I thought. He was a gangster's aide de camp, opened the doors, fetched the car, went out for drinks and made himself scarce when he got the sign, but he wasn't just the garden variety. He was a real smart boy." Brammin paused, and when the silence had matured I asked the man's name.

"I don't know. He answered to Sebbie R. It wasn't polite in those circles to ask for an ID card. What I do know was that he was a thorough son of a bitch." The old man's eyes turned angry, and emotion tightened the sagging lines of his chin. "That bastard crippled one of our drivers. Smashed his face in and ran over his legs with the truck."

"But no conviction."

"Our driver was afraid to testify, and there were no other witnesses. Can't blame the fellow. He had a family. I wasn't so brave myself. I'd had enough. I wasn't going to deal with people like that, and I wasn't up to fighting them. New World offered me a job, and I jumped at it."

"What about this Sebbie R.?"

"Last I heard he went to the university, then on to one of the big eastern law schools. Mob money for tuition, I'm sure. It's possible he reacted like me and decided he'd had enough violence to last a lifetime, but I don't think so. I knew him, and I knew his type. I'd seen him around since he began running errands at fourteen. He was a violent kid, and the fact that he was smart enough to see the advantages of legitimacy wouldn't have changed him. But he saw the advantages, all right. After I left Chicago I never heard any more about him. Not even a whisper."

"Probably wound up on Wall Street."

"So I assumed until I went to a regional Rotary Club meeting a few months ago. There was a big do for all the service clubs that had participated in the annual charity drive and a Sarasota mansion was loaned for the event. I wouldn't have gone, but my golf partner had had a hand in the planning: the usual thing, we all stood around with weak cocktails in our hands. Fred insisted on introducing me to our host, so we went up front where the VIPs were buzzing around a man with a face like a cadaver. He looked as if he'd been hauled out of the ground, and he had an odd voice, as though he were whispering from far away and the vibration was being amplified. Throat cancer, I heard later. They were falling all over him and praising his house to the skies, but he ignored most of them and just watched the crowd. He had cold yellowish eyes, and he didn't say much until Fred said to me, 'Your nephew knows Cheri, doesn't he?' Then the sick man pricked up his ears and asked my name again. I had the funniest feeling at the time. Not recognition, certainly — forty years or so make an awful difference in everyone — but almost a sense of *déjà vu*. But even that wouldn't have made me think twice — I've been to thousands of cocktail parties and sooner or later one of them is going to remind you of an earlier evening. It was our host's reaction. Poor old Fred is very dense about the more subtle social signals. He kept on about this and that — Rod and what a charming girl Cheri is, that sort of thing — and then he asked, 'Weren't you from Chicago originally? I've been telling Henry here that I thought you were an old Chicagoan. You haven't been back for a long time, have you, Henry?'

"Our host muttered something about school in the city and left, quite abruptly, with two young men who'd been hanging about in the background. Rude exit, but none of the others seemed to notice that. Just the top guy's manner. But I noticed, and when I started seeing the two young men around in places where I wouldn't have expected them, I began to make a few inquiries about Mr. Vladimir Sebastian."

"And he turns out to be one Sebbie R. from Chicago."

"No. He turns out to be nobody. No one knows anything about him except that he retired from a big law practice quite a few years ago and that he has been important in the land business here and in one of the banks. Beside that, no one knows — or no one's saying."

"A man of discretion."

"Absolute, until quite recently. Opening his house for charity parties, parceling money to this and that, and now, of course, the museum. You'd heard of that, hadn't you?"

"Yes, I had. He's gotten a lot of ink over it. Donating a museum isn't exactly the thing to do if you've anything to hide."

"That's what puzzled me. I would have forgotten about it, if I hadn't been afraid of Rod's getting involved. I was afraid of that when I heard about him and Cheri, and more so when I saw the style he was affecting. And then there's Sebastian's young men."

"What about them?"

"They're just around. Alone, together — I keep seeing them. Anytime I go somewhere unusual, I can expect them. Sometimes I think my car's being followed, but never too far. Once in a while I'll see them drive by the club here or pull out of the parking lot when I'm getting ready to leave. I've wondered about my phone occasionally, too."

"Have you had that checked?" I asked quickly.

"No. I've been trying to ignore them."

"The best plan. He can't be sure you've recognized him."

"That was my thought. Otherwise he'd have taken a more direct approach."

"Possibly. There's something else, though," I said.

"What's that?"

"Rod's probably pretty far in debt to this man. That may be the trump card."

"So I suppose, but if that's all there is to it, what happened to you last night makes no sense."

"No. I think we'd better find out what Rod is supplying for Mr. Sebastian. That's our ace."

Brammin shook his head. "I never cared for gambling. I want you to go home. I don't want to be responsible for your getting hurt."

"Then you shouldn't have consulted me in the first place. I wouldn't worry too much. If Mr. Sebastian is as cautious as he seems, the two fellows in the car are in hot water today, and he's not apt to try anything very uproarious just before the museum opening."

"That's an assumption."

"All we have to go on at the moment. I wouldn't think you'd feel good about leaving Rod to his own devices — not if Sebastian's the man you think he is."

My old friend switched on the golf cart, and we purred up a long meadow away from the lagoon. Big white clouds were gathering in lumpy rows over the palms, and the dry yellow fairway was as hot as an oven. The sandy soil looked parched, and the dark pines shimmered in the dazzling afternoon light. We rode all the way to the seventeenth in silence, then stopped to let an aged foursome negotiate the last tee. "I've sometimes regretted I didn't stay in Chicago," Brammin said.

He saw my surprise.

"Not for the business opportunities; I did far better at New World. But I've felt I ran away and left the people further down the line to deal with the thugs. I learned a lot from that — about my own limitations. Now I'm not so sure again."

"I think at your age you can be excused for not wanting to mount a crusade. There's really nothing you could do to Vladimir Sebastian. I'm surprised he doesn't realize that."

"Age has nothing to do with it," Brammin replied testily.

"That's just television thinking — all that crap about senior citizens and the golden age. The rules aren't rewritten for you at sixty-five. I would imagine Sebastian feels the same way. He'll react as if he were going to live forever, instead of his probable four or five months."

That unpleasant thought might be accurate.

"All right, then, here's what I'd suggest. Let me see what I can learn about Vlad Sebastian — and whether or not I can discover the connection between him and Rod. Give me a day or so. You said yourself you couldn't identify him as the Chicago thug. He may not be. If he isn't, leave Rod to handle his own affairs.

Brammin considered this as we rolled toward the clubhouse. "And how do you propose to do this?"

"I have sources. I'd also like to meet Sebastian. Can you get me an invitation to a party where he's likely to show up?"

"That girl of his runs nonstop entertainment. The museum's been a bonanza for her. I'll find out."

"Good. If I can meet him within a day or so, I'll stay; otherwise, I'll fly to D.C. and then come back."

"This is taking up a great deal of your time."

"Yes, but it's well spent. Between you and me, I get tired of office work and that's what most jobs amount to: facts, figures, phone calls."

"I think you ought to settle down."

"As you say it's not just a matter of age. Call me as soon as you can arrange an invitation. That would be better than a more direct approach."

"I'd be interested to know how you'd handle him," Brammin said drily.

"Carefully and with a good deal of inspiration. You can let me out here. There's no need for us to be seen together."

"I'll call you tonight, and I would go very easy on the inspiration," he added. "It always seemed to me that you relied too heavily on that."

The cart moved smoothly away, growing smaller and darker

against the endless sunlight, its occupant sitting stiff and up-right beneath his white straw hat. Yet he was clearly fragile, his shoulders slightly stooped, the tendons and muscles about to lose the long battle with fatigue and gravity. My remark about his age had offended him, but perhaps that was for the best. He had been disturbed about Rod; now instead he was angry. As for myself, I was uneasy, which, I suppose, is what private investigators are paid to be.

Chapter 5

"Nope, not here. Try his house."

"All right. Thanks."

The man at the newspaper office hung up, and I redialed. I was not having the best of luck with my male friends. Brammin had landed me in what looked like a family mess with Organization overtones, and Harry had been out having lunch again with Baby. In Sarasota, the phone rang a long time, and when Hillary finally answered, his growling, distracted voice suggested that his day hadn't gone too well, either. Maybe Theresa wasn't the miracle worker I'd assumed.

"Hello Hillary. It's Anna."

"Anna?"

"In Ibis. I stayed on a few days."

"Oh, sorry old girl. Mind wandering. I've been working on a rather difficult piece."

"The same one you told me about?"

"Yes."

"I'd like to talk to you about that. I've come across something that might help you."

"That'll be the day. I'll tell and you'll take."

"Not necessarily, but if you're not interested — "

"We won't talk about it now," Hillary said quickly. "Are you free this evening?"

"Yes. Shall I come up?"

"No, I'll drive down. Let me get a piece of paper."

I gave him my address.

"What time is it now? Four-thirty? With the traffic, I'll see you in about an hour, Anna."

"Right."

I went to the kitchen and made a very large gin and tonic. Then I remembered Hillary's problem and went out and bought a six-pack of Coke and some lemonade. I was virtuously sipping the latter when his car swung into the apartment lot.

"I'm in back, Hillary."

He unfolded himself from the small car and strolled across the cracked cement of the courtyard to where I was relaxing on the establishment's only chaise longue. On the way he took in the peeling stucco, the rampant shrubs, and the weary lawn chairs. "Your taste for exotic Americana continues to amaze me," he said.

"Client's request. Do you like it?"

"I suppose I could. Very Humphrey Bogart." He picked up a glass and opened one of the cans of lemonade. "This for me?"

"What the doctor ordered."

He gave a wry smile, poured himself a drink, then sat on the grass next to my chair and deposited his head in my lap. I raised my eyebrows. "Comfortable?"

"Damned uncomfortable."

"I should think so."

"I'm in trouble."

"Theresa caught you with the neighbor's wife."

"Never."

"Never? This is pretty cozy at the moment."

He smiled ironically. "I'm lonely — and you're an old friend."

"Too old a friend."

"I persuaded Terry to visit her mom in Lauderdale for a week."

"Opening all sorts of possibilities."

"Yes. Sorry, though, old girl, none of them are nice."

"You're not going to confess some horrid new habit, are you?"

"I wish I had one. The truth of the matter is that someone's after me."

"We have something in common."

"Do we? Now that's interesting."

"I told you I had something worthwhile."

"An understatement as usual." He took a sip of lemonade.

I sat up and crossed my legs Indian fashion, dislodging Hillary. "I wouldn't want anyone to get the wrong idea," I said. "I don't want to be offered as an alternate target."

"I hadn't thought of that, and that's the truth, but I had to get Terry out of the way. Not a good situation at all."

"I had the impression she thought all that was behind you."

"Oh, yes. One reason she was so keen to move over here. Not that there was any real trouble in Miami. Well, nothing a reporter doesn't expect — obscene phone calls at home and abusive ones at work. A few threats, too. The Cuban community is positively Renaissance — plot and counterplot. They could have given John Webster a few pointers."

"I'm sure your wife was right to worry."

"I suppose. What wives are for, eh?"

"She's made a big difference to you," I said seriously.

"Yes, she has. That's why she had to visit Mama in Miami. I see a pattern developing that I don't much like. For one thing, someone's been trying to discredit me. A rumor's been around that I've been drinking again. Complaints about my work, too, and I've had difficulties with the New York television people about financing my latest project. Hard to trace, rumors, but it seems I've made myself unpopular with someone who has interesting connections."

"Any idea who you're looking for?"

"Whom."

"What?"

"Looking for *whom*. When I think of the time I spent on your grammar."

"There were other attractions, as I remember."

"Still are, dear girl," he said, patting my knee, "but I'm on the straight and narrow."

"I'm glad to hear it. Now, what else besides these rumors?"

"Odd things. I was nearly run over one evening, and since then I've had the feeling I'm being followed. That sounds paranoid, but I have no doubt about it. Terry's noticed too: strangers around the neighborhood, people hanging around our cars when we're downtown at work — that sort of thing."

"Any candidates?"

"No, that's the peculiar thing. Unless you buy my wife's theory of Cuban gangsters or revolutionaries — same thing in her book."

"But you don't."

"No. I had generally good relations with the community, and their approach tends to be direct. Someone calls at your door with a thirty-eight and flowers are sent to your funeral. This is a more subtle approach all together and far too long after the fact."

"What about the business in Guatemala? Anything interesting you haven't told the rest of us?"

"That's occurred to me. I've gone over it a dozen times. You don't forget finding the bodies of people you know. I think I can remember every detail. It's all very vivid in my mind, but nothing seems significant. There's little chance of the case being solved anyway. The murder of two archeological site guards in a country where half the population is living hand to mouth? The temples are one of the few things they've got that can be turned to cash. Who's going to care? It doesn't make sense."

"All right, that leaves the museum story, doesn't it? Have you learned something you shouldn't have about Mr. Vlad Sebastian?"

"Do I detect a certain professional interest?"

"Personal and professional. Someone ran my car off the road last night, and one of his employees is the most likely prospect."

"You'll have to tell me more than that, Anna. I always thought your driving was suspect."

"Well, what have you told me so far? Mostly ancient history. I've got my client to think about."

"They pay the bills, but don't tell me you put them ahead of your precious hide."

"This one's special. He's one of my oldest friends and a person who takes things seriously, Hillary. Not like you and me."

"And he has gray hair and you've always preferred older men."

"Right on the first, but not the second. I don't want him to wind up in the New York *Times* magazine section as an important detail in your latest exposé."

"Everyone worries too much. Including Mr. Sebastian. My piece on his museum is finished. He comes off quite well."

"But there's something else."

"Well, I owe my friends in Guatemala something. I'm preparing another documentary on the art market and on the major collectors. No reason why a few poor bastards who loot graves should bear all the onus, is there? The big collectors and the big museums don't have especially clean hands where antiquities are concerned. A few things I'd found out about Vladimir Sebastian made me think he'd be a good prospect. But no. He's clean, as they say here. In fact, he's dreadfully fussy about the provenances of his pictures and objets d'art and his big holdings are in the Impressionists. Pretty safe unless he's having them stolen to order and then he'd hardly risk donating them to the state."

"What did you learn about Sebastian? No one seems to know a thing about him before he entered the land market here."

"Something from you first. Why were you run off the road? You weren't hurt, by the way, were you?"

"Nice of you to ask," I said, and Hillary grinned. "I was following a station wagon away from an antique shop."

"Sounds risky."

"A very special wagon — a real old estate job with wood

panels and round headlights that lives out in a fancy neighborhood on one of the keys."

"And this aging behemoth turned on you and forced you off the road."

"No. The aging behemoth has an ultra modern engine. It got away from me and the next thing I knew I was being tailed by two reckless types in a black Chrysler." Hillary's curiosity was obvious. "Sound familiar?"

"Like the car that nearly sent me to the angels. Dark road. I was walking to the store. He approached without lights. I assumed it was an accident at first."

"In my case there was no doubt of their intentions."

"I'm more interested in that antique shop you mentioned."

"After you tell me about Vlad Sebastian."

"All right, fair enough. Your previous informants are correct: he doesn't exist earlier than fifteen years ago."

"That still gives him time to get into trouble."

"So it does, and he changed his name early on. That much is clear. The papers are on file in Chicago. Before that, he had some unpronounceable Rumanian surname. Sebastian was his given name, but even that's uncertain because his original birth certificate was destroyed in a court house fire."

"Opening opportunities."

"Seems to have. This was when he began practicing law. I've been trying to flesh out that part of his life. He claims to have had a practice, but he doesn't seem to have appeared in court very often."

"That's where the big money is — in nonappearing law."

"Must be. Fifteen years ago, he became a partner in the land company that, incidentally, is connected to a bank in which the Teamsters have an interest."

"You have been muddying the water."

"And several undesirables have surfaced, but none of them are directly linked to Mr. Sebastian. His hands are almost ostentatiously clean."

"But you don't believe that."

"A nonpracticing lawyer who goes from the Chicago slums to a Florida palace with no visible means of support but a land company? He'd have been a good story, but he didn't fit the pattern I need for the new script. I wrote up his museum opening, hinted here and there about a mysterious past, and left it at that."

I nodded.

"Now for the antique shop. It's not for a story. You can trust me, Anna. When I'm sober," he added with a touch of bitterness, "my word is perfectly good."

Despite this touching declaration, I extracted a few more concessions before I told him about Cheri Sebastian and Rod Brammin.

"The good-looking young guy who hangs around all the time?"

"Good-looking would cover Rod. Tall, well built, dark eyes. Not pretty by any means. Drives a red Corvette."

Hillary knew him, and I explained about the *Melody* and the boxes I'd seen unloaded.

"And whatever this stuff is, you think it's going to Sebastian?"

"No proof, but it looks that way. The wagon was what convinced me. Your wife said he collected classic autos and one of the car buffs around here told me that the old man not only won't ride in anything newer than the forties, but insists most of his staff use the vehicles, too. He likes to be surrounded by antiques."

"What do you think the Brammin kid is bringing in?"

I hesitated. "Drugs, I suppose. It's the big growth industry down here, isn't it?"

"But you're not sure?"

It was a trifle awkward to explain that I thought run-of-the-mill dope smuggling suited neither Rod Brammin nor Vlad Sebastian. "Just a feeling. The crate and the boxes — they don't fit somehow."

Hillary looked thoughtful but kept his ideas to himself. He'd never been one of your eager collaborators.

"So," I said. "There's where I am at the moment. I'm angling for a chance to meet Sebastian — and have a look around his garage for that wagon."

"Ah."

"This can work both ways. If I can find out what Brammin is supplying, my client will have some leverage with Sebastian — all for a good cause, of course."

"I think you're reverting to your old habits, dear girl, but if it gets me out of trouble I'll go along with you."

"No scruples?"

"Few enough to tell you you're wasting your time waiting for an invitation. Cheri Sebastian runs an open house every weekend. One just shows up, grabs a drink, and joins the throng. Nobody ever checks the guest list. You should do a better job of your background work."

I got up, dusted off my slacks, and put on my sandals. "Thanks for the tip."

Hillary picked up another two cans of lemonade. "Do you mind? I always bring my own now. Hostesses either serve trashy punch or nothing but booze. The Sebastians are the latter case. Some of their regulars are never sober."

"You're coming?"

"I wouldn't miss it. If your theory is correct, I may soon meet my newest enemy."

Chapter 6

Iᴛ ᴡᴀs ᴊᴜsᴛ ᴀs Hillary had described, a perpetual party, with strings of colored lights between the palms, and music, and bright crowds eddying about the terrace or emerging from the shadows like new species of tropical flora. Sebastian's house was a massive pink stucco building that opened in the back to a large and beautiful garden. Against the pale walls, jacaranda trees rose in a lavender mist, and gold trees dangled their yellow blossoms, while a dozen brilliant varieties reflected the lights of the long windows. Farther back in the scrub beyond the garden, fleshy plants raised their spikes beneath the ragged banners of the palms, and when a breeze came up from the Gulf, the hanks of dead leaves and fronds made a dry rattle, an unprogrammed addition to a band that was adding Latin to rock to produce a bouncy, slightly synthetic rhythm, as if the musicians had lost their convictions playing too many society galas.

Hillary parked his car at the tail end of the string of Jaguars, Cadillacs, Maseratis, and Corvettes that decorated the curving drive, and as we approached the lawn we could see the inland waterway beyond the trees with a boat dock and a cabin cruiser. From the top of the house, I imagine one could see the breakers of the Gulf. As Hillary opened a lemonade, he asked, "Like it?"

"Bit hard to maintain."

"I like this," he replied, with a gesture that encompassed the night, the garden, the house, the sound of ice clinking in glasses and a fancy band, of conversations in high, excited voices and the rustling palmettos. "I love society. I really do. Even here."

"Polite or otherwise?"

"No, I mean it. Unfortunate that Terry loathes this sort of thing."

"Sensible woman."

"You both fail to appreciate the nuances. What would Proust have been without the Faubourg and all those wretched hostesses or Anthony Powell without his house parties and the bohemian set? It's all here, and the nice thing is this lot have the time and money to do what they please."

"Not a combination I find attractive."

"But you're a moralist. Yes, yes you are, even if you're inconsistent. You believe in innate depravity. Well, so do I, of course — any reasonable person does — but I don't find it depressing. Hello, hello, Philip. Caroline! Oh, lovely," he called to a passing couple, who returned his salutations with metallic giggles.

"I notice you've become keen on these parties only since your reformation. Sure your enthusiasm's not just smugness?"

"What a frightful thing to say and very unkind. You'll fit right in here. The truth of the matter is I've always loved these affairs, but I used to pass out too soon. Now that I'm sober, I can enjoy them longer than anyone else."

"Does that hold true for your writing, too?" A waiter passed with a large silver tray, and I stopped him for a cocktail. Since Hillary seemed set to discuss some of his more eccentric theories, I felt I deserved one.

"In a way. Poor Terry has enabled me to indulge other vices — including a taste for needling the powers that be. But don't you love this — look at it — Cheri thinks nothing of inviting fifty or a hundred people for the weekend. She's charming you know, a natural leader, but flawed." He returned to his lemonade.

"In what way?"

"Needs followers. She has no capacity for being alone. Her

father's just the opposite. Right now, he'll be in one of two places — either right up at the top of the house — " Hillary pointed to a balcony, half-hidden behind a fat balustrade — "or in his chapel."

"His chapel?"

"He's rumored to be religious," Hillary answered drily. "It's in a separate building beyond the garden. In any case, he does not join in the festivities. Not ever. He is always alone, even when he is the host."

"I'd heard he's accompanied by a pair of flunkies."

"A flotilla's more like it, but that's irrelevant. He hasn't the slightest need for human company. But Cheri — oh, there she is. We'll give her a miss for the moment. Do you know she's taken a great liking to me?"

"That's not totally unprecedented."

"Well, in a way this is. Completely platonic — or maybe strictly business describes it best. I used to think she could tell me about her father, and now she has the same misapprehension about me."

Another group of revelers passed us, and Hillary appreciatively sniffed the sweet, marijuana-laden cloud hovering around them. "Good stuff," he said. "Someone here must have an unending supply."

"I can't stand the smell since I gave up cigarettes."

"Serves you right for pursuing clean living. What about a sandwich? Then we'll wander toward the garage." He stopped to greet some acquaintances. During his work on the museum story, Hillary had obviously met an enormous number of people, and as we left the buffet line I remarked on this.

"In-depth research," he replied.

"Carried on mostly at cocktail parties, I suspect."

"Precisely where the art trade is conducted — except for the poor sods who actually produce the goods."

His explanation wasn't wholly convincing; it seemed to me that Hillary had insinuated himself too thoroughly into the Sebastian circle for a mere magazine story. We passed from the yellow lights around the terrace to the dark, soft night that lay just past the rampant hibiscus and oleanders and the hedge of plum boxwood bordering the lawn. As we started down the gravel drive, Hillary drew me into the shadows. "Wait," he cautioned.

"What is it?"

"Papa Sebastian's eyes and ears are out. They always are at these affairs — keeping the guests away from the great man."

A quite extraordinary figure approached. He was slender, elegantly turned out, perfectly tanned, and so exactly resembled a men's store mannequin that he might have been a model come to life. His face was frozen, expressionless, as though flesh and bone had been replaced by some more durable material, and a pair of chill, flickering eyes that did nothing to soften the overall effect. Hillary saw my expression and gestured for silence as the young man passed, leaving a faint scent of musk to complete a disagreeable impression.

"That's Marcus. He knows a lot about the collection. Not the most genial chap."

"What happened to his face?"

"Acquired by long practice, I suppose. He takes great pains with his sun tan. And cosmetic surgery, too, probably. Very vain, our Marcus."

"Where are the cars?"

Hillary pointed to another pink stucco building just past the track leading to the waterway and the dock. A few couples were sitting by the edge of the water, and there was a large, noisy group poised on the end of the pier.

"These parties must complicate Marcus' duties."

"They do, indeed." Hillary indicated the first row of doors. "These are the old cars, as I remember. We'll have to be quiet, because the chauffeur's family lives above."

"I'd think it would be all hands on deck for this many guests."

"Hope you're right." He tried the door of the first bay, but it was locked.

"There should be a regular door somewhere." Around the side of the garage, an outside stair led to the apartments above, and below was a screen door that proved to be fastened from the inside.

"Locked?"

"Just hooked, I think." I opened my purse for the jackknife and the penlight that comprised my entire breaking-and-entering kit. Being in business for myself, I couldn't afford any crazy stunts: prosperity seemed to have entailed respectability. "Hold this, would you?" I opened the blade and slid it up the screen, flipping the catch. "Anyone in sight?"

"No one fit to notice anything."

"We're just desperately keen on antique cars, remember."

I opened the door. A long row of square-nosed shapes filled a darkness broken only by faint reflections from the highly polished radiators, the deep enameled chassis, and the large, faceted lamps. Near my foot, something soft landed with a plop, then another. "What's that?"

I switched on the flashlight. A large toad flopped away like a sack full of marbles. "Ugh."

"The secret of Sebastian's success," Hillary said.

"Never mind being clever. What's this?"

"A Mercedes. Beautiful car, isn't it? It's a 500K from 1935." He stopped to admire a detail on the hood.

"Come on, Hillary." Some type of touring car, a spectacular Silver Cloud, then, next to a two-seater with rakish lines, the heavy, square wood body of the station wagon appeared. I checked the front, but I had been sure from the first. "This is it. There can't be another one just like it." I ran the light along the side and into the lush leather-and-walnut interior. "Better watch the door."

"Don't take too long."

I eased open the latch on the back window and ran the light around the compartment. Not even a speck of dust.

"Anna." There was a warning in Hillary's whisper.

I lowered the light, then, when no sound corroborated his alarm, opened the rear door and shone the beam along the back and down the running board. There were a few dry bits of straw, which I wrapped in a handkerchief.

"Anna!" This time, I could distinguish steps on the gravel. I switched off the light, shut the car carefully, and edged to the back of the garage. In the feeble light from the yard, I saw Hillary reach across the screen door to push down the hook as the approaching steps resolved into two men talking about jai alai. Thanks to Joey, one had had a good night at the fronton, and while he tossed around four and five figures, the other pulled at the handle of the screen door.

"It's all right. Angela's home. I see the light."

"Pays to check," the other replied, and I could hear him testing the overhead doors in front. Then the footsteps faded. Hillary and I waited a few minutes before making a soft-footed exit. "Better see if you can hook it again," Hillary said, and we fiddled with the door until we managed to flip down the catch with my knife.

"Not the most expensive hardware."

"That's so he can afford the two touts," Hillary said. "Find anything?"

"The car had been cleaned."

"To be expected." He waved at some of the party on the boat dock. A few were splashing in the water, and, from the laughter on the pier, the others sounded likely to join them. "Now to find Cheri," Hillary said. "The terrace, I'd think. Yes, there she is." He pointed to an animated figure sitting on the edge of a crowded table. Our hostess wore lilac silk pajamas and a good deal of flamboyant makeup that intensified the sharp, dramatic lines of her face and hid a somewhat sallow complexion. Her gestures were quick but graceful, and little ripples of laughter ran about the circle near her. Cheri demanded the center of attention, and she knew how to direct the spotlights. When Hillary caught her eye, she came forward to greet him with a kiss and drew him over to say hello to Rod, who was lounging against the railing of the terrace. I received an intelligent, appraising glance.

"You're visiting Sarasota?" she asked.

"In the process of settling in. I remember you, Rod, from your shop the other day. I was looking for a screen."

"Oh yes, of course," he replied politely, but I had the feeling he would rather not discuss the shop. "Any luck yet?"

"Not so far. Perhaps I'll have to try Miami or West Palm Beach." In the background Cheri giggled at something Hillary said, and the inner circle of her admirers shifted slightly: we were the newcomers, and they were anxious to see how we were to be placed. I recognized the sulky blonde and her red-haired date from my visit to Rod's apartment. They were smoking elongated cigarettes and, despite their world-weary expressions, following our conversation avidly.

"Have you seen Cheri's father's collection?" the girl interrupted. "He has some really rare things."

"Not yet. We've been admiring the outside of the house," I said.

"You should ask Cheri to take you round. It's like a museum," her friend put in.

"That's why Rod's so persistent," the blonde teased. "He'll be Father Sebastian's chief antique dealer."

For different reasons, this irked both Cheri and Rod.

"My father has all the antiques he needs," she snapped. "And anyway, Kippy, Rod sells decorative pieces. Not the sort of thing Dad buys at all."

The blond girl made a face. "You'll lose a customer, Rod. She's not going to promote your business."

"Never mind, Kippy. I'll see you do all the advertising," he said, and turned his back on her. She had raised a sensitive subject and Cheri hadn't helped. Based on what his uncle had said, I guessed that the great Sebastian fortune was at once desirable and humiliating to him.

Kippy pouted. "No one's in a good mood tonight. We really ought to go somewhere different for a change."

No one took up her idea immediately, although there was an interested murmur, which Cheri quashed. "We *are* going somewhere different," she announced, turning with a flourish. She was just a trifle too much: too quick, too sharp, too made up, too nervous, but her announcement brought an anticipatory shifting of chairs and drinks.

"Rod's going off on his boat, aren't you, darling, and we're going to persuade him to take us all." She made another sweeping gesture, which appeared to take in the entire compound, the party on the lawn, and the revelers down by the pier. Actually, the invitation was clearly for the inner circle only, and I noticed that several guests looked apprehensive, either at the idea itself or at the prospect that they might not be included. Rod appeared annoyed.

"That sounds terrific," someone said, and several of the women began making what could have become very elaborate plans if Rod had not cut them off.

"Sorry. No riders this trip. I told you, Cheri," he added pointedly, "that the engine needs repairs. I've got to take it north." He smiled at the other guests, covering himself with a layer of smooth good humor. "I don't suppose any of you really want to see the Panhandle."

"There's always something wrong with the engine when we want to have fun," Cheri complained, "yet you can make a three-week sail by yourself every other month."

"I use it hard," Rod admitted in a controlled voice. "That's why she needs an overhaul, and why I can't take a party along." When he set his face, he didn't look like an easy man to convince, but Cheri attempted to get around him with a joke.

"You have no imagination! Pensacola, Apalachicola — all those rough sailors and hijackers and smugglers — and with a 'failing' engine — I think it would be fun."

"The sailors might be fun," Hillary said, "but the other two are hard on a party — "

Cheri was not to be put off the track. "So what's wrong with the stupid engine?"

"I'm not sure. It's running very heavy."

"You're far too secretive about that damn boat." She dropped her voice to add, "I'll ask my father; he'll know. He's got an interest in it after all."

This was clearly a high card, and a few of the more discreet guests edged away, as though they were used to sudden quarrels and outbursts.

"It's entirely up to you," Rod replied, his flat voice suggesting he had his own resources. Perhaps they'd been over this ground before, but if he had more to say we didn't hear it, because Hillary began a long and involved story about a run-in he'd had with some Miami crooks. Apocryphal or not, it was enough of a distraction so that Rod and Cheri decided to postpone their disagreement.

"No reliability among thieves," Hillary concluded.

"No reliability period," Rod said. "Listen, I'm sorry about the trip," he continued, turning on the charm, "but this came up at a bad time. You can't imagine the hassle I had today."

"But you'll tell us," Cheri said sarcastically. She was not completely mollified, but she didn't quarrel just for a diversion. I wondered what she'd wanted to discover. That Rod had managed to keep his sailing destinations secret from her suggested an interesting relationship.

"Sally's boyfriend moved to Orlando, and she's going with him — as of this morning."

"My God," someone said in mock horror, "that sounds serious. By the way, who is this Sally?"

"Sally — my assistant — the one who minds the shop, types the letters and keeps the bills straight."

"Oh, Sally who does the work."

"Someone has to."

Rod laughed but he didn't care for their teasing. He was probably the only one in the group who had to earn a living, and money was his weak spot. "Yeah," he said. "And I've got to take the boat up North, and I need someone to replace her. She left everything in a mess, of course, and this is the end of the season."

"Stay home," was Cheri's advice. "You worry too much about that boat."

"Somebody should volunteer to help Rod," the blond girl said, and Cheri shot her a look of real dislike.

"What about you, Kippy, and then the rest of us can go sailing. You were seasick last time anyway, remember, and we had to change the bunk covers." Cheri played rough — there was no doubt about it. But not with Rod. She was clearly fond of him and not in as strong a position as I would have expected. That was interesting, too.

"It blew up a storm!"

"You shouldn't sail if you can't stand a bit of weather."

"Besides, I don't know anything about antiques," Kippy proclaimed with some spirit. "I don't even like that old junk."

"Then there was that time at the regatta. It was really too funny when you fell — "

"Rod needs a typist," the red-haired youth interrupted. "I thought there were agencies — "

"I know someone who could be in your shop tomorrow," I said casually, "if you're really looking for help."

"There you are, Rod!" Kippy said. I had an ally, dubious but enthusiastic. "That's just what you need."

"Yeah?" He looked at me curiously.

"A friend of mine. She's a thoroughly trained secretary, and she's worked for an art gallery. We drove down here together. She's been looking for work, and she doesn't want a business office."

"I am in a bit of a spot," he said carefully.

"So give her a try," Kippy insisted. I wished she'd shut up.

"You have such interesting friends, Hillary," Cheri remarked. "He knows absolutely everyone, doesn't he?" she asked the group.

"But not Anna's friend, I don't think." He glanced at me and raised one eyebrow.

I ignored him. "Just a thought," I said. "People with experience are usually hard to get, but perhaps around here — " I picked up another drink. "Let's go down by the water before it gets any later, Hillary. You really have a beautiful place, Cheri. I'd like to walk around it."

"Don't bother now. You can't see much at this hour. Come back anytime during the day. Someone will always be here to show you around. Besides," she turned on a radiant smile, "I'm ready to shoot some pool. Hillary owes me a rematch."

This was a popular suggestion. Cheri led Hillary and the rest away triumphantly, but Rod lingered behind. He must have been suspicious. Must have been, if Sebastian were behind Hillary's near accident. But he couldn't be sure about me. Perhaps they hadn't mentioned the woman in the car. Or perhaps they hadn't figured she'd have stayed around. He leaned against one of the tables and drained a cocktail glass, his eyes wary and curiously furtive. His confident manner was only one of many, I observed, and there was something elusive about him, as if he had not quite settled into one distinct personality but kept a stock of selves in reserve. After a moment he spoke. "Could your friend come by around twelve-thirty or one? I'm leaving early afternoon."

"I'm sure that would be fine."

"It would maybe only be temporary. I'd want to see if she worked out."

"Of course. She'll appreciate the opportunity. She's hoping to get back into something connected with the arts."

"Good." He stuck his hands in his pockets and rocked casually back on his heels. His bright eyes strayed from my face to the lawn and then out to the Gulf. "Nice of you to mention her," he said.

"Not at all. I'm doing my friend a favor."

"It's difficult sometimes to explain business to people who don't need to work." I got a rueful smile. I was being confided in and subtly flattered.

"I can imagine." He was a most attractive man, but I couldn't help thinking his charm had an ounce of calculation in it, especially when he took my arm in a friendly manner.

"I should go join the game. Won't you come, too?"

"I'll walk back with you, but no pool tonight. I want to see if I can get Hillary mobilized to go home. I didn't bring my car."

"Don't worry. It's early yet, and John seems to enjoy a party."

"That's my impression."

"Well, stick around. You're here to get acquainted, after all."

"Unfortunately, moving entails a lot of work, and I have things to do tomorrow. I can't loaf on the beach all the time."

"No, too bad," he said, as we walked along the side of the house. "What do you think of Florida?"

"Very sunny. It's hard to tell otherwise. How do you like it? You're not a native, are you?"

"No, I haven't lived here too long, either." He released my arm and took a last look at the sea, now a mere luminous band under the stars. "The water's nice," he said cautiously.

"Yes, but otherwise the area strikes me as a bit dull."

"You have to get in with the right crowd."

"You seem to have managed that."

"I'd better put in an appearance at the game," he said, as if on cue. "Sure you won't change your mind?" We had reached the rear terrace, and I could hear the click of sticks and balls, and Cheri's laughter.

"Not tonight, thanks. Ask Hillary to come out, would you?"

He smiled. The request pleased him, perhaps because it would annoy Cheri, who had made a great fuss over Hillary. "See you tomorrow," he said, and disappeared inside. A few minutes later, a tall, thin silhouette appeared, puffing a very fragrant joint. "I'm rather good at pool, you know. Last time we played, I took two hundred dollars off Miss Sebastian."

"We're all familiar with your misspent prime, Hillary."

"Cheri isn't. My picaresque existence is a source of considerable interest to her."

"For itself or for some resemblance to Papa's?"

"There's the Freudian question, but she won't have a chance to confide in me tonight, will she?"

"Sorry, but I've some arrangements to make, and they've got to be finished tonight."

"Rod intends to hire your friend! I wouldn't have believed it. You are persuasive — or he's got a death wish or both. Who is the lucky lady or is that what you're about to arrange?"

"You don't need to know everything, Hillary. Let's just say I have exactly the right person in mind."

Chapter 7

THE PHONE rang in the workshop, once, twice, three times. I had already tried our house without success, and I glanced impatiently at my watch: nine-twenty. Air connections are poor between D.C. and western Florida, and even with the best of luck it was going to be difficult to make Rod's by lunchtime. Come on, come on, I thought, but the wretched machine buzzed monotonously, and I was about to give up when Harry came on the line.

"Hello. Helios Workshop."

"You're keeping late hours."

"Hi, Honey! Where're you calling from?"

"I'm still in Ibis. I must get hold of Baby. Is she there?"

"At this time of night? We don't pay overtime, you know."

He sounded defensive. "What about those curry suppers?" I asked. "And those lunches?"

"Hey, what is this? Who are you checking up on? Baby or me?"

I'd gone a bit too far: Harry was still Harry. So I backed off as gracefully as possible. "I figured you might know where she is."

"I know what you thought. You haven't been away that long. Have I asked you anything about Hillary?"

God bless the righteous. "Not yet."

"How is he anyway?"

"All right at the moment. We were at a party tonight."

"Oh." One of those significant oh's.

"Strictly business."

"Did I say anything?"

Talk about getting off on the wrong foot. Why is it that when
you love someone and miss him and want to say something nice
it never comes out right? I took refuge in business. "Harry, I've
got to reach Baby tonight, okay? Because she's to be on the
early flight into Tampa. Write that down, would you?"

"Who the hell's she working for, you or us?"

"You at the moment, but I really need her, and I've half-
hinted at a job for her."

"Anna!"

"I know, I shouldn't have, but she's a sharp kid. She's really
cut out for the work. And Harry, I've got to have someone I can
trust in a Sarasota job by one tomorrow. Explain to Jan it's only
a loan."

"You'd better talk to him yourself — you know how he is
about — "

"All right, all right. Tell him I'll pay the Kelly girl —
or whoever replaces Baby — and her salary, too. Now, do you
have any idea where she'd be?"

"Try her apartment." Flat and fed up.

"I don't have the number." Ditto.

"Hold on."

I could hear him rummaging through the clutter on his workbench, then a door opened and closed. Finally he returned
sounding more like himself. "Got a problem," he said.

"Not an unlisted number?"

"No, but there are two or three possibilities. She's moved,
and I remember the one time I phoned her, I had to call some
girlfriend's house to reach her."

"Great. Give them all to me. She's got to be down here tomorrow. It's really, really important — maybe for Hillary, too. I'll
explain everything when I get home."

"Listen, why don't I try to call her, while you call Jan?"

That was a good idea, because if he couldn't locate her, he'd probably know one of the printmakers who could. My suspicious nature lifted its ugly head, but fortunately I was able to ignore it and be appreciative. "That would be great. Thanks, dear. So, how are things going?"

"Not too bad. I'm getting set up for tomorrow. We've had a struggle with a new batch of ink that came in, and I'm trying to find the right colors."

He sounded tired. I wished I were home. I'm not good at long distance. "Don't work too hard."

"Naw, you, either. I'll see if I can find Baby. What plane's she to catch?"

"There's a Delta at seven-fifty A.M. that goes through Atlanta. That's the best. It arrives at eleven forty-five, and I'll meet her at the Tampa airport."

"I'd better write that down."

"And clothes. Tell her the most conservative rags she owns. Enough for a couple of days. Got that?"

"Yeah. Anything else?"

"No, I'll fill her in when she arrives. Thanks, Harry. I'll see you in a couple of days, I hope."

"Hurry back — and straighten that out with Jan, will you?"

"I'll do it right now. Good night, dear."

The receiver clicked at the other end. Now I could hear the shredded leaves of the palms swishing against the jalousie windows. The breeze was up, and the lights of the neighborhood bobbed in the black tropical foliage like ships on a rough sea. I was annoyed with myself. Paranoia is useful professionally, but it makes its insidious way into your personal life, and jealousy is its opening gambit. Damn. I shook my head, dialed D.C. again, and spent the next ten minutes on high finance with Jan Gorgon: my bill to Old Brammin was going to be spectacular.

It would have been nice to think my old friend would get his money's worth, but the next morning as I waited for the eleven forty-five to land, I wasn't so certain he would. Plans never look as good in the morning as they do the night before, and when

I saw Baby come padding up the long incline in a Navaho-inspired sundress, I had a moment of real uncertainty. Perhaps this was asking too much — she was, after all, something of an unknown quantity, and the job was not without risk. There would be problems for sure.

"Hiya, Anna."

"How're you doing, Baby?"

She glanced around the crowded, stuffy airport. "This sure is the pits."

"Have you any luggage?"

"Just this." She held up a large tote. "Harry said you'd be in a hurry." I recognized the bag: it was an old leather one that had been lying around the workshop.

"Right. Let's go." I felt marginally better: she could follow directions — even if they were Harry's.

"That was a goddamn early flight."

"No other way. You're to be in Sarasota and ready to go to work within an hour."

"Christ!"

"Provided you're hired."

"I'll be hired. Why shouldn't I be?"

"Well, let me have a look. Drop about five pounds of the jewelry and the top two inches of mascara, put a plain T-shirt on under that serape, and you may pass."

"They give the same shitty advice at Katy Gibbs," Baby said, snapping her gum.

"Also: no gum and not so much as a 'damn' until you're on your way home."

"Who the hell am I working for — the Sisters of Mercy?"

"No, much worse: a fancy antique store with a mobster holding the mortgage. If the clientele doesn't inspire you, just remember the owners. Got that?"

Baby expressed herself on this point, but she chucked the gum and disappeared into the washroom. When I started hollering for her five minutes later, she emerged looking as close to innocent youth as she was able.

"You can work on your hair in the car," I said. "We'll be lucky to make Sarasota by one."

"This guy's a hair fetishist?"

"Alas, no. Sorry to disappoint you, but it's the nice, rich, blue-haired ladies who come to the shop that I'm thinking about. They'll at least expect your hair to be combed."

Baby paused at the car door. "We're getting one thing straight right now: what's in this for me?"

I threw her case into the trunk. "Fifty a day on top of your regular salary, plus all expenses, of course."

"Seventy-five," she countered flatly. "You won't get anyone else on such short notice."

How's that? The kid was a natural. "Fifty. Regard it as a tryout for a better job."

"Seventy-five. You said the mob's involved."

"Fifty. They're only silent partners."

"I don't go for less than seventy-five."

"Fifty, if everything runs smoothly. Seventy-five, if there's trouble."

"A deal," said Baby, and she got into the car. "What do I have to do?"

The Torino's engine turned over with a smooth purr: it was a better machine altogether than my last, unlamented rental. "The first thing you've got to do is to be hired at a place called Key Antiques. Rod Brammin, the owner, is going to be away for a few days and needs a last minute replacement for his assistant. You'll mind the shop, mail the bills, record sales. Nothing more complicated than you do at the workshop."

"No sweat."

"None at all. Did Jan remember to give you that reference letter? There's a couple more in the envelope on the seat. Take them all with you."

Baby flipped through the pages. "My," she said in mock amazement, "you've said some nice things about me."

"I'll mean every word, too, if you can find out how Key Antiques makes its money."

"A little action on the side, huh?"

"The owner's bringing in something from Latin America, probably from the Yucatán or Guatemala. Brammin goes off on long mysterious sailing trips and leaves wooden crates about that are too big to hold anything he sells. I want to find out what he's smuggling and where it's going."

"Boatloads of grass!" Baby said admiringly.

"Possible, but I'm betting against. What I want you to do is to be on the alert for anything that doesn't look right. No matter how trivial. I just can't predict what may turn out to be important. Try to have a look at the books, but don't be surprised if there's nothing there. He will undoubtedly keep a second set that you won't be shown, and I don't want you to take unnecessary risks. Remember that."

"Okay."

"We'll have to pick up on little things — a suspicious customer, bits and pieces of stuff in odd corners, bills that don't make sense. Tell me everything you notice: customers in the shop, deliveries in or out, remarks made. All right?"

Baby dragged a pink comb through her thick, tangled hair. "Yeah. What's this guy like?"

"Tall, dark, and dangerous."

"Ah."

"That is strictly out of bounds. Besides being responsible for your safety, I have a certain professional reputation which you'll protect if you're working for me. Understand?"

"Okay, okay, just a misunderstanding."

"You've seen too many TV shows."

"We can't all be culture freaks," she said.

I didn't dispute the truth of this observation, and while Baby toned down her lion's mane, I fought the traffic between Greater Tampa and St. Armand's Key. By five after one, my new wheels rested a block from the antique shop, and Baby and I were settling the final details of our approach. "You drove South with me, that's important, and you've been scouting the employment agencies."

"Un-huh."

"You're interested in the arts."

She nodded.

"Can you drive?"

"I had driver training."

"Can't be helped. I'll get you a car. You're going to share my apartment in Ibis, so if he asks for your address give him that, but don't volunteer it."

"Why can't I stay at a motel in Sarasota?"

"Because you've supposedly moved down here, and because I want to keep an eye on you — for your own protection."

She checked the shop front and glanced in the windows. "Does this guy trust you?"

"Almost certainly not, so be careful."

"Seventy-five," said Baby, "I can see it's guaranteed," and she pushed open the door. Rod appeared immediately from the back, dressed for the boat in shorts and a sweatshirt. He seemed impatient and on edge, although he immediately composed his handsome face into a smile for our benefit.

"I had almost given up on you," he said.

"We had a flat tire, and neither of us has changed one in years." I introduced Baby. "June Quigley. Rod Brammin."

"How do you do," she said, offering her hand with a shy gesture that was perfect. She had a technique, I must admit. Then she answered questions about her typing and bookkeeping, identified a piece of Sandwich glass and some export porcelain, and very properly admired a fine example of Japanese lacquerwork. Rod was impressed by her knowledge and, I suspect, recognized a fellow adventurer. More important, he was in a hurry. He skimmed the letter I'd extorted from Jan Gorgon, nodded, and said he'd check her other references when he returned. Then he escorted Baby to the back room where an electric typewriter sat amidst a pile of unanswered correspondence.

"You can start on these," he said. "No need to worry about the shop today. One of my friends has come for the afternoon to help." With this he nodded toward Sebastian's male model, who was sitting in a canvas director's chair smoking. When we were introduced, Marcus rose and shook hands lethargically, then slid back to his seat. Except for his frigid eyes, he seemed exhausted, as though the effort of maintaining that perfectly impassive façade were sapping his vitality. I avoided Baby's look, and she went to the desk to begin a businesslike examination of the paperwork.

"What about postage?" she asked.

"There are stamps in this drawer. If you have any other questions ask Marcus. He knows the routine," Rod said, and with a nod to the impassive figure in the chair, he collected his sea bag. "Think you'll manage?"

"No trouble," Baby said. "Can you pick me up, Anna?"

"What time does the shop close?"

"Six," Rod said.

"I'll be here," I promised and followed him out onto the street, where he swung his duffel bag onto his shoulder.

"I think she'll work out," he remarked without looking directly at me. "Thanks. I needed to get away."

"Thank you. She's delighted with the chance."

Brammin's restless eyes wandered down the street to settle on some far distant point. He was in a hurry, yet reluctant to leave. Ten years earlier I would have suspected some attraction of mine; now I recognized indecision. "Nice day for a sail," I remarked.

"Wish I was going farther. Tell June I'll be in on Saturday."

"A quick trip."

"The museum opens Sunday. I'm supposed to be back for that."

"I'd forgotten. That will be quite an occasion."

"It certainly will." He looked at me intently for a few seconds, then smiled. He was an odd mixture of virility and coquetry, a man out of his time, in a way. He would have made a successful courtier at some elegant and dangerous court. "See you then, Anna."

Shifting his sea bag once more, Rod set off rapidly, his head bowed slightly, as if, like Marcus, he was wearied by dancing attendance on the Sebastians.

I was a bit done in myself and decided to have lunch.

Afterward, walking down the bright, hot street toward the car, I heard someone call my name.

"Anna. Anna Peters!"

I didn't recognize the voice, but I remembered the Lamborghini, which slid to a stop beyond an unbroken row of Chryslers and Cadillacs. Cheri stood up and waved, oblivious of the traffic behind her.

"Can you come out today?"

"Today?"

"Didn't you see Rod?"

"Just briefly," I said, squeezing between the parked cars. "He was in a hurry to get away."

"I told him especially to ask you to come out," she said in an exasperated voice. "You'd like to see the grounds, wouldn't you?"

"Very much — if it isn't a bother."

"Not at all. I'm not busy today. Come on."

A brace of horns erupted behind us, and I clambered into the car, which took off like a racehorse, its powerful motor muffled by the Latin music pouring from a quartet of speakers. As we flew across the bridge and keys, gliding like princesses in the sleek silver machine, I decided that men must find Cheri attractive. She was no beauty, but she had what might be as good, a striking, almost eccentric, presence. The wind uncurled her thick dark hair and set it like a pennant behind her. The lavender shirt matched her cool eyes, and as she drove, concentrating on the road and obviously enjoying the car, her high, bare forehead and slightly hooked nose created a clean, intriguing profile. Add a couple of million dollars, and it wasn't hard to understand why Rod Brammin was interested. Her response to him was a touch less predictable, and while I considered this, conversation lagged, but pleasantly. Idle chatter was replaced by the rushing wind that thinned out the monotonous pulsations of the music until we reached the narrow road up the base of the key. The big pastel houses glittered in the brilliant ocean light, and what had seemed a jungle at night was now revealed as a thin screen of wind-ravaged palms behind which the Gulf lay in gold and silver bands.

"Have you known John Hillary a long time?" Cheri asked.

"Yes, a long time."

"From before he was married, you mean?"

"Oh, yes. I knew him up North, and he's lived in Florida for several years now."

"That's right. He's a fascinating man."

"He'd be pleased to hear you say that."

"No, I mean it. He knows so many people, he can get on with so many different types."

"A man of the world."

"Do you know his wife?"

"I've met her. She seems very nice."

Cheri was noncommittal. "I don't know her."

"You haven't known him too long, though, have you?"

"I met him at a party — oh, when was it? Well, just after that TV special. Did you see it?"

"Yes."

"Some of my college friends are very into the Third World. They all watched it, of course. They thought it should have taken a more Marxist analysis."

"Of murder?"

She hesitated. "Murder?"

"The tomb guards were killed."

"They're a part of the overall picture. I mean, exploitation is the real issue, isn't it? I agree with that," she added quickly. "But he didn't do too badly. To tell the truth, my friends were terribly impressed with meeting Hillary."

"Was this at one of your parties?"

"I don't remember." She frowned slightly as if that were a question she'd like answered. "There are so many, but I don't think it was at our house. Anyway, he was there, and he's quite a lion when he wants to be." She gave a quick, impish grin. She was more into Society than the Third World, and, like most good hostesses, she bagged her lions whenever the chance presented itself.

"He's done a piece on the museum, too, hasn't he?"

"Oh, that! Yes, it's funny, isn't it, my father doesn't care for him, but Hillary's still the only reporter he's ever really talked to."

"How do you know your dad doesn't like him?"

"He doesn't like reporters. Daddy isn't a publicity seeker. I've had a hard time convincing him to do anything in the community. It's really just since his illness — he's had cancer, you know."

"Yes, I had heard. I'm sorry."

"He sees I can't stand sitting at home. And isn't it foolish to let this go to waste?" she added, as the Lamborghini swept around a final corner, revealing the house and gardens moored amidst an ocean of lawn on which sprinklers were sending up rainbow arcs to preserve the opulent green. There was a pervasive rotten egg smell from the sulfur-laden water, but the house looked even more impressive than it had at night, standing bleached and monumental in the burning white light. With the day, the lush vegetation seemed to have retreated behind the high pink walls of the garden, where rampant and multihued, it was gathering its forces to engulf the noble tile-and-stucco structure.

"That's quite a building. Is it old?"

"Fairly — by Florida standards. It's from the thirties, but the Italianate style is old enough. The details are quite authentic; the original owners brought back cornices and columns from Rome and had copies made. And then they went Spanish on the sides."

"It fits together though. And it's withstood storms all that time."

"Obviously. We're on the wide part of the key here, though.

Some of the newer houses are much more vulnerable." She parked the car below the terrace next to a Silver Cloud, and the chauffeur waiting beside it jumped to open the door.

"Daddy hasn't gone out yet?"

"No, Miss Sebastian."

A brief frown, of annoyance or anxiety. "I'll see him tonight."

"I'll tell him, Miss."

"We'll start with the garden," she said to me. "This place has been on the House Tour a number of times, and everyone really likes the garden best." Her smile was quick and bright and perhaps a trifle nervous, but she could be charming when she chose. Cheri knew how to focus all her attention on a person, and few can resist this rare form of flattery. And then she was thoughtful, taking pains to point out what might interest her guest: a rare hibiscus in the garden, the little Velásquez infanta in the hall, a mechanical clock with moving figures in the library. "It doesn't work anymore," she said, running her fingers over the glass bell. "Daddy used to wind it for me. The waves would come up and move the boats." She looked at me over the transparent dome for an instant then moved on to point out other treasures, the perfect guide. Unlike some of her young friends, I sensed a purpose behind this attention, and I suspected that it was the same one that lay behind her fascination with Hillary. What she hoped to discover, I had no idea, but Cheri struck me as a sort of social chemist, searching for the right human ingredient to add to some compound of her own devising.

"Are you interested in antique cars?" she asked when we emerged from the house.

"Not especially."

"Me, neither. I'll spare you that."

We stood talking for a minute by the door, and I noticed a building I hadn't spotted before. In the foliage beyond the garden was an asymmetric brick tower with what might have been a fancifully interpreted battlement. "What is that building?"

"Construction," Cheri corrected. "It's actually a sculpture."

"It looks like a tower."

"I'll show you inside. There's an artist over on the East Coast who's been building those things for years. Dad bought a design that would be large enough for a room and turned it into a chapel." That touch of religious extravagance seemed to please her. "Sounds medieval, doesn't it?"

"A little."

"Not that he's religious, but I suppose a lot of people who built chapels weren't. He uses it as his own secret place. Of course, he's always insisted I go to Mass."

"Parents have been known to do that." Sebastian must have quite an appetite for solitude, if even the immense and isolated mansion were not private enough for him.

At the bottom of the garden, Cheri brushed aside the soft tentacles of the vines and unlatched a metal grille. A white sand path wound between the palms, cactus, and palmettos to the structure, which, set in a clump of Florida pines, had been cleverly placed so that the full effect of the building was reserved until you were almost upon it. Basically, it was an oval tower, larger on one side than the other, and decorated with a nonfunctional battlement and a rounded dome top that had been left half unfinished to suggest a ruin. The trees had been pruned to give the modestly scaled construction an illusion of greater height and, standing alone at the edge of the wood, the tower made a curiously evocative addition to the landscape, suggesting some Provençal or Moorish relic and hinting at other architectural associations I could not immediately identify.

"It reminds me of a ziggurat," Cheri said, pointing to a decorative band that ran up the sides like a ramp.

"Half-pyramid and half-tower," I suggested.

"Whatever it is, Daddy's very fond of it," she said, trying the narrow door. "We're in luck. Ordinarily it's locked. Daddy is very fussy about visitors in the chapel, but we can take a peek if I can find the light."

High in the tower wall some irregular openings sent shafts of light into the shallow, semicircular room, illuminating a

dark wood carving of the Virgin that stood against the rear
wall. A single black wooden chair and a tapestry hanging behind the statue completed the furnishings. I was surprised both
by the asceticism of the room and by its size and shape.

"I can't seem to find the light."

"Never mind, it's easy enough to see."

"Oh, here it is." She snapped on a ring of recessed spotlights
in the pointed buff ceiling. I commented on how tiny the room
seemed in comparison with the bulk of the total building.

"That's one of the things Daddy liked about it, but the size
is pure accident, a consequence of the structural design. The
artist usually makes them solid and smaller. The frame had to
be reinforced as it was," she said, indicating the steel ribs showing against the brickwork.

"It must have been fun to watch it going up."

"I suppose. I was away in Europe at the time. I'd hoped it was
to be a playhouse, but instead it's out of bounds."

"A nice setting for the statue, though."

"Seventeenth-century Burgundian, I think."

"Late sixteenth century." The voice behind us breathed
rather than spoke, the words issuing with a harsh, metallic
sound as if an air current were being forced through the bris-
tles of a metal brush. Vlad Sebastian had come soundlessly
down the path to stand just outside the door. He was dressed
as if for a meeting in a light gray suit, and he leaned on an
elegant cane with a heavy ivory handle. Despite his small size
and an appearance of delicate emaciation, there was something
commanding about his figure. His head had gone all to bone
with his illness, and pain had furrowed two long trenches that
ran from just below his pouched eyes to the wrinkled line of his
jaw. Perhaps to hide some scars of the disease, he wore a white
turtleneck in the intense heat, but his most striking feature
was the pair of large yellowish eyes set deep in his worn gray
face. They surveyed his own wreckage and everything else with
a stony, reptilian detachment.

Cheri seemed startled to see him, but I feigned innocence and
remarked on the beauty of the sculpture.

Without replying, Sebastian stepped carefully over the threshold. His legs were stiff, and I realized that the cane was by no means an affectation.

"Cheri doesn't often bring visitors here." He turned to his daughter, a question in his eyes.

"Anna asked about the building," she replied. "This is my father, Anna. Daddy, this is Anna Peters, a friend of John Hillary's."

The old man stared at us both with his flat, unblinking eyes. He struck me as being at once intellectually curious and emotionally indifferent.

"You remember John," Cheri began, but he waved his hand irritably.

"You will excuse me," he said, "I have an appointment and I would like a little time here first."

I glanced at my watch. "I should be going. Thank you for showing me around, Cheri." I nodded to the old man as I passed.

"I'll see you at dinner," she said to her father, then she joined me on the path.

"I hope we didn't disturb him."

She shrugged. I had the feeling she dealt with him cautiously, but from policy, not fear. "There's nothing around there," she remarked when I walked toward the back of the building.

"I'm curious about how the top was finished off." I smiled. I was trying to smile a lot, like a proper architectural enthusiast. There were no openings on the far side, just a sheer, smooth curve of brick. Behind us, the door of the chapel closed, and Cheri seemed vaguely annoyed or perhaps puzzled. I had the sense that she had just made a new move in some obscure contest between them, and I was not surprised to find her hospitality running short.

"I suppose you'll want to get back into town." It was a conclusion, not a supposition. I was the counter that had been deployed, and now I was no longer useful.

"Yes. I promised to pick up my friend after work. She doesn't have a car yet."

"You must bring her along this weekend. I'll see you get an extra ticket. We're going to have a party in honor of the opening. After all, she's enabled Rod to go off on that important business of his."

"He said he'd be back on Saturday."

"Of course. My father expects him here. Daddy doesn't like to be disappointed," she said, with a slow, cold smile.

When she smiled like that, Cheri very much resembled her sinister parent.

Chapter 8

"JESUS H! " Baby said as she dumped the saddlebag that held her indispensables onto the table.

I looked up from the stove. "A hard day?"

She elaborated. Under the profanity, I glimpsed that Marcus was the root of her grievance.

"Has he been bothering you?"

"Bothering me! They'd have to dissect him to find life." She sat down, her bracelets clattering against the Formica top. "What the hell's for supper?"

"Cold soup and a steak. Think you can manage that?"

She made a face and began picking bits out of the salad. "An awful lot of cholesterol. You ought to try some of that health food shit."

"That's just how it strikes me." I snapped open the broiler and turned the meat. Why is it that good investigators are so often prima donnas? At her age, I ate anything.

"You buy any mangoes?"

"In that paper bag."

Baby walked to the counter, her sandals slapping on the floor, with a soft, slovenly sound that annoyed me. Nothing. Four days, and nothing has turned up. Nothing at all. She rummaged in the bag and examined the fruit. "You ought to try these," she said.

"You ought to wash them. You'll get some kind of stomach crud."

"You never know who's been handling them," Baby sneered in a prim, nasty voice, an echo, I assumed, of the aunt who seemed to have mixed her up pretty well, and took a large bite. Then she went to the icebox. "Only one cruddy beer?"

"I don't drink them."

She didn't pursue the conversation but stood at the window, staring out over the courtyard.

"Were you followed?"

"Nope."

"Don't worry then." When I'd accepted Old Brammin's job I hadn't realized it would entail being cook and nursemaid for a troubled kid. I wasn't cut out for youth counseling. "Have some dinner."

Baby sat down. She didn't like soup, but despite the cholesterol she could do justice to beef. "Any more?"

"Finish it."

"I'll have some ice cream," she said when we were done.

"Help yourself."

"I'd rather have butter pecan."

"Buy some tomorrow."

"I'll need money."

Baby preferred her fee daily. She did not have what you could call classy manners. I handed over another fifty.

"You never carry small bills?"

"I came prepared."

She stuck the money in her pocket, dished out the ice cream, then sighed in resignation when I took out my notebook and pen. "Not a goddamn thing today," she said.

"Let me be the judge of that."

"All right, all right. Marcus was there when I arrived."

"What time was that?"

"Quarter of eleven."

"What does he do all day?"

"Not a — " I looked up. "Not a thing. Marcus sits in the back room and watches."

"Does he handle the customers?"

"He let me do that today."

"So he stayed in the back?"

"Yes."

"Were you alone in the office?"

"No way."

"But you are in the front of the shop?"

"Yeah. I disturbed the dust." Baby pantomimed a dainty operation with a feather duster.

"No sign of a second storeroom or closet or anything like that?"

"I told you yesterday, what you see is what there is. The storeroom at the side is half-empty."

I flipped back to my notes from the previous day, but I hadn't forgotten anything. The storeroom housed a workbench and tools, lumber, and several chests and bureaus. Baby had managed to examine the furnishings on pretext of admiring the fittings, but found nothing in them.

"He's creepy. I can't stand him. He just sits there."

"That's what he's being paid to do. Brammin and his friend aren't sure about us."

"It would have been easier to close the shop."

"That might have raised other questions."

"I doubt it," Baby said. "We sold only two things today."

"You hadn't mentioned that. What did you sell?"

"A figurine of a monkey."

"Hollow?"

"And empty."

"What else?"

"An old sword."

I jotted this down without enthusiasm. If Marcus lurked in the back room all day, any clues to Brammin's or Sebastian's involvement must be there. "No sign of straw or grass — I mean, real meadow grass?"

"I'll look."

"Check the storeroom." I wished I had heard the report on the straw sample I'd sent off. Probably the university botany department couldn't tell me much about it, but it was worth trying. Baby appeared discouraged. "Something will turn up." I said, "Now we'll go through the day. You arrived at quarter to eleven —"

That was about the time that I had met Henry Brammin. He was no happier than other clients who have had to wait for their information. We sat on a bench and watched the sea while I explained Baby's fortuitous employment.

"Not quite above board," he commented.

"Neither is smuggling."

"You haven't proved that yet."

"Haven't proved anything, but your nephew is entangled financially with Sebastian, and I'm convinced that he is paying off his obligations in kind. There is no other explanation." I described the party at the Sebastians' and told him I had found the old station wagon in their garage.

"That's what I was afraid of."

"Your nephew returns on Saturday. We should know by then what he's handling. After that you can decide what to do."

"What about Sebastian?"

I summarized what I had learned from Hillary and from a long series of telephone calls to Chicago, Boston, and New York. Brammin shook his head when I mentioned the collector's purported original surname. "Never heard of it," he said.

"Anyone ever mention if Sebbie R. was Rumanian?"

"I assumed he was East European and Jewish."

"He raised Cheri a Catholic, but then he seems to have gone to considerable lengths to eradicate his past."

"The only thing against this fellow is his reaction to meeting me."

"Yes. Apparently he overreacts to any sign of interest." I mentioned Hillary's difficulties, and Brammin sighed.

"We seem to have stirred up a fine mess." He stood up, sat down, twitched off his hat, and made up his mind. "I'm going to see Sebastian. You've given me enough information already. I won't continue this cloak and dagger business. There's been too much of that already. I'll tell Sebastian I'll settle Rod's debts and put the boy on a sound financial footing. That's the last thing I'll do for Rod."

"You don't think you'd better consult your nephew first?"

"This will be between Sebastian and me. I want an end to this; it will be worth the money."

"Take a good lawyer with you and don't meet at Sebastian's house."

He nodded briskly. "I'll invite him to my lawyer's office. I think he'll come, what with his museum opening."

"And he'd settle for sure if you knew what he was buying."

"We'll have to do without that. This has gone on long enough. You were nearly hurt; you've had to employ someone in Rod's shop. I want my nephew out of this business now. You can't deal with these people with their weapons. This has nothing to do with a lack of confidence in you or with the cost, Anna. I appreciate what you've done."

I was afraid he might be taking a bigger risk than he realized. "I'll tell you what," I said. "There's still another two days before Rod is due back. If Baby leaves before then, they'll be suspicious. I'll pick up the tab for the next couple of days if you'll postpone seeing Sebastian."

Brammin thought this over. "Very well, but I intend to call him late tomorrow afternoon and set up a meeting for the next day."

"All right, fair enough. We'll find something more, I'm sure of it."

"So am I," my old friend said, "but two days is all. I'm not willing to wait any longer for bad news."

The next morning, Baby departed for work, leaving dirty breakfast dishes in the sink, piles of cosmetics in the bathroom, and cigarette butts everywhere. I closed the door to the kitchen, threw away all the ashtrays, and dialed D.C. After spending some time on my neglected business, I turned to the baffling matter of Vlad Sebastian. I was just about to contact the

Sarasota land records office for more information on his real estate speculations when the phone rang.

"Hiya. Anna?" It was Baby.

"Yes."

"How about lunch? Just us girls."

That was the sort of phrase Baby never used. Someone was listening. "Ladies' lunch? Sounds like fun."

She giggled. "You can treat."

"My pleasure. What time?"

"Marcus says one-thirty. Is that okay?"

"I'll pick you up."

She was waiting in front of the shop, doing the crossword in the morning paper, and, instead of crumpling it into her bag, she set the Sarasota *Herald-Tribune* carefully on the seat between us. "I think I've found what you're looking for."

I stabbed on the brakes and reached for the newspaper.

"Underneath. I hid it in the paper. It's a bill from Gulf-Line Marine Warehouses in Apalachicola. It's so enormous, I almost showed it to Marcus, thinking it was a mistake."

At the first traffic light I had a look. "Whew! How long has the stuff been stored? See if you can tell while I find a place to pull over."

"Five weeks, but there's a carry-over. It looks as if he's had a balance for a while. It's one of those Xeroxed bills that they take right off the ledger."

There was a fried chicken restaurant ahead, and I made a sharp turn into the lot, stopping by the public phone booth near the curb to examine the bill. "I think this is it. Go get something to eat, Baby. Here." I handed her money, then dived for the phone.

"Gulf-Line Marine Warehouses."

"I'm calling from Key Antiques with regard to our latest bill. I think there must have been some mistake."

The woman in the office checked and assured me that everything was in order. I insisted on speaking to the manager.

"What do you mean a mistake? Do you know how many tons

of stuff you've had sitting here? I don't care what you're selling, lady, these ain't no trinkets. Two compartments he's taking up. Yeah."

I checked the tonnage.

"Yeah, at least a couple. I ain't kidding ya. Them machine parts weigh — "

"Machine parts?"

"That's what it says on the label. Hold on a minute, I'll check."

He was back in a few minutes. "Don't worry about that bill," he said affably. "It's all settled. We got a new girl in the billing department who'd already sent out the charge, but it's been taken care of. That load went out Tuesday night."

Damn! We were two days late. "And the bill's been paid?"

He laughed. "You don't take it away until you've paid for it. Key Antiques, right?"

"That's right. If Mr. Brammin took care of it himself, that's fine. It was Mr. Brammin?"

"That's what he called himself. If he's got the money and the receipt, he gets the goods."

Several tons of machine parts, huh? That's why Rod had gone north, but whatever was in those boxes wasn't machinery. I glanced over at the fried chicken stand where Baby was working her way through a box of the Colonel's best, while a man with too many muscles and not enough shirt attempted to attract her attention. Not machine parts at all: in an instant, I made the connections. I had Rod Brammin, all right, but Hillary was in serious trouble, and as fast as I could find the number, I dialed the paper.

"Newsroom." Over the man's voice, typewriters clattered like a troop of cavalry.

"John Hillary, please."

He set down the phone and yelled. "Hillary in?" "Naw, he's not in yet."

"Do you expect him today?"

"He's part time. He may be here later."

"If he comes in, ask him to call Anna Peters immediately. Yes, P-e-t-e-r-s. Don't let him leave. Tell him it's important."

The man gave a bored assent.

"He's to speak to me before he goes home."

"Has there been an accident or something?"

"I hope not," I said, hung up, and dialed the house. The phone only rang twice, and when someone lifted the receiver without speaking, I was pretty sure Hillary had company. "Is Mr. Boycott home?"

"Who?" It was an American voice.

"Mr. Boycott at three-six-six — five-one-five — "

"Nope, wrong number." The connection was broken abruptly. I listened to the line buzz, aware that the phone booth was stifling and that the black asphalt sea around the chicken bar was shimmering with an almost hallucinatory light. A friend, a casual acquaintance? Possible. Hillary, as Cheri said, knew all sorts of people. How long to get to his house? I searched my bag for the map. Not there. I ran to the car, found the map in the glove compartment, and flopped it open on the hood. Hillary's place was at the back of beyond. Where the hell am I anyway? I thought, squinting to decipher the street sign. If the man wasn't a passing acquaintance, he was probably not alone. Sebastian's people worked in pairs. I traced the network of streets: it was a long way and even if I got there in time I wasn't sure exactly what I could manage. None of the possibilities looked good, and I returned to the phone and dialed the local police.

"Police Department, Sergeant Leroy Morris."

Under the circumstances, it wasn't too hard to sound frantic. Taking a deep breath I screamed, "I think we got a rabid dog."

"Where're you calling from?"

"It's acting very strange, shaking his head, and its eyes look funny."

"Where is this, m'am?"

I gave him the street, but not a house address. "It's a big black German shepherd, drooling, too. What? It's down by our neighbor's house. The Hillarys'. Fifty-three. Yes, yes, I can see it now. You've got to hurry, the children will be back from school any minute."

"Your name, please."

"Oh, it's gone out of sight! It's in the next yard. I'll see if I can keep an eye on it." And with this, I dropped the phone on the policeman's questions, advice, and directions, and turned to the next problem. "Baby!"

"Coming."

Should I risk letting her return to the shop? Not if Sebastian's goons were at Hillary's. But what if I'd jumped to the wrong conclusion? There was danger for everybody in spooking them now.

"Any luck?"

"We hit the jackpot. You've done a good job."

Baby grinned. "What now?"

I took out another twenty-five dollars. "Your fee goes up."

"They know about me?"

"Not yet, but they may find out. I'm not sure if this is a false alarm or not. Can you make an excuse to get out of the shop this afternoon?"

"Sure."

"If there's a problem, I'll call you and ask about some article in the shop. You get yourself out of there, grab your car, and drive straight to the airport. Don't even pick up your clothes, just get on the first plane out and make a connection in Atlanta. Don't delay."

Baby nodded.

"Understand?"

"Sure."

"Good. Get in quick and I'll take you back."

I dropped her at the corner of the boulevard. She looked like a little gypsy amid the glossy shop fronts and option-laden cars, and I had to remind myself that she was tough and capable.

Hillary was the more immediate problem. I tried not to worry about him as I sped over the causeway, cutting recklessly from one lane to another, until I reached the mainland and the traffic backed up. Sarasota had been built in layers, adding the outer green and blue and white ring of the luxurious waterfront gardens, beaches, and condominiums to the acres of tinted glass and revolving signs and architectural incongruities of the shopping areas; which not so many years before had been tacked onto the faded pastels of the old districts, with their peeling billboards and shabby shops and street corners where tired men drank beer and soda pop. I took some wrong turns there, but finally the streets led into the trees and grass and bungalows of the suburbs, and I found the ramshackle neighborhood with the overgrown yards. The edge of the road was coated with white sand, there were bare patches on the lawns, and, over everything, the heat laid a somnolent curtain, silencing even the dogs. Sixty-five, sixty-three. The next few mailboxes were uncommunicative. There it was. I recognized the flower tubs. No cars. I turned in a drive farther down the street and parked next to an empty lot. Chickens clucked in the scrub and the lush strings of a studio orchestra announced an afternoon soap opera. I hesitated for a moment, then crossed to the house.

The Hillarys' front door was under an overhang of the roof and further shaded by a clump of leathery greens resembling a monster philodendron. I glanced over my shoulder to check if the neighbors had noticed my arrival, but except for a boy on a bike there seemed to be no one around. Still I delayed, apprehensive, then gently turned the handle. The door swung open soundlessly. Inside there was no movement, no suspicious step or rustle but something had gone wrong. There was broken glass in the hallway where a picture had been ripped from the wall and smashed, and water and earth where a flower pot had been upended. When I crossed the hall, I felt sick. The living room had been destroyed, couches and chairs overturned, pillows slit, mirrors smashed, curtains torn. Hunks of plaster had been gouged from the walls, the books had been dumped from the cases near the fireplace, and tiles smashed on the floor. The dining room was littered with broken glass and splintered wood, and, beyond the archway, the kitchen floor was awash in the contents of the icebox and cupboards. Eggs and eggshells dripped down one wall and dishes and glasses lay shattered over the countertops. On the table, still intact, two bottles of bourbon, both open, one half-empty, added a sharp alcohol scent to the odor of souring milk.

I picked my way through the rubble to the bedroom. The bureau drawers had been emptied but the destruction was not nearly so complete. They had either been disturbed or successful. The adjoining bathroom was a mess of shattered glass and oily fluids, and in the sink, scarlet and unmistakable, was a spatter of fresh blood. One of the bastards had gotten cut, I hoped, but the conjunction of blood, glass, and destruction raised other fears. I tore through the bedroom, opened the closet, peered under the bed, then checked the guest room. I thought I heard a sound, stopped, and lifted one of the blinds. The window glass was hot, the silent yard outside edged green and purple with the shadows of the trees and the half-enclosed shed that served as garage and storage. I dropped the shade and ran, skidded on the slime of egg and milk in the kitchen, grabbed the countertop to keep from falling. I remembered a hundred little things about Hillary, how much I'd liked him, how much he still amused me, how much he'd been able to do with his life. I found myself swearing — and bleeding, too, because one of the sharp china shards was sticking into my palm. I withdrew it and licked off the wound then, leaning against the wall for balance, made my way out of the wreckage of Hillary's home by the unlatched screen door. Had they left that way? There was no sign, and I hurried to the shed. A clutter of garden equipment, mowers, rakes, shovels, a pair of water skis, a broken-down boat dolly, and all the usual detritus of suburban life formed an obstacle to a wide closet fronted with sliding doors. These were half-open and protruding from one corner were a pair of sandals affixed to a very long pair of legs.

"Oh my God! Hillary, what's happened to you?"

Clearing a mower, a rake, and something that serrated my ankle, I grabbed the nearest foot and pulled. There was a sudden clunk and a clatter and a couple of years of old *Geographics* fell in a white and yellow avalanche. Hillary raised his hand to his head with a groan.

"Hillary!"

"If you'd let go of my foot, I could get out of this damn hole."

I released him. "Are you all right?"

"I was until I fractured my skull on that board." He crawled from under the bottom part of the closet, straightened up, and aimed a vicious kick at the shelf, which obligingly collapsed, spilling a mildewed volume of the *Encyclopaedia Britannica* and dislodging a palmetto bug. Hillary wiped his face. He had not quite lost his usual sangfroid, but he was plenty shaken. "Well, old girl. I didn't hear you come in. I thought the goons had come back." As he spoke, he slipped a narrow envelope into his shirt pocket.

"Was that what they were after?"

"Hmmmm? Oh this? The hand is not always quicker than the eye. Yes, I'd guess it is. Part of it anyway. Have you been inside?"

I nodded. "I'm sorry."

"Thorough chaps. They'd have found it if they'd gotten this far."

"They were interrupted."

"So I assumed."

"The police appeared. A rabid dog scare."

"I hope it wasn't a Dalmatian; Max is very fond of his."

"A large, dark German shepherd, last seen in your yard."

"I'll be on the lookout. How did you happen to know?"

"When I called your house, a stranger answered."

"And why did you call?"

I produced the bill. "Baby found this at work today. There's only one heavy item Rod could import that would connect with you."

"Not too bad, although it took you a few days."

Hillary has never been willing to give me much credit. "You, I suppose, knew earlier."

"I suspected earlier, and I knew this morning. This noon to be exact." He took out his wallet and produced a letter. "I shouldn't have been reading your mail, but you didn't tell me there was anything in the station wagon."

I snatched the letter. It was from the university botany department. The grasses were of a distinct type, indigenous to certain regions of Guatemala and Yucatán. "Q.E.D."

"I had stopped by your apartment," he explained.

"And I'd left a message for you at the paper." I folded the letter. Some birds fluttered through the shrubbery, and we both stood still, listening. I could hear my heart whispering in my ear. Hillary placed his hand on my shoulder. "Are you all right?"

"Just scared. There was blood in the bathroom."

"Not mine, I am happy to report." His voice wavered a little, and I put my arm around him. He leaned his head against mine for a few seconds. "I don't know how I'm going to tell Terry."

That brought back present problems. "You'd better tell her fast and have her contact her cousin or whatever he is on the police force. And I must call Baby."

"Then," said Hillary, "I think we'd better get the hell out of here."

Chapter 9

HILLARY took a cup from the litter on the counter and held it to the light. The thin china was translucent and delicately patterned: probably a wedding gift. He sat it with sad care on the sill and began sweeping the shattered remnants of the set into the trash, when he noticed the bottles on the table. He lifted one, sniffed it, then poured a little into the china cup and examined it critically. I was anxious, but said nothing.

"What do you suppose is in this?" He held out the cup.

"It smells fine." I went to take a sip, but Hillary stopped me.

"I wouldn't drink any of that, if I were you. Of course, they no doubt know it's poison to me anyway, but no point in taking chances." He gave a bitter smile and tipped the bottle, empty-ing the bourbon into the sink. "You didn't think I could do that, did you? But right now, I'd far rather find those bastards than get drunk." He started dumping the second bottle and added, "The phone's in the hall — if it's still connected."

I found it on the floor, replaced the receiver, and dialed Key Antiques, hoping this wasn't the day Marcus decided to exert himself.

"Key Antiques, may I help you?"

"There's been some trouble, Baby. Remember I'm a customer calling. Pay attention and answer with something about the shop."

"Yes, I'm new, but I think you have the right place."

"Leave as soon as you can. I'll send on your clothes."

"We'll be open the usual hours tomorrow," Baby said, "but we're closing early today."

"Is that for real?" I asked quickly.

"Yes."

"Marcus' idea?"

"Yes, that's right. Come by tomorrow — "

"Someone called him?"

"Yes."

"Go right to the airport and see you aren't followed."

"Very good," she said in a smooth saleslady voice.

"Be sure to let Harry know when you get back, because I'll call him."

"Isn't that the truth," Baby said, "prices keep rising all the time." With this hint she said good-by. As long as Baby kept her mind on profits, she wouldn't have any trouble with her nerves.

I called Old Brammin next, but my friend was already out on the course.

"He just began his round fifteen, twenty minutes ago," the starter said.

"Would you leave a message that I called? And ask him to wait for me?"

There was a fiddling and fussing at the other end. My eyes wandered across to the ruined living room, then to a few pieces of glass near the toe of my shoe and a note pad on the floor. I picked it up. The top sheet of paper was gone, but the ball-point pen had dug through to the lower layers. Curious, I held a page up to the light and discovered that my name and address had been on the pad. It was a good thing I'd warned Baby not to stop by the apartment.

The starter returned. I spelled my name for him twice, reiterated the message's importance, and hung up.

"Your turn, Hillary."

No answer. I waded back to the kitchen, where he was attempting to coax a covey of egg yolks onto a dustpan. I closed the open icebox door and started picking glass from mounds of mustard, butter, and mayonnaise. "I'll do some of this; you'd better call Theresa."

"I'm postponing that as long as possible."

I threw the empty milk cartons in the trash and scraped two smashed tomatoes from the linoleum. Really this was ridiculous. "What are we doing this for?" I asked. "We've got to call the police — we can't remove half the evidence."

Hillary shrugged. "This will smell."

"And I've got to drive back to Ibis, but I'll help you clear this mess later. The police will be done by that time."

He paused for a moment. "I thought we'd try for that cargo," he said, overly casual. "You could get the money, couldn't you?"

"I'd thought of that, but we're two days late. Brammin — or someone — has already picked it up. The *Melody* is due in tomorrow, and probably the crates are safe in her hold."

"We don't have the evidence, then."

"I have enough to tell my client, and this disaster should satisfy you. You'd better call the police, warn your wife, and find somewhere safe until — "

He cut me off. "My idea is that we'll find Rod Brammin's cargo, preferably on Sebastian's property."

"That's your thought, huh?"

"Yes."

"And you propose to straighten this mess, tell Theresa there was a slight earth tremor, and pretend nothing else happened?"

"I believe I can link Sebastian's contacts to the murders in Guatemala. Wrong — I'm convinced I can — if we get the goods."

"A big 'if' — and I have my client's interests to consider. This isn't going to be a pleasant surprise for him."

"On the other hand, there are worse surprises."

"Meaning?"

"Ahhh!" said Hillary. Tipping the dustpan at precisely the right angle, he sloshed up a glob of albumen and milk, which he propelled neatly into the sink. "Meaning that Rod Brammin and I share an unfortunate ability: we can connect Mr. Vladimir Sebastian, collector *extraordinaire,* with a crew of jungle cutthroats who hack the glyphs off Mayan stelae and coincidentally murder state monument guards. Now, if they'd found my photographs, which presumably record something significant, there would be only one link between Sebastian and the men who haul the statues to the *Melody.*" Hillary ran water in the sink, wet a sponge, and began to sop up the milk on the floor. "Things are going to get sticky now, and the question for them is, can they trust Rod any more than they can trust me?"

Precisely. "And don't forget the other question: will they try to prevent you from publishing your story now that they've tipped you off?"

Hillary worked diligently on the floor. "We were discussing your client."

"They may be back."

"Most likely." He wrung out the sponge.

"You'd do better with a bucket."

"You always were full of good ideas."

"I hope *you* have some," I said. "Suppose your wife returns unexpectedly? She won't be happy, and, worse yet, she won't be safe. She must be warned and you've got to get your ass out of here."

I thought for a moment I'd triggered an explosion of bad temper, but I was wrong. Hillary leaned back on his heels and said, "Max has a place — a shack in the interior near one of the ranches. He worked out that way when he first came from Jamaica. I can stay there."

"Until when?"

"Until you let me know that the stones have arrived at Sebastian's."

"All I have to do is to stick around, observe Rod, and locate Sebastian's very private collection."

"*You're* the expert," he said. There has always been a certain rivalry between Hillary and me, a sense of competition, which ultimately made any intimate relationship unstable. "I'm quite willing to do my bit if something strenuous is required," he continued, "but until then, I'd only attract the undesirables. As for my house, I'll ask our neighbor to phone the police. Terry and I will simply be out of town."

"They'll contact Terry's family in Miami."

"I'll call her, I'll call her. But it's not really very easy to know what to say." He looked around regretfully. Yes, this was bad luck. She had helped him to become strong and sober, and then his virtues had destroyed their home and endangered them both.

"There's no other way," Hillary continued. "What would you tell the police? That Rod Brammin's been storing heavy boxes in an Apalachicola warehouse and that Vlad Sebastian has a mysterious past and a love of art, and therefore one or both of them has begun a vendetta against you and me? Be reasonable. Vlad Sebastian is important around here. Unless we can go to the police with a statue in our hands and all the steps filled in, they won't be sympathetic, especially since Sebastian's crowd has gone to some effort to discredit me. That's what the bottles were left for — I'm supposed to have done this myself." Despite his calm voice, Hillary was compressing his anger into determination. "Even if the story breaks," he added, "you know who'll be blamed."

I did indeed. "Rod Brammin."

"Right. And that's what you'd better tell your client. His young friend travels with tough company."

That was on my list. "Tell me one other thing, Hillary. You wrote my address down by your phone the other day, didn't you?"

"Was it still there?"

"No. That seems to be the one thing they got."

He let out a sigh.

"So how big is this hut in the woods?" I asked.

"Not big enough," he snapped. I gathered this was one thing he would not tell Terry.

"We'll worry about that later," I said, because Hillary simply had to be moved. "Let's visit your neighbor."

He chucked the sponge in the sink, took a last unhappy survey, and went into the bedroom. When he returned he had his shaving kit, a toothbrush, and a jacket. "Mosquitoes," he explained and, without another word, went out. Around the side of the garage, we squeezed past a row of white-skinned punk trees, avoided a thorny cluster of shrubbery, and entered a neat, square yard with a swing set in one corner and a big Dalmatian tied to a clothes line. The dog barked and wagged its tail, until Hillary went over to quiet it down. A tall, thin woman with a skin like chocolate velvet and elegant hands appeared at the back door. She was wearing a bright apron over a pair of jeans, and she had a serene, effortless smile.

"I figured that was you, John. I always know when Daisy stops barking."

Hillary held his finger to his lips and motioned me toward the house. The woman made a quizzical face, then stepped aside and let us in. "What are you up to now?"

"Emmie, this is Anna Peters, an old friend of mine from D.C. Anna, Emmie Hamilton. Are the kids home?"

"Dave's at Little League and Lucille's at the beach."

"Good. Somebody busted up the house."

"No!"

"Yes — nearly a total loss."

"I never heard a thing!" She went to the back door and strained to see through the trees. "Course I was out — "

"That's not important, Emmie. It's done and I know why. I stepped on tender toes for a story I'm researching."

Emmie looked exasperated. "What did Terry move you over here for? That woman'll have your hide."

"I'd rather it be her than the people who're currently interested," Hillary said seriously, and Emmie's face went still. I wondered to what extent he had confided in her and Max.

"Can I help?"

"I want you to call the police." She nodded. "And say you stopped by and found the mess. Terry's in Miami, but you can be vague on that. I can't have her coming back here no matter what the cops want."

"Where are you going to be?"

"Can I borrow the shack? It'll only be for a couple of days." Emmie hesitated.

"Max won't mind."

"It's not that, but what should I tell the police?"

"That you don't know where I am. I'll keep in touch, but I can't stay here." Hillary glanced out the kitchen window. "They're almost sure to be back."

She opened the kitchen cabinet and took out a key.

"Thanks, Emmie."

"You better watch yourself, John."

"Not to worry. Now come with us, we'll show you the damage. The back way'll be better. No one should know that Anna and I have been here. You won't mention that to Terry, either, will you?"

Emmie's loyalties were divided. I decided not to say anything.

"I don't want her to worry," Hillary persisted. "And she must not come back — not for a few days."

"I don't suppose I'll be talking to her anyway," Emmie said, and with that Hillary had to be content, no matter how awkward he felt. After she had seen the house and gone to phone, we headed for our cars.

"Where'd you leave the MG?"

"Up the street. Where will I meet you?"

"You'd better give me directions to Max's place."

He would rather not have. Perhaps the rumors about Theresa's temperament were correct.

"They found my address in your house," I reminded him, "and by this time they know my car."

"All right, all right. Stop at the burger place down the road, and I'll draw you a map."

With this we separated and, a quarter of an hour later, equipped with a hastily sketched map to a ranch near Myakka Head, I left for my rendezvous with Old Brammin. Another hour of crawling traffic, and I arrived at the golf club, disenchanted with relaxation in the sunshine state. Brammin's threesome was still on the course, and rather than hang around the minuscule clubhouse, I crossed the road to the narrow white shore that curved under the gray-green fringe of palms until it disappeared in a blue-white glare. The wind was surprisingly strong; on the golf course not a hundred yards away the air was still and sultry, the lagoon without a ripple. On the shore, the loose sand blew in sheets just above the ground, and the terns hovered precariously over the surf, the gusts requiring continual shifts in their balance. I felt like that — or, more precisely, like a juggler who has tossed too many oranges in the air and watches their implacable drift out of the tidy orbit of his hands. Never mix business with friendship. My concern for Henry Brammin and Hillary had spread to Rod, who was probably a fool, and to Baby, who looked out for number one. I felt responsible, and I was trying to sort out to whom and for what, when Old Brammin asked, "What has happened, Anna?"

"A lot, all bad," I said, starting to get up.

"Sit, sit. I'll join you. I've been walking all afternoon." He eased himself down onto the warm sand and adjusted the brim of his hat against the declining sun. "Well?"

I outlined the day's events and described what Hillary and I had pieced together of Rod's traffic in antiquities.

"Let me get this straight," his uncle said. "Rod is using his boat to bring old Indian rock carvings from Guatemala." His voice was gently incredulous.

"Not just any old carvings. The Mayan sculptors were among the greatest in the world, and their finest work is priceless. Artistically, that is. Even quite inferior examples may be important scientifically."

"Why is that?"

"Because many of their sculptures are stelae or bas-reliefs

with a combination of pictures and hieroglyphics. The Mayan language has yet to be completely deciphered, so every example is potentially significant — and most useful *in situ.* The lintels and stelae — those are free-standing bas-reliefs — have inscriptions, dates, historical incidents, chronologies. When they're cut apart and dispersed, it becomes impossible to use the context to help decode the message."

"I understand. But without approving of Rod's business, it does seem a natural extension of the antique and art trade."

"Oh yes — from Roman times. Napoleon filled the Louvre that way, and André Malraux was busted for taking sculptures from Cambodia. But unfortunately for all of *us,* Rod has involved himself just at the time when governments are beginning to clamp down on the trade. Not many of the vulnerable countries can afford to guard their monuments properly, although they try. The Guatemalan government had hired guards for the site where John Hillary and his crew were filming six months ago. Two of the guards were murdered by a gang of looters who removed a rare stela and an assortment of glyphs which they hacked off other sculptures."

After a tense pause Brammin said, "And Rod was involved with these thugs?"

"That we don't know. He may not have any idea where the shipment originated and probably he wasn't implicated in the killings. I would think not, somehow: he probably dealt with an intermediary further up the chain. But, and this is the serious consideration at the moment, I'm certain he can connect Sebastian to stolen antiquities — at the very least."

"What about your friend — this Hillary whose home was vandalized? What does he know?"

"That's the odd thing — he doesn't. Or rather, he didn't know he had any information until someone started harassing him, trying to discredit his work. Now the business with his house. Hillary thinks there must be something on his photographs or in the outtakes of his film. Or else Sebastian or one of his people panicked. If that's the case, Rod is really more vulnerable.

He's the only link to our rich, respectable connoisseur-philan-thropist."

"Yes," Brammin said, eyeing me curiously. "What do you intend to do?"

"I don't know."

Foolish candor. He looked shocked. A client is still a client, even if he's one of your oldest friends.

"That's your profession," he said.

"It's by no means an exact science. Every so often you have to wait for an idea. That's what I'm doing at the moment."

Brammin pulled out a cigar, cut off the tip, and lit it up. "Have you any advice for me?" he asked.

"Your case is simpler. You have Rod to worry about. Find out when he is expected home and meet him with a good lawyer. The story must break — I hope you understand there isn't any way I can prevent that. I have no influence over Hillary, and, even if I had, things have gone too far. His house was almost gutted; the police had to be notified. He will undoubtedly do a follow-up on his original report and the story will be out. Even if he didn't do it, someone else surely would."

"If he has information about a capital crime, he has no choice," Brammin said firmly. "I did not hire you to hide my nephew's criminal activity."

"But possibly we can minimize Rod's part. You said you were willing to settle his debts. That's the hold Sebastian has on him — or one of them."

"I will do that and I'll find a good criminal lawyer." He looked down at the sand, and picked a bit of loose tobacco off the end of the cigar. "I am not happy about it, though," he said after a minute. "There's the Sebastian girl, too."

"Yes. I'm not sure that she knows anything."

"I suppose that's the other hold Sebastian has on him."

"Perhaps. My opinion is that he and Sebastian offered each other adventure and danger as well as money. There are not many opportunities for that anymore — especially not for a man of Sebastian's age and condition. And then he made it possible for Rod, not only to keep his boat but — "

"To sail off in search of buried treasure."

"It's long been popular," I said.

"Where does that leave Miss Sebastian?"

"Miss Sebastian is otherwise inclined." I pictured her as unenthusiastic about treasure hunts.

Brammin smoked for a time, while I watched the wind sift a fine layer of sand over the toe of my shoe. I had answered his questions, but I was dissatisfied with the job. Nothing had been neatly resolved and all the loose ends were dangerous — or at best, highly troublesome.

"I would set everything in motion today," I said finally. "See your lawyer, get his advice. And — " this wasn't so easy — "I'd make arrangements either to have someone keep an eye on your house or to stay elsewhere with a friend. There is a security firm in Sarasota that would have guards. They would be a good investment for a couple of days, and I'm through as of this afternoon. You've found out what you wanted to know."

"There still isn't proof," Brammin said. "Not in the legal sense."

"If Rod ships the artworks from Apalachicola in the *Melody,* that's that. Maybe he will confide in you. It would be better for him, though, if they wound up on Sebastian's estate. Of course, if Rod has sent them direct, we'd need to search Sebastian's house — perhaps even the new museum."

"Are there grounds for a warrant?"

"I doubt it — not with someone as influential as Sebastian. But from your point of view, we've got him in a good position. Any more suspicious incidents, and he opens himself up to an investigation. He doesn't have much freedom of movement. And that's to Rod's benefit."

"Temporarily. There's still your friend."

"That's why you have to make your plans about Rod right away. His buccaneering ends tomorrow."

"And you're flying home when? Tonight, tomorrow?"

"I might stick around for a day — at my own expense, of

course — just to see what turns up. Cheri has invited me to her party for the museum opening tomorrow night. I thought I'd go."

"You'd be better off home."

"But then there's Hillary," I said, "and he's an old friend, too."

Chapter 10

THE SUN swung behind the pines and shot long, red rays through the foliage to dye billboards and store fronts and to glitter over the acres of parked cars and the shiny plastic of the revolving signs. I stopped twice along the main highway, once to buy a newspaper, once to pick up a box of fried chicken, soda, and a melon. Then I turned east, out of the alternating bands of glare and shadow onto a flat, sunlit road that ran straight through the orchards into cattle country. Past the tacky highway souvenir shops, the few blocks of small houses, and the inevitable trailer park, the land was empty, hot, and drab. The slick northern fringe of the coast disappeared, and the old South returned, lonely, agricultural, poor. The miles of shopping centers and malls contracted to battered rural stores flanked at their quiet crossroads by small square white schools and low houses with sagging porches and dirt yards. Sometimes there were citrus orchards, gloriously glossy and perfumed, but, left to its own devices, the land was at once overgrown and exhausted. The dusty gray-green grass and palmetto scrub formed a monotonous carpet, from which a few tall pines opened like eccentric umbrellas. Grazing beneath them were herds of thin, exotic cattle, bred from Indian Brahman stock to resist heat, flies, and pests. Some were almost purebred, white, humped, and huge; others, odd Hereford, Angus, Holstein crosses with patched coats and hunched shoulders, or unrecognizable gray and spotted beasts with big horns and hard constitutions, that ambled among white flocks of egrets. The pastures were interrupted by swamps, dark and lush, and, above, the enormous sky filled with tier upon tier of flamingo-colored clouds.

I drove fast, keeping one eye on the rearview mirror, although traffic was sparse, consisting mostly of dusty pickup trucks. When a white station wagon lingered behind me for several miles, I cut off onto a side road, but the driver did not follow. I had apparently passed beyond Sebastian's orbit, and by the time I found the narrow road leading toward the ranch, there was no one to watch me turn. A quarter of a mile farther, a dirt track branched toward some trees and a bare wooden sign announced private land. I nursed the car over the potholes to a neglected property on the edge of a dense thicket of pines.

There were two buildings under swaybacked roofs, one, a shed with sliding doors, both closed; the other, a wooden cottage raised on pilings. Two windows and a door opened onto a wide front porch that held a single chair and an old freezer. The cottage was narrow, no more than a room's width, and topped by a metal chimney. The evening light glowed in the windows, washed the bare, gray boards with rose and touched the trunks of the pines with sienna, but it was a desolate spot, hot and faintly ominous. You would have to be very fond of fishing or of weekends with the boys to spend much time there.

I pulled the car alongside the shed, disturbing doves, which flew into the pines with whistling wings. In the house were two rooms: the larger held a table, four wooden chairs, and a line of empty shelving across the back wall; the smaller was a kitchen with a cast iron stove, a linoleum-topped cabinet, and an enameled basin. There was no sign of Hillary. In the shed, I found the black MG, and stood listening for a moment, oppressed by the stillness. Behind the buildings was a yard with a pump, a privy, and a couple of grapefruit trees, then several old live oaks, hung with moss. Through their gray twilight was the thicket that marked the end of a large scrubby pasture. This was further separated from Max's land by a barbed-wire fence that straddled a shallow pond. A couple of dun cows grazed on the opposite shore, and grackles squabbled along the mudflat. On a rock on the near side, Hillary sat fishing with a cane pole, a .22 rifle resting on a gunnysack by his feet.

I called to him and he waved.

"Put your car in the shed."

By the time I wrestled open the loose, heavy doors and parked the car, he had returned to the house, the pole over one shoulder, the rifle in his hand.

"Prepared for all eventualities," I remarked.

"Quite the American woodsman," he joked, but his strong, square jaw was set and his face was tense. He was afraid, like me, and the red, slanting light heightened the lines under his eyes and at the corners of his mouth. "But no catfish tonight," he added. "I hope you brought provisions."

"Fried chicken. I've never enjoyed cleaning fish."

"No taste for life in the woods?"

I looked around the yard. The sun had dropped below the scrub, draining the colors from the house and trees. Everything was graying and losing definition, and the swamp insects were setting up a steady hum. "I can't say I like this."

He set the pole down and leaned the rifle against the side of the house.

"Is that yours or does it come with the place?"

"Max thought I should have it. He came by the paper before I left. The police have been and gone and are checking our house regularly."

"What were you doing at the paper?"

"A little session with the photography department."

"Find anything?"

"Not really. Maybe you'll see something. I've probably studied the prints too many times."

"I'll have a look — after the Colonel's finest."

"Before the grease congeals, don't you mean?"

"You'd have gone hungry," I reminded him, and began to unpack the car. By the time we went into the house, the sky was

dark and the cabin darker. I groped my way to the table and
set down the food, while Hillary rattled in the kitchen cabinet
for the oil lamp. When he struck a match and touched the wick,
a warm orange glow spread around the room, sending the
moths into ecstasy.

"That's better."

He hung the lantern on a nail and closed the front blinds.
"Do we need anything else?"

"A big knife for this melon."

He found a carving knife, laid it on the table, and sat down.
I opened the Colonel's best and apologized for the warm soda.

"The locals travel with ice chests."

"Probably not on such short notice."

Hillary got up for a knife and fork: he had never accepted
American table manners. I watched him neatly dissect a
chicken breast, then a leg. He ate his melon with a fork. There
was nothing much to say about that — or about anything else.
Once we had been lovers, then casual friends, then acquaintances meeting after a long time and many changes. Present
danger made us colleagues in a dubious enterprise; neither of
us had a clear idea of what that might entail.

I remarked that the soda was flat.

"What I like is that Dr. Pepper."

"Too sweet for me."

"But I can't indulge in the dry stuff."

I nodded. Awkward ground again: I might as well ask the
question that had been bothering me. "Did you talk to
Theresa?"

"Indirectly."

"What does that mean?"

"She was out, and I couldn't wait long enough to catch her,"
he said shortly. He would have preferred to tell me nothing, but
he must have decided that wasn't feasible, because he continued, "I spoke to Luccio, her cousin. He's a detective with the
Miami police. A very competent chap."

"She'd mentioned him."

"He knows whom to contact in Guatemala if we can get evidence." He gave me a sharp look, as if he suspected that I'd withheld something.

"I don't have anything else. My client is going to meet Rod tomorrow with a lawyer. I believe he's expected by early afternoon."

Hillary frowned. "I wish you'd left that alone. Rod might dump the sculptures. That would be the quickest way to destroy the evidence."

"Not with my client around. Besides, unless Rod is implicated at the other end, he won't be in serious trouble — especially if he can return the sculptures."

"I'd still rather you had left it alone."

"That would have been irresponsible. I was hired by someone interested in Rod's welfare. I didn't want to get in your way, but you can't expect me to drop my client, either."

"And who are you working for now?" Underneath Hillary's clever, flippant manner was a hard, determined man, harder and more determined than if he hadn't wasted a decade in Washington bars. Life had a certain urgency for Hillary, and it was just as well that he had picked up the amusing mannerisms he had.

"My job finished today."

"Then why didn't you go home?"

"My client asked that, too. I said an old friend had asked me to locate some stolen goods."

Hillary folded his hands on the table and leaned forward belligerently. I inspired mixed feelings, and he needed to see how far he could push me. "How much?" he asked.

"I want you to go easy on Rod and to keep his uncle's name out of your — whatever you're preparing. Mine, too."

"Always an angle."

"So what do you think you are — one of life's deserving charities? I'm not asking for any great ethical compromise, but I don't want to see Rod take the blame if you can't connect Sebastian to the antiquities traffic."

"Sebastian's the one I'm after."

"Good. Then what's the problem?"

"I'm not making any deals with you, Anna, that's all. Because if Rod was involved in Guatemala — "

"That's a goddamn different story."

We stared angrily at each other across the table for a few seconds, then let our eyes slide away to the fluttering insect shadows and the lamp's long orbits of gold and yellow.

"All right," Hillary said after a few minutes. "Nothing on the uncle. Rod takes his chances."

"The trick is to prove Sebastian's receiving the stuff. That's our main worry. That and what's on your pictures."

Hillary lifted a leather satchel from the floor, and while I cleared aside the greasy chicken wrappers and cans, he laid the prints out on the table.

"I took these on my first visit to the site, when the program was still in the talking stages," he said, arranging a sequence of aerial views. The green jungle rolled like the sea or a rich, porous tapestry over which the shadow of a small plane moved like a dragonfly. "See these?" He pointed to green humps in the forest.

"Yes."

"These are sites. Buildings, pyramids, temple complexes."

"Under all those trees?"

"Yes. They look like little mountains, but they are man-made."

"Incredible they were ever found."

"Aerial photography helps, but the rain forest is very thick," Hillary said. He laid another snapshot on the table. This one was a clearing. From the jungle floor, studded with tree stumps and splintered saplings, three thin, white pyramids emerged like rotting teeth in a green mouth. A few small trees and bushes still clung to their steep sides, and what had once been stairs up to the temples on top were now landslides of broken and dislodged stones. "The workers must keep cutting all the time or the clearings fill in again. It's a continual job."

Another snap. "This is a gound-level view of the largest pyramid. They're fairly far along with its reconstruction." While he pointed out stages in the work, I examined the picture curiously. It was a very tall structure, built in narrow tiers with a wide stair rising to a small rectangular building with a single door. The roof of this temple was as big as the building itself and ornamented with a filigree of fanciful designs.

"How high is this?"

"It's not one of the biggest. Some reach twelve stories. This is about eight or nine."

"Of our stories — like a skyscraper?"

"That's right. I've climbed it."

"And what are these?"

"Stucco decorations."

"Not stone?"

"No, it looks like stone, but that's fine stucco. Those are god masks — they're very abstract, and these are designs of serpents. The feathered serpent is a common motif throughout the area. Often it's so stylized and elaborated, you almost have to be an expert to see it."

His long fingers traced the curving body of a serpent, vaguely Chinese in feeling. The creature was magnificently ornamented, some of the stylized feathers ending in grotesque heads, and the effect was fanciful and hypnotic, like the rhythmic patterns in an oriental rug.

"This is where the university team stays during the working season; the guards are there year round. They're quartered here." He pointed to a long, white barracks. Behind it, the shadow of a pyramid rose against the jungle.

More pictures: close shots of elaborately carved lintels, of the curious glyphs — monkeys, grotesque gods, ornate heads, strange, organic shapes all worked into the handsome patterns that count off long dates with fantastic accuracy. And there were stucco wall decorations and stelae and altars, boulders covered with an impenetrable mesh of decoration. Smiling workmen with broad Mayan faces stood with their tools in the plaza before the pyramid, and a young woman in a kerchief carefully cleaned a sculpture. The series ended with a last aerial shot.

"Marvelous," I said, "but hardly anything untoward."

"This pack has more." He opened another envelope. "The site has only recently been opened to visitors. The tours will help support the maintenance and protection of the monuments. We wanted to include that, and I shot pictures of the first tour group."

The long shots were much the same, the tourists visible only as black specks at the base of the soaring pyramids.

"Did you get these enlarged?"

"No definition." He handed me some larger prints. "I had several closer shots of the group enlarged."

I studied the prints. The visitors were a motley crew arrayed in everything from full jungle kit to sundress and sandals. A few looked obviously American, like the lady in the pink pantsuit; the rest were universal tourist. They might have been from anywhere. "Can we assume this person is American?"

Hillary shrugged and laid out additional photos. I scrutinized each face. The lady in pink had sharp features. The man in Bermuda shorts carried a cane. The Latin with the mustache had a long lens on his camera. The enlargement process brought up a variety of details but seemed to blur the person's features in the process. Personalities became elusive; the greater the enlargement, the less recognizable they seemed. When we completed the pack, I shook my head. "I'm not as familiar with the Sebastian crowd as you are. Is there anyone you recognize?"

"Yes, but I wanted you to look first. Try again." He moved the lamp nearer, and I turned over the pictures slowly, concentrating on every detail. It must have taken half an hour, but the result was the same.

"No luck. I'm sorry."

Hillary reached over and selected a photo. "This man," he said. "I've a feeling I've seen him."

The man was heavy, his pants tight over an ample behind, his short-sleeved shirt strained at the shoulders and armpits. He had dark, tightly waved hair, and he stirred no recognition whatsoever. "None that shows his face?"

"No. And — it may be just imagination — I have the feeling, the memory, that he avoided the camera."

I peered at the photo again. The visitors were on the central plaza, standing in a semicircle around their guide, who pointed toward some object beyond camera range.

"What are they looking at?"

"The stela that was later stolen. This was the first tour — the first chance anyone had to walk up and inspect the goods, so to speak."

I looked again. The plump man still suggested nothing, but I noticed something about the figure next to him. I leaned closer to the light and squinted. The other man was thin, and his face and body were shaded, probably by the shadow of the stela. I could make out a dark pair of slacks, a loose print shirt. Only his bare arm was plainly visible. He was gesturing toward the stela, perhaps directing the other man to take a picture, for there appeared to be a strap around his companion's neck. "A camera strap, do you think?"

"Most of them had cameras."

I stood up and tipped the print.

"You need glasses."

"This is a poor light."

"Vanity," he said, needling me.

I ignored him and sat down, puzzled. There was a link bracelet on the man's arm. I'd seen one recently.

"Does anyone around Sebastian wear a bracelet?"

"Marcus wears everything."

"This isn't Marcus. Damn. I know I just saw one of those. It's not jewelry, it's one of those medic-alert things. You know — for diabetics and penicillin allergies. They wear a little disk that describes their problem in case of emergency."

"There must be a lot of those down here. Half of Florida's chronic."

"Yeah, but I've the feeling — " A menacing insect was quartering the room, its hard wings scratching the walls each time it landed. Memory balked. "Maybe you're right. I'll go through them again in the morning."

Hillary gathered the snapshots into neat piles. "I think I'll make coffee. Do you want some?"

"All right. I'm going to get my sweater. It's chilly."

I crossed the back yard, stepping cautiously until my eyes adjusted to the darkness. The swampy ground beyond the trees was alive with frogs, and brilliant stars hung like ornaments above the pines. The door of the shed opened with a loud metallic rasp, and I waited to see if I had disturbed anything, but there were only the oblivious frogs, until, returning, I heard a more suggestive sound: a powerful car approaching along the dirt road. I ran for the shack, but Hillary had heard the motor, too, because the light went out. I reached the shadow of the house as a large sedan with low beams went barreling past, leaving a ghostly cloud of dust. Hillary opened the door. "Did you get a look at the car?"

"Big, dark, and expensive. Doesn't belong here."

"It's going on," Hillary said. "I can still hear it."

I shrugged. Short of leaving, there was nothing to be done. "It probably belongs to the ranch."

"Let's hope so."

Hillary relit the lamp and poured some instant coffee. Then he sat on the floor with his back against the wall, the rifle within reach beside him.

"Are you a good shot?" I asked.

"Yes. I learned at school. We had a rifle team."

"How wholesome."

"We were to be officers and gentlemen. What about you?"

"My education was strictly plebeian. I can't shoot at all."

"Oh? I'm surprised — in your business."

"Firearms are more nuisance than they're worth most of the time. I'm in the business of preventing trouble, after all."

"The feminine touch," he said, teasing.

"Don't knock it. Femininity reassures the clientele."

"I don't feel particularly reassured."

"You're not exactly a voluntary client."

"No. It's not that I don't appreciate your efforts, but this is going to get me into trouble with Terry."

"She'll get over it. Think of the story you'll have — and I don't take any credit line. Part of the service."

He grinned and relaxed enough to tell me a funny story about an earlier collaborator of his. In return, I described my trials with Baby. Baby suggested Theresa again, and Theresa, Harry.

"Why don't you two get married?" Hillary asked.

"The voice of bourgeois propriety."

"I'm serious. I'd think it would simplify your financial affairs."

"You *have* turned straight and narrow."

"What's the problem?" he asked, unruffled.

I shrugged. "Cowardice, basically. I don't want to change anything."

"Marriage is good for the soul."

"This is just what I've always wanted to do," I interrupted. "Spend a night in a godforsaken swamp with a marriage advocate."

"It's not my fault you can't forget my charm."

We both laughed. Subsequently we devoted a good deal of verbiage to friendship between men and women. We really spent an edifying evening, which goes to show how inventive you can be when sex is taboo and sleep is elusive.

At one o'clock the lamp sputtered out of fuel and Hillary didn't bother to fill it up again. He put his satchel under his head and stretched out on the boards, the rifle next to his hand.

"Is the safety on that thing?"

"No. I'll put it on the other side," he said.

I heard him rustling in the dimness. From the swamp a bird called in a hoarse, troubled voice over the monotonous insects.

I folded my sweater into a pillow, curled up facing the door, and closed my eyes.

A purple sound exploded out of the darkness, turned into a red sun beyond my eyelids and then into a painful white light that filled the doorway of the shack, obliterating everything but the sick panic that dried my throat and compressed my chest. There were figures in the light, three or four dark shapes wavering against the night sky. Their feet sounded on the bare boards of the floor, and the open door flapped violently against the wall. I struggled to get up, groping on the floor for some weapon, some distraction, but Hillary was quicker. Even half-blinded I saw the movement as he reached away from me toward the rifle, but the figures behind the lights were quicker yet, because the sound of a shot filled the room, knocking Hillary back against the wall and sending a red wash of blood across his temple. I screamed in horror, reached for him, touched the empty lamp and, half-crouching, hurled it into the lights and dived after. Something swung out of the glare and amorphous darkness. A dull, heavy pain ran up the side of my head, drove sharp and keen into the bones, and snuffed out light and reason.

Sound, it preserved. And smell. The boards of the shack smelled like pine resin and old dust and shook as heavy feet tramped back and forth over my exposed brain. Although muffled sounds echoed around my head, I couldn't force my eyes open. My brain seemed to be floating on its own, unable to process more than snatches of its surroundings. Voices, without meaning. Smell. A new, funny smell. Like camping trips as a child. But dangerous. Something dangerous. Perhaps it was blood, Hillary's blood, running down the cabin wall, and the brain wanted to scream, but there was no scream, no answer. Suddenly the whole world tilted violently. I was being rolled over and over in the darkness and with every lurch I felt nauseated. There was light and spinning. I was on some sort of carousel, deathly sick and calling out, but soundlessly. Then there was a loud noise. A banging. Feet. The dangerous smell. I couldn't get up, couldn't open my eyes: my brain was elsewhere or my eyes were elsewhere, but the smell was dangerous. The smell and a new sound, whispering, insinuating. My head seemed to be generating lurid disks against a green-tinged darkness as the whispering came nearer, nearer and hotter. There was heat. Fire! I was on my knees and the fire was a hot orange-gold wind close, very close. "Here! This way! Get up!" a voice cried. I crawled toward it, sick, through sparks and a roar like the sea, a roar engulfing like the surf at night. But hot. My head sagged, and I fell away from the heat and whispering, stumbling down steps, being dragged, falling.

I smelled the earth and opened my eyes. An orange curtain shot toward the stars; at its base the shack burned red and black, resinous boards squealing and whining like dying animals. "Hillary!" I screamed. "Hillary!" I pulled myself up, had to get up, but someone restrained me and I fell back into oblivion.

When my eyes opened again the night was paling into dawn. The air stank of smoke, but the sheets of flame had vanished. I was lying on the cool damp ground, and Hillary was half-sitting, half-lying beside me on the grass. His face looked dark. I put out my hand and found the whole side of his head was wet.

"Jesus!"

"I'm all right," he said, his voice strange and shaky. "The bullet just grazed me. I was only out for a minute. I opened my eyes and thought I was dead."

"Why didn't they shoot us both?"

"Accident. It was to seem like an accident."

"They talked about that?"

"That's right."

"And they poured gas around the cabin. I couldn't do anything, but I could smell it."

"You've a real glass jaw, my dear. I thought I'd never get you out of there."

I shook my head. My brain had become attached to some heavy rotating object and refused to order events logically, but my eyes were beginning to focus and the dawn was far enough advanced so that I could see the dark red furrow along the side of Hillary's head. It was nasty, although not too deep, and still bleeding profusely. "We'd better stop the bleeding."

"I haven't worked on that yet." He wiped his jaw with a trembling hand and closed his eyes. "Making me feel queasy."

"Loss of blood." I crawled over beside him and started unbuttoning his shirt. "Let me tear up your shirt."

"You're supposed to rip your petticoat."

"Stop being a comedian." I tore the sleeves off his shirt, folded them into a pad, and pressed it over the wound. "Hold that right there. I'll get some water."

The pump was beyond reach of the fire, but close enough so that the last hot sparks danced around my feet and settled in my hair. I wet a strip of cloth and returned to wipe the blood off Hillary's face. "Is it stopping?"

He lifted off the compress. "What do you think?"

"Looks a bit better. All we can do is tie it up."

I fiddled with the scraps of cloth until his head was bandaged, then I sat on the ground, feeling sick.

"Put your head down. That helps."

"I'll be all right in a minute." The dizziness, fear's aftershock, came and went, but the night grew clearer and so did my brain. "I suppose the cars are gone."

"There's no shed left."

I focused my eyes in that general direction. All that remained was a foul-smelling heap. I patted the pockets of my slacks and was surprised to find I still had money and credit cards.

"They didn't take anything," I said.

"Only the pictures."

"Any duplicates?"

"The negatives were in the car."

"Shit!" I got up, stuck my hands in my pockets, and began to stamp around the yard. Hillary sat nursing his wounded head and looking miserable. Total cost of our excursion, excluding personal injuries: one shed, one cottage, one late-model rental car, one aging MG, and two sets of photographs.

"Nothing for it but to go to the police," Hillary said with a show of decisiveness.

I kicked a half-burned hunk of paper, the remains of the evening newspaper I'd bought but never read.

"There's no way either of us can show up at the Sebastians' after this. Maybe the police will find something to link him with — " Instead of completing this forlorn hope, Hillary stopped to fuss with his bandage. I poked at the newsprint. The top page, brown and soft as dust, wafted from a photo of a sharp, elegant face with a stiff smile.

"We'll stop on the main road and call. Or would it be quicker to walk back to the ranch?"

I brushed away the burned fragments and began to read the caption and the accompanying story.

"What are you doing, Anna?"

"Listen to this, Hillary! We're home free. 'Socialite Cheri Sebastian poses with some of the handmade costumes which will enliven the Beaux Arts Ball Saturday night. The ball is part of the weekend festivities marking the opening of the Sebastian Fine Arts Museum. Created by local art students, the costumes will be auctioned to raise funds for a regional fine arts scholarship. The ball for three hundred invited guests will be held at the Sebastian estate — ' "

"Ordinarily I'd be delighted," Hillary interrupted, "but somehow I'm not in the mood for a party that ends with the sale of students' papier-mâché."

"No, no, that's not the important thing, you idiot. It's a Beaux Arts Ball — like the old artists' parties — a costume party. We can walk in, search the house, check the guests. She even gave me an extra ticket." I started to laugh rather foolishly.

Hillary snatched the crumbling newsprint. "Poor Cheri," he said after a moment. "She has no idea what she's getting into. She really thinks she's invulnerable."

"Like us," I said, looking at the ruins of the cottage and the shed. Smoke from the fire hung in an acrid cloud. We were shaky, sooty, and muddy, and blood was staining through Hillary's bandage.

"Like us," he agreed.

Chapter 11

"How's your head?" I asked Hillary.

"Aching. How's yours?"

"Ditto. You'd think they could put the sun in storage for a day or two." Shielding my eyes with my hand, I squinted against the white morning glare. There was nothing behind us but the straight dusty road, the weedy drainage ditches, and the endless miles of palmetto scrub. More of the same lay ahead. We had walked since dawn without meeting a single car.

"You were interested in Sebastian from the first, weren't you? The rest about art smuggling was just a bluff."

"Not entirely," Hillary replied. "After what happened in Guatemala I wanted to expose the 'respectable' people who profit from an illegal traffic. I still plan to do that. But everything I learned about the Mayan thefts suggested that the stela had been stolen to order. It was too large an operation, and the thieves had been too well equipped and organized for ordinary looters. A number of details pointed to an American client."

"How did you find Sebastian?"

"That was pure coincidence, as I told you before. I was asked to do the museum story and his reluctance to discuss his past, combined with the quality of his collections, made me wonder about him. Aren't you impressed by his taste? He buys everything himself — there's no paid collector."

"I haven't seen the museum yet, but his personal collection is certainly individualistic."

"That's my point. And he's an old thug, I'm sure of it, although he's covered his tracks." Hillary stopped to wipe his face on the front of his torn shirt.

"Do you want to rest?"

"Maybe for a minute. I feel a bit shaky — delayed reaction." He folded his long legs and settled on the side of the road. "Sebastian's a very intelligent man. Have you met him?"

"Just momentarily."

"Probably the best way, I saw him hit Marcus with a cane one day."

"What did Marcus do?"

"He got out of the way and assured me later that it was most uncharacteristic behavior."

I remembered Henry Brammin's description. "I suppose you can't hide a violent personality forever."

"No. The funny thing, in retrospect, is that although I was sure he was a crook, I didn't connect him with the Guatemala incidents or with my own problems. I assumed Terry was right — that I'd made an enemy in Miami."

"Then there's Cheri."

"Oh, yes. She's a real little Psyche." When I looked puzzled, he added, "I forgot you didn't have a classical education. Psyche married Cupid, but wasn't supposed to discover his identity. Cheri's afraid there's a skeleton in the closet, and she's trying to find out what it is. Ironic, when everything her father's done for the last few years has been for her benefit."

"No personal vanity involved?"

"His vanity doesn't need anything — certainly not parties and museums. He's dropped his cover for Cheri, and she's not satisfied."

"She's in a precarious position."

"Even crime has to have drawbacks," Hillary said. Then he scrambled to his feet. "What's that? Isn't that a car?"

A white plume of dust lengthened over the palmettos behind a battered gray truck approaching very fast.

"You don't suppose it's our night visitors?"

"In that heap?" Hillary shaded his eyes. "Only one man."

I stepped into the road and waved. The truck showed no sign of slowing. I moved farther onto the asphalt and shouted. The driver hit his brakes with a screech, swerved around us, and stopped. "My friend's had an accident," I said. "Are you heading for Sarasota?"

A pair of thick, rimless glasses glittered in the morning sun. "You should stay the hell out of the road. You're liable to get run over that way."

Behind the glasses was a large round head fringed with white hair. The rest of the driver's physique was equally geometric and uncompromising. He had an impressive bulbous nose, a straight mouth, and a square chin seamed with wrinkles. Large square hands tapped an impatient rhythm on the wheel, and as he looked me up and down the lenses of his glasses magnified a pair of belligerent, accusatory eyes. "What happened to you, fellow?" He raised his head slightly and shifted his square shoulders as if, despite his advanced age, he was ready for anything.

"Motorbike tipped over." Hillary touched his bandage delicately. "I took a bad spill and wrecked the machine."

"How come your ladyfriend here walked away unhurt?"

"I was testing the machine. We'd had some problems with the engine," Hillary replied smoothly.

The old man sniffed. "Sure got mighty dirty just watching. And that ain't grease, neither."

"No, it's soot," I said. My nerves were not at their best.

"That's the truth, anyway," he said and, reaching over, opened the door. He looked hard at Hillary who gave a delighted smile.

"Get that damn door shut right." I closed it and pushed the lock. Satisfied with this, the man put the truck into gear, and as soon as the protesting vehicle had managed third, he floored the accelerator and set us bouncing over the narrow road at an alarming rate. Hillary braced himself against the back of the seat.

"Do you drive this way often?"

"Four times a week for the last thirty years," our benefactor snapped. He drove slightly hunched over, eyes fixed straight ahead, and he was allergic to the brake. "Go in to the shopping center," he continued. "Nothing but crap nowadays at the country stores. Soda pop and potato chips and preserved meat. Full of poisons. They put in every damn thing." His expression darkened.

"They have to be tasted to be believed," Hillary agreed.

"You foreigners don't know anything about American food. Hell, they eat anything we send over there. We're keeping them multiplying on our surplus, when the average man here can hardly afford groceries."

"The earth will soon be flooded with Englishmen," Hillary said wickedly.

"Lucky earth."

"Whole country's going to hell," the old man continued, swerving the truck to avoid a dead dog. "Corruption, immorality. Free sex. Legal pornography. They took the prayers out of the schools and put the pornography in. What do you expect from a country like that?"

"Nothing too much," Hillary admitted, hastily bracing his hand against the dash to keep from jolting through the windshield.

"Greatest country on earth going down the drain. Hell, Europe's been rotten for a hundred years, and Asia for centuries. The rest of the world isn't even civilized. Lot of barbarians."

"You meet a few of those everywhere," Hillary commented.

The round glasses turned toward him for an instant. I wondered if he had passed the burned-out shack and also if I could finish the run into town without getting sick. Every bounce of the truck seemed to aim straight for my stomach.

"You married?"

"Yes, I am."

"Not to this dame. No ring, I noticed."

"It's a long story," Hillary said. "Stranger than fiction."

Reaction to this was delayed by a crossroads where we skidded sideways onto the main road. Hillary and I clung to the frame, but the old man, impervious to Newton's laws, remained stolidly hunched behind the wheel. The highway provided more scope. The red speedometer needle crept over sixty-five although the truck frame shuddered with the effort, and our passage was marked by near misses and gusts of black exhaust. Our driver was indifferent. Speed limits were part of some ill-defined conspiracy also affecting a business that he was careful not to specify. We must have provided a certain loathsome stimulation, because he refused all appeals to stop until we reached the center of the city. By that time, his driving had nearly terrified us into submission.

"Christ, what a kamikaze," Hillary said as the truck roared away from the sidewalk. He leaned against a lamp post for support.

"It's fortunate he doesn't drive a better truck."

"I used to wonder who bought the old *National Enquirer.*"

"Now you know. Real American Gothics like that one."

"Is my head bleeding again?"

"A little. We'll find a drugstore and buy bandages — unless you know a doctor who doesn't report gunshot wounds."

"They tend to have slightly later office hours," Hillary said. "This way." He gestured toward a side street. "I think there's an Eckerd's along here. If I could stand that ride, I can survive your idea of first aid. The old bastard knew something."

"Sure he did. I imagine he passed the shack."

"Lovely man."

"We made his day. Vice and bloodshed right in his own county. What more could he want?"

On the next block we spotted a public bench and, beyond it, the drugstore. Hillary slouched down on the seat, exhausted. "Get me aspirins, too, would you?"

"Right, and bandages, a clean shirt, a hat, maybe?"

"A hat?"

"You'll have to rent us a car. I've now lost two within a week. They'll put me on the never-never list."

"A car. And costumes for Cheri's party." He pivoted about, depositing his feet on the bench, and lay back with a groan. "Anything else?"

"Don't get arrested for vagrancy. We cannot afford any more delays."

"No more delays," Hillary agreed. He propped himself up on one elbow. "Just hurry it up with the aspirin."

I did. Also with the disinfectant, the adhesive tape, the gauze pads, the extra-large-size Panama hat and the two T-shirts, one adorned with a pelican exhorting us to "Visit Sarasota," the other by an anthropomorphic orange proclaiming "Florida: the Sunshine State." I dumped half the bottle of disinfectant over Hillary's head and rebandaged the wound, which did not look nearly as messy as it had in the predawn light. Then we retired to the rest rooms of a nearby diner to emerge dressed like a pair of besotted tourists. Hillary plunked his hat over the bandage, ordered coffee and toast, and began consuming aspirin.

"Leave some for me, will you?" A couple of my teeth moved with suspicious ease, and I had discovered a nasty bruise along my jawline. I could foresee a bad day in the dentist's chair.

"Better eat something," Hillary said, but the smell of frying eggs and sausage made my stomach quiver, and when the short-order cook dropped his spatula the clatter made me jump. The shock of awakening in the cabin, the violent explosion of light, sound, and pain, kept sliding in and out of consciousness, as if the brutality and speed of the experience had prevented it from being completely assimilated. We had nearly been burned to death, and a smell of smoke and ash lingered to prove it. When I ran my hand through my hair, little pieces of soot fell down the white T-shirt and wafted onto the counter.

"Odd scalp condition," Hillary remarked, then stifled a laugh by cramming a piece of toast into his mouth. His fingers trembled slightly, and he turned to the morning paper to restore his composure. While he read yet another account of the Sebastians' extravagances, I picked at his leftover toast. The bread had a greasy aftertaste, but it helped fill the vacuum created in the instant that the cabin door had banged open.

"Do you want some more?" There were red rims around Hillary's eyes and a faint greenish tinge to his tan, but as long as he kept a grip on himself he still looked remarkably nonchalant.

"No, I'd better call D.C. and check on Baby."

"I'd forgotten about her," he said.

"So had I until I began functioning again."

It was approaching ten, too late to call Harry at home, and when I dialed the workshop Jan answered. "Helios Gallery and Workshop."

"June Quigley, please." I really didn't want to talk to Jan.

"She's not in this morning."

Damn. "It's Anna, Jan. Did she get back all right?"

"What the hell have you been up to, Anna? Baby's gone for half the week, calls me to pick her up at the airport, then announces she's taking a day off to recuperate. Nobody else can type around here, and the damn Kelly Girl couldn't tell a silk screen from an etching. Baby's not your employee, you know."

"Yes, yes, I'm sorry, Jan. But as long as she got back — "

"I've told Harry, this can't continue. I predicted there'd be problems — " Jan's accent began to get heavier, and I was preparing for a fine burst of Slavic rage when the operator interrupted. "Your time is up, ma'am."

"Put in more money," Jan yelled. "This is business. We're going to get this straightened out — "

I thanked the operator and hung up. Hillary was waiting outside the booth. "Is everything all right?"

I nodded.

"Good. Now the costumes." He flipped open the yellow pages, and I went to get more change. When I returned with the dimes, he was already deep in negotiations, which he interrupted to ask, "How do you fancy a mermaid?"

"Not at all. Sequins are itchy."

"There's not much left. Even the gatecrashers want to come prepared — Yes? That will be fine. Yes. The last one? We'll have to take it. Make that eleven-thirty, please. No, no, you can charge it." He held out his hand, and I gave him my Master Charge. There were some reassuring noises at the other end after he had read off the numbers. "I think we're all set," Hillary said as he put down the receiver. "A limited selection, rather clichéd, I'm afraid."

"What are they?"

"What is described as a 'Spanish-Mexican outfit, suitable for Italian bandit choruses,' with a large hat. No one else had anything with a hat."

"Fine."

"And one harem outfit in purple, 'diaphanous, but in perfect taste,' according to my informant."

"Terrific."

"It was that or the sequined fishtail, old girl."

"Let's hope it's not too diaphanous or they'll spot me by the bruises."

"They won't believe their eyes," Hillary replied with a certain grim satisfaction, then he flipped to the auto listings and reserved a car. Forty-five minutes later we arrived at the costumer's in a flaming red Dodge and received two large boxes from his much depleted stock.

"The party doesn't begin until dark," Hillary remarked as we threw the boxes in the trunk. "That leaves us a certain amount of time to kill."

"Somehow I don't feel much like the beach."

"I was thinking more of sleep, preferably uninterrupted." He surveyed the block. "I can't get rid of the feeling that we're going to run into someone we know."

"That could be very unlucky."

"Where do you want to go, then?"

"My apartment. That's the last place Sebastian's crew would expect us. I really should be there anyway in case my client calls. We want to know when Rod arrives."

Hillary considered this. "What about the car? The super might notice it's a different one."

"Leave it down the street. If we go through the rear door we should be perfectly safe."

"All right, but you drive. I feel distinctly woozy." He climbed into the back seat, closed his eyes, and didn't open them again until I parked on the street behind the apartment. One of the small houses on the block had been closed up, and by cutting through its overgrown yard and squeezing past a ferocious cactus, we came out at the rear entrance to the apartments. I had the key to the back door in my pocket.

"Shall I go up first?"

"If you like. I can check the parking lot in front."

"I'm sure they've been and gone," I said, and I was right. The shades had been thoughtfully drawn in all the rooms, resulting in pale, tangerine-colored shadows, very pleasant to aching eyes. The people who had drawn the shades had done their work thoroughly, but quietly. No smashed bottles or overturned furniture, but my suitcase had been upended on one of the beds, and Baby's prized cosmetics had been opened and discarded.

"Missing anything of value?" Hillary asked.

"I'd made a few notes on the case, that's all, and, of course, they'll have guessed that Baby was a plant."

"They left your camera, anyway." It was a cheap Kodak, loaded with color film. I had not had time to take vacation pictures of the beach for Harry.

"A robbery would have looked suspicious."

"When we were found tragically incinerated."

"I wonder if they'll try to arrange that discovery — or just leave it to chance?"

Hillary shrugged. He wandered into Baby's room, pulled off his shoes and flopped down on the bed. I watched out the back windows for a while, then put the chain lock on the front door of the apartment and checked Hillary. He had fallen asleep, but his breathing was even and his color had improved —

probably no concussion. That was a relief. I stretched out on my own bed to listen while a mockingbird sang endless, elaborate variations. The sound distracted me from the menacing purple circles that floated across my retinas and from psychic echoes of slamming doors and tramping feet and the insidious hiss and crackle of fire. I woke once or twice, but there was only silence or the peaceful sounds of a suburban afternoon beyond the soiled orange shades, and I fell back to sleep instantly, to be awakened suddenly and for good by the telephone. I sat up, uncertain where I was until the room took shape. I was in Ibis and it was late afternoon and the phone was on the wall in the kitchenette. I lifted the receiver and waited.

"Anna? Is that you?" It was Henry Brammin.

"Yes, it's me. Have you seen Rod?"

"I thought you'd gone home. I haven't been able to get you. I'm worried about Rod. The *Melody* was expected in just after lunch. I stopped by the marina and met Cheri Sebastian, who was there to pick him up. Nervous little thing, you know her, she went in and tried to contact him by shore-to-ship telephone. No luck. Then she tried on the marine band. Nothing."

"But it's a long sail. He's not all that late, is he?"

"No, but she'd talked to him last night. He said he'd made unusually good time and that if anything changed he'd put into shore somewhere and drive down in time for her party. He wasn't far off Port Richey last night."

"Where's that?"

"Just above Tampa. He should have been here hours ago and if he's still on the water he should have answered our calls."

"And the Gulf 's been calm?"

"Like a pond. Ordinarily I wouldn't be worried, but she was upset. She had been keeping in touch with him, and she insisted he should have been here by one or two at the latest."

"Who was with him? Did Cheri mention that?"

"No, in fact, he seems to be confiding in her less and less —that's what I read between the lines. Usually he took a professional sailor with him, a local fellow named Peter, and sometimes Marcus, a young employee of Vlad Sebastian's — "

"I know Marcus."

"No more need be said then. Or, if Marcus isn't free, he takes another oddball, an older fellow who does gardening at his apartment building."

I hadn't been afraid for Rod until then, but the mention of the gardener set off nasty little warning bells. Vlad Sebastian didn't leave much to chance; one of his men was always around to protect the investment. "Marcus didn't sail with him. He was minding the antique shop just yesterday."

"Must have been the other two."

"Can't you find out for sure?"

"I can try. Of course, anything could have happened. He could have changed his crew up in Apalachicola. Those ports always have guys hanging around the docks looking for a job."

"Or a ship."

"That's what has me concerned. A lot of funny things have happened around Apalachicola lately. The *Melody* isn't the first yacht to go missing. If Rod doesn't show up this evening, we'll have to inform the Coast Guard."

"I agree. By the way, did you take the precautions I suggested yesterday?"

"Yes. I feel like a damn fool."

"That's a small price to pay. You'll be talking to Cheri, won't you?"

"Yes, she said she'd call me if she heard anything."

"Fine — just don't mention that you've spoken to me."

"I wasn't planning to — but why not?"

"Because there are three or four people who think I'm dead, and I want my resurrection to surprise them."

Chapter 12

"Do you think Rod's in the Gulf?" Hillary asked as he struggled with the black string tie which completed his "Spanish" attire. The tie went around the collar of a loose white shirt. The rest of the ensemble was black — black bolero jacket, fitted black pants, black boots, and a black sombrero with a scroll of silver braid and some black ball fringe like the trim on an overstuffed sofa. I had darkened his orange sideburns with Baby's leftover eyebrow pencil, and with his hat off Hillary had a suspicious particolored appearance, completed by the large, white bandage.

"It's a possibility."

"I can't get this thing straight."

I glanced from the conveyer belt of highway lights to see that the tie was all askew. "I'll fix it for you when we stop."

"Why are these bow things only tieable by women?" He gave another tug, then destroyed the effect by jerking open his collar, seeking relief from the heat. Costume parties in the subtropics require a commitment to frivolity. Hillary looked parboiled in his regalia, and I was sweltering in a tent of purple cheesecloth designed for a harem habitué of cool blood and substantial girth. I drove with the diaphanous sleeves rolled up and the veils tied back, because it was one of Hillary's less practical affectations that he had trouble with American-made cars.

"How are you betting?" I asked.

"About Rod?" He was silent for a moment. "Still afloat, I'd guess. He's no innocent, and he's more capable than you realize. But I won't be surprised if he doesn't show up. It isn't safe to have something on Papa Sebastian."

"He's not the only one."

"You're forgetting we're dead, eliminated in that convenient camping accident."

"I was thinking of Marcus and company. And that gardener who sometimes sails with Rod. I told you — I'm sure he's the man in your picture. As soon as Old Brammin mentioned him, I remembered the bracelet. It rattled against his clippers."

"My picture that was."

"Maybe we'll be lucky and get another. No one seems to have noticed who left with Rod last week. Maybe the gardener didn't go — or he could have driven back early from Apalachicola."

"Hopefully. But, as I was going to say, they're loyal soldier types. Rod's another matter entirely."

"I'd assumed he was trying to join the family. Otherwise why Cheri?"

"That's unfair — she can be charming."

"And a pain in the rear, too."

Hillary shrugged philosophically and began to fiddle with the air conditioner. "Sometimes that's part of the attraction."

"More likely her millions are the attraction. That thing isn't working, is it?"

"Not unless you like your air lukewarm."

"When we get on the key road, we can open the windows."

"We'll have to or you'll wind up with one dead Pancho Villa."

"You should complain."

"Hmmm. That costume does not really suit you. Very Desdemona's-death-scene."

"That's a cheerful omen."

"She has some glorious music," he replied and began to hum in a thin falsetto.

"Shut up, Hillary, and watch the signs. Is it the next turn?"

"No, one more."

Neither of us was feeling too sharp, and our silly conversation was mere bravado. It was that or snapping at each other. Hillary and I have always been too much alike, evading fear as well as other emotions by flippancy. For happiness, we need completely different types, either intense personalities like Theresa or serene ones like Harry. Otherwise we turn hard and superficial and hurt ourselves and other people. In retrospect, we really weren't a good team, because each of us maintained a pretense of unconcern which provoked the other into recklessness.

"Turn here," Hillary directed. A few minutes later, the water appeared behind the palms and the sea breeze blew up. When I stopped the car, we could hear it whistling over the surf Hillary put on his mask and his sombrero, and I fixed his tie. "Better keep your hat on straight or your bandage will show."

He checked the effect in the mirror, then helped me pin the veil, which I had reinforced with a strip of material taken out of the hem. That left my eyes visible, but I had rescued a pair of Baby's long false lashes from the trash. "All right?"

"I wouldn't recognize you. Are you sure you can keep your eyes open under all that nylon?"

"About as long as I can tote the rest of this rig," I said, starting the car. Our precautions proved far-sighted; Marcus was checking the guests at the foot of the drive. We were directed to a lot below the lawn, and I left the keys under the front seat. "In case we have to split up."

"Right, and I'll take the camera," Hillary said, "just in case."

"Only a picture, though. No settling of debts tonight."

"Don't worry, old girl," he said smoothly. "You're letting this Zorro suit give you ideas. Wait a minute — one of your trailing things is caught." He untangled my sleeve from a branch, and we proceeded across the lawn to the party.

The house and garden were even more brilliantly decorated than they had been on the previous weekend, and rows of Japanese lanterns were reflected in the waterway. The band seemed noisier, too, and the voices a little shriller, as if some jealous sprite had included a hostile brew among the concoctions at the bar. Everyone seemed to be in a rush, and cowboys and gypsy princesses, space cadets and clowns, fantastic birds with feather heads atop chorus girl tights, grotesquely masked kings and animals, robots and gangsters brushed past us in a frenzy of movement that left sequins winking on the lawn and vivid pink and green feathers fluttering along the tables. The whole flamboyant mob seemed in a hurry to get somewhere else, from the buffet tables to the dance floor, from the dance floor to the bar, from the bar to the promenade by the water, as if engaged in a bizarre treasure hunt. Perhaps they were, because there were continual outbursts of laughter and shrieks of surprise and discovery and wild bits of clowning and promiscuous fool-ishness hidden behind the papier-mâché and mesh and veils and the elaborate masks that a bevy of ravishingly dressed women carried on sticks like dowagers' lorgnettes.

"Bit of a zoo here tonight," Hillary said. "Half of them are flying on one thing or another."

"We seem to be on the lunatic fringe. I suppose the sober citizens are nearer the house."

"They'll be at the bar trying to reach the same heights. Our best bet is the kitchen entrance. The hangers-on have their own canteen."

We made our way through the revelers on the terrace. The long windows were all open, and inside, on the marble floor of the ballroom, the dancing was in full swing. Half the masks had been discarded and lay in bright, amorphous piles around the edge of the floor, while their costumed owners gyrated in fantastic groupings borrowed from every continent, era, and fashion. The chandeliers glittered overhead in crystal extravagance, but the paintings that usually lined the walls had been prudently hoisted out of reach, and now and again we caught a glimpse of Marcus or of one of the other functionaries prowling in the background. "I don't see Cheri," I remarked.

"Still trying to raise Rod, I suppose."

Behind the ballroom was a hall that led to the living rooms

and a library, all sprinkled with guests. The library opened
onto the back terrace and the walled garden, where a group
was playing tag and hide-and-seek amidst the trees and shrubs,
running about like elf children in their weird finery. Whenever
they left the lights near the terrace, they were swallowed up by
the shadows of the enormous spiked plants, and beyond the
walls the palms rattled in the wind like witches' laughter. It
was remarkable that some overstimulated adolescents and a
few dozen yards of imitation satin could produce such a fanciful, even sinister, impression. I glanced toward the upper stories of the mansion. "This should be to Papa Sebastian's taste."

"Not if they ruin his flowers," Hillary observed with satisfaction.

We walked through the trees at the back of the garden until
one of the guards directed us away from the path leading to the
chapel and the garage. We returned along the kitchen side of
the house where a huge fan was pumping out heat and the
smell of roast turkey. Through the open door we could see the
harried cooks and the overloaded waitresses running in and out
with trays for the buffet tables.

"No sign of him?" Hillary asked.

"Nope."

A swing down toward the water proved no more productive,
but then there was a great commotion everywhere, and eyes
one almost recognized winked behind the slits of a mask then
vanished, and a familiar gait was disguised by cardboard armor
and tinsel mail. After the heat of the day, even the breeze along
the inland waterway felt cool, and we soon followed a group of
underdressed visitors back to the terrace. Hillary picked up a
plate and began to nibble on the turkey and the hors d'oeuvres.
"I don't think he's here."

"Maybe he and Rod both disappeared."

Hillary made a face. This was preposterous, I agreed, and
although I wasn't hungry, I took a roll and salad and went to
sit on the wall. Something clinked. It was only someone empty-
ing ice from a glass onto the stone terrace, but behind, only a

few feet away, stood a sour-faced man with round shoulders. He wore an open shirt and a cheap jacket, and when he put down the cigarette he was smoking I noticed a flash of silver around his wrist. I got up as unobtrusively as possible and went around the table. Hillary had his back to me, talking to an acquaintance, and, just before I reached him, a very realistic satyr pushed past me, spilling some of his drink down my arm.

"Oh, sorry! Mary Ann? Is that you? Jesus, girl, you left your costume a little late, didn't you? I swear I saw that number last winter at the Civic Opera. Frightful mob, isn't it? Impossible to find anything decent."

I smiled, nodded, edged past him. "I'm not Mary Ann."

More apologies. He was one of those aggressive apologizers, who browbeat you with regrets, explanations, and amplifications. Hillary's black sombrero bobbed above a sunrise of plumes. I pushed past a Viking queen and an unmasked Darth Vader. A dark costume entered the ballroom, but by the time I reached the house, Hillary had disappeared, and I could not locate him in the swirl of costumes, faces, and masks. I retraced our earlier route through the back rooms, the garden, and down to the shore. Several times I thought I saw his black hat, but it was always something else. When I returned to the terrace, the gardener was gone, of course, and Hillary had not reappeared. I didn't trust him. He always had some scheme of his own, and he preferred not to reveal his plans. That must drive his wife crazy.

I took a glass from a tray, sipped a little of the dry bubbly, and watched the upper floors of the house. The rooms were lit, but the wide balcony, the high balustrade, and the potted plants concealed their interiors. The back of the house was the same story, although some of the rooms were dark. Perhaps they were out of bounds for the party. I put down the glass, and walked into the foyer and through the hall to the main staircase. People were running up and down to the upper floor or loafing on the pink marble steps, or wandering along the upper gallery admiring the pictures. I fell in with a group examining a Degas pastel and waited until the bedroom designated as a powder room was empty. From the tour Cheri had given me, I remembered that the room was strikingly pretty with cerise walls and green lacquered furniture, but the important thing was that it connected to a dressing room with a French door onto the balcony. This was locked, but in my evening purse, I had a small screwdriver, a knife, and a short piece of wire. Except for keeping my veil out of the way, I had no trouble opening it, and I was just putting away the tools when I heard a step in the outer room. I jumped up and snapped the purse shut, but, before I could arrange my veil again, Cheri appeared in the doorway. She was beautifully dressed in pale blue, with her hair done up in feathers and brilliants, and she carried a white satin mask. Her eyes were very bright, as if she were close to tears, and her face was pale. "Oh, Anna! I've been wanting to talk to you." She reached behind to pull the door of the dressing room shut. "Have you heard any more about Rod?"

So she wasn't involved. Poor girl. "Someone mentioned his boat was late," I said. "I hope there's nothing wrong."

"No one tells me anything. I can't even find out who went with him. No one knows anything! You'd think they ran that marina with their eyes shut."

"Did you ask Marcus? He was at the shop the afternoon Rod left."

"Why would he mention his crew to Marcus when he didn't to me?" she asked resentfully. "He hardly knows Marcus."

"Yet Marcus minded the shop for him."

"That's different. That's business."

"Perhaps the boat is business, too."

"The *Melody*? Some business. It's always needing repairs." Cheri put down the mask and took cigarettes out of her evening purse. "Want one?"

"No, thanks." I waited until she blew out the match and said, as if as an afterthought, "Surely your dad wouldn't have invested in it if it weren't a good buy."

She looked up sharply.

"You mentioned that a week ago," I said, all innocence, "when you were discussing a sail up to Apalachicola with Rod."

"Oh, that. Dad loaned him money for repairs, that's all."

"Your dad's very generous with Rod."

"Why do you say that?"

"Rod lives rather well — considering his assets. He wouldn't have either his shop or his apartment, would he, if he weren't dealing with your father's company?"

"You do hear a lot, don't you? What else do you hear about Rod and my father?"

"That the relationship between Rod and your father is strictly business." She started to say something, but I held up my hand. "Oh, no doubt they met through you and no doubt there was a certain amount of parental indulgence, but Rod is costing your dad a bundle, and you can be sure he's getting something in return."

Cheri's curiosity momentarily outweighed her indignation. "What could Rod give my father?"

"There are a number of items that a man with a ship like the *Melody* can acquire. Some of them are illicit. Those are the expensive items — ones that would balance out a fancy apartment, marine bills, and rent on a first class shop."

"I don't believe this!" Cheri exclaimed, very much the aggrieved hostess. "I hardly know you. You're a guest in my house, and you're telling these lies about my father and Rod — "

I interrupted her. "You're a bright person, Cheri, and, even living here, you must know money doesn't fall from heaven. Hasn't it ever puzzled you how Rod stays afloat financially?"

"No!"

"Now that's a lie, and I'll tell you how I know. You're awfully interested in my friend John Hillary. Even though your father disapproves of him."

"Hillary's a delightful man. No jealousy like an old flame, I can see."

"You see what you want to see. Hillary is delightful and smart, which made him undesirable from the start. But the thing your dad doesn't like — or Rod either — is that Hillary's a crime reporter with considerable expertise and a very good investigator on top of that. Sooner or later he will find out whatever is to be found. You realized that and that's why you've cultivated him. You'd like to be the first to know."

"That's a lot of shit," Cheri shouted, her face very white.

"Because then your father and Rod will not be able to conduct their business secretly and you'll know where you stand. I don't blame you at all. You're in a very unfortunate position."

"This is all — imagination. You don't know what you're talking about." Cheri's anger was not completely convincing, but her alarm was genuine.

"On the contrary, I make it my business to know what I'm talking about. I have only partial proof, that's true, but in the last twenty-four hours the circumstantial evidence has nearly overwhelmed me, literally. If I were you, Cheri, I wouldn't lose any time in notifying the Coast Guard. Because either something's happened to Rod, or — "

There was a knocking in the bedroom and Cheri hastily opened the connecting door. "What is it?" Her voice was harsh.

"Miss Sebastian?"

"Yes, just a minute, Marcus."

I refastened my veil like a woman in purdah.

"It's time for the fireworks, Miss Sebastian."

Cheri glanced back to me. "We can wait a while for those."

"It looks like rain. If we hold off much longer, they're apt to get wet."

"Oh, all right. Go ahead. I'll be down."

"I need the keys for the boat."

"They weren't in the shed?"

"No, Miss."

"Wait a minute," she said as she went out. "I'll get them for you, but leave them in the boat. Arthur will want to clean up the frames on the shore afterward." I heard her go into the hall, issuing orders and directions, then made my exit to the balcony. Below, the party made patches of color on the lawn. Then came the jagged band of the trees and across the key road, the silver line of the surf and the black nothingness of the sea. The air smelled like rain and the breeze blew the veiling back against my mouth. I crossed the front of the house, went around the corner and down to the darkened rooms overlooking the garden. The first was closed, its air conditioner rumbling. The next few were shut, too, the glass covered by such heavy drapes that it was impossible to tell if anyone were inside or if the lights were on. From one room, though, I thought I heard voices, and when I found that there was a narrow little window open close to the far end of the building, I tucked up my purple skirts and squeezed inside. Then I pulled the window shut, in case someone else went exploring, and stood squinting in the darkness until I identified the dim rows of shapes as racks of elegant men's suits, shirts, and jackets. Underfoot were rows and rows of narrow, perfectly polished shoes. I felt my way forward in the closet and opened the door softly. The next room was a small square dressing room containing a beautiful carved armoire, an inlaid chest of drawers, a set of silver brushes, and an elaborate mirror. Heavy floor-length velvet drapes shut out the night, but a small light had been left burning, and I could see that there was a bathroom on one side of the dressing room and a suite of rooms branching off on the other. Sebastian's wing had been designed as quite separate from the rest of the house, and through this promising territory I picked my way, opening all the closets in the handsome sitting room and examining the small sculptures displayed in Sebastian's king-sized bedroom. Aside from a few pre-Columbian ceramics, there was nothing suggestive; in fact, there was almost certainly no place for a stela weighing a ton or more.

Past the bedroom was a storage area lined from floor to ceiling with wide, shallow drawers for prints and drawings. I had flicked on the overhead light to make sure of the contents, when a sound in the next room made me hastily switch it off. There was another sound, soft and muffled by the smooth, thick carpeting, the drapes, the ample, comfortable furniture, and the fabric-covered walls, but unmistakable, nonetheless. Someone was in the adjoining room. I peered through the keyhole without success. There was someone, though, moving very stealthily, and once in a while making a clinking sound as if handling small pieces of metal. Each time, all movement stopped for an instant as if the person were making every effort to be unobtrusive. Suspecting it might be Hillary, I turned the knob and inched the door open until I could see into a room lined by shelves filled with leather-bound books. Flanking the windows were a number of collector's cabinets holding porcelain and figurines. One stood next to the door to the storage area, almost blocking my view of the left-hand side of the room. In the center was a leather chair and an elaborate desk with a bronze sphinx holding up two lamps. Behind the chair was a figure in a gray cape or shirt that moved suddenly, revealing a monstrous red demon face and shortening my breath in spite of myself. The man turned slightly, then, reassured by the silence, he reached into a square, brassbound chest and proceeded to remove some coins, which he transferred to a leather bag. I heard the click of a lock or a hinge closing. Then the man took out a knife and, holding a small jewelers' box up to the light, pried the catch. He put away the knife and pushed the demon's face farther back on his head before emptying the contents into his sack. Rod Brammin was not lost at sea after all, and I was about to ask if this was how he usually collected his share when the door on my left opened. The demon face swung around like a jack-in-the-box, and Rod jumped up, one hand on the desk. Then he straightened his shoulders and relaxed. "Evening, Marcus."

The outer door closed. I flattened myself against the side of the wall and strained to see through the narrow opening. Marcus strolled into the center of the room, one hand in the pocket of his cream-colored slacks, his face perfectly composed. "What are you doing here? These are Mr. Sebastian's private rooms."

"Come off it, Marcus. It's perfectly obvious what I'm doing."
Rod knelt down on the floor. He dumped a noisy handful of
coins and boxes into his sack, then stood up, kicking the door
of the chest shut. "I'll be on my way now," he said.

Marcus reached for the telephone on the desk, but Rod was
quicker and, by the look of it, stronger. He grabbed Marcus'
wrist. "Later. Just tell the old pirate I've taken my severance
pay. Don't worry. This will be adequate. He won't need to mail
a check."

Marcus pulled away, brushed some imagined dust from his
jacket, and straightened the medallion he wore around his
neck. "You wanna die, be my guest," he said.

"That has already been decided — or were you left out of that
plan? Peter and Arthur had to bring the sculptures back by
truck. Surprise! But there were a couple of guys down at the
dock who would crew back with me. Do I look stupid, Marcus?"
he demanded, his voice rising dangerously. "Do you think I'd
go anywhere with wharf rats I didn't know? Particularly ones
Vlad recommended?"

"What did you do with them?"

"I discouraged them," Rod said coldly, then he fastened the
neck of his sack and slung it over his shoulder, pulling the cape
around him.

"Did you sail back alone?" Marcus' eyes were quick in his
still face.

"That's another thing you might tell Vlad. I'm keeping the
Melody. Fair enough, isn't it? He keeps Cheri; I keep the ship."
Although Rod smiled when he said this, he did not seem a
happy man. "The store is his, too. I can hardly take that with
me. You might persuade him to let you run it. Antiques suit
you, Marcus. You're a bit of a curiosity yourself." He took out
his knife and opened the blade, then he detached the phone
from its jack and severed one of the wires. "Talk to him later,
all right? I hadn't planned for you to arrive." Rod gave another
faint, unhappy smile, and, leaving his large knife open on the

desk, stared thoughtfully at Sebastian's assistant. Marcus moved his hand slowly up to his medallion again. This time, Rod understood the reason for this uncharacteristically nervous maneuver and lunged across the desk. Marcus was quick enough to pluck a tiny revolver from his jacket pocket, but Rod seized his arm, throwing him off balance and tipping the ornate empire lamp off the desk. With his free hand Marcus began hammering at Rod, and he must have been stronger than he looked, for Rod gasped and reached for the knife. I opened the door further, uncertain whether or not I dared intervene, when they began to fight in earnest. They dropped to the floor and struggled savagely, flinging each other against the book cases and the furniture. The gun went off, shattering the glass front of a cabinet, and then Rod's knife rattled against the side of the desk. They struggled over this for a moment, and Rod seemed to have been slashed, for there was blood on his face when he stumbled, his hands on the floor. Marcus leaped and kicked him viciously once, twice. Falling back from this attack, Rod grabbed the bronze lamp, and swung it waist high. It caught Marcus in the ribs, knocking the wind out of him and forcing him against the desk. While he struggled for breath, Rod swung the lamp again. The cord ripped from the wall, and the bulbs flared out as the sphinx hit the side of Marcus' head with a thud. In the sudden darkness, someone fell. I heard labored breathing, then the clinking of the coins in the leather bag. I retreated hastily through the storage room to behind a lacquer screen in the bedroom, but no one came, and I heard nothing more.

After waiting several minutes, I crept back and opened the door. Silence and darkness. Switching on the light in the print room to survey the damage, I entered Sebastian's private library. There were books on the floor and broken glass. The sphinx lamp lay on its side with one bracket twisted. The chair behind the desk had been toppled over. Marcus' little gun gleamed on the pile carpet; so did the medallion, which lay just to the side of his head, but it was rapidly being covered by the thick stream of blood issuing from his mouth. I felt for his pulse and tried to find his heartbeat, but his expression remained noncommittal: there was no sign of life. I stood up, snatching my trailing drapery away from the expanding mess. Had I touched anything? Too much. I retraced my steps, hastily wiping off the handles of the print drawers, the doors of the cabinets in Sebastian's bedroom, the doorknob in the closet, the sides of the windows. Anything else? No time, I'd have to take my chances. I ran back through the suite, remembered to switch off the light in the storage room, eased open the main door of the library, and found myself in a short empty corridor. At one end was a stair down, and when I reached the bottom, I could hear the noise of the party. One door led to the back, obviously to the kitchen area. The other opened into a crowd of people who were laughing and complaining and shaking rain off masks and costumes and exclaiming over the sudden downpour that had put a premature end to the fireworks and driven everybody indoors. Everyone, that is, but Hillary and, presumably, Rod who must have made an inconspicuous exit in the midst of all the confusion. I pushed my way through the hall and into the ballroom, where I caught a glimpse of Cheri. Outside, cars were starting up and people were running back and forth with umbrellas. In the ballroom, the musicians were packing, except for one clarinetist who warbled bouncy pop variations. There was no sign of Hillary. I completed one more circuit, then ventured onto the terrace. It was wet underfoot, but the cloudburst had dwindled to mere spits of rain, and the gray morning sky echoed with the boom of the surf. Cigarette butts and empty glasses littered the flagstones and a few men and women stood with their masks off, smoking, while several young couples in swimsuits ran barefoot across the wet grass. A line of headlights traced the Sebastians' curving drive and the key road, but even these had begun to thin out. The party was over, and the frenetic hilarity of the evening had left the remainder of the guests reflective, even melancholy. They talked slowly in quiet voices, filling up the damp air with cigarette smoke as though reluctant to taste the night odors of salt, sulfur, and swamp. From the bottom of the lawn, I spotted our car, nearly alone in the lot, and, anxious, I returned through the emptying house to the garden. Some of the staff were relaxing around the corner by the kitchen: soon one of them would go upstairs and discover Marcus. That thought made me hurry past the formal flower beds to the iron gate in the back wall. It was beginning to drizzle again, and the path toward Sebastian's chapel and the other outbuildings was unlit. I followed the white sand between the dark trees and shrubs for a time before I heard voices, or rather, a voice: Hillary's. I darted forward, stumbled over my purple skirts, and had a near miss with a large spiky cactus. I stopped, ripped off my veil, and wrapped up the trailing costume like a sarong. To hell with the Near East.

"Tell the old bastard I'm here," Hillary said in his least pleasant voice.

The reply was indistinct but clearly negative, and it was followed by a brilliant flash of white that illuminated the roots and branches of an immense banyon tree and revealed Hillary and Arthur, the apartment gardener, near a tool shed. Hillary discarded a flash cube and returned the camera to his pocket. "Thank you," he said primly. "For my album."

The gardener demanded the film, but Hillary declined with a few suitable remarks and started to leave. Arthur reached into the tool shed and produced a machete. I yelled a warning. Surprised, he hesitated, then charged Hillary, the blade swinging. I ran toward them as Hillary dodged behind first one bush, then another. There was no doubt that Arthur was adept with the weapon: it severed a large cactus and effortlessly topped a palmetto. I picked up a shovel, intending to swing it like a bat. But despite his unprepossessing appearance, the gardener was surprisingly agile, and I was hampered by the trailing sleeves and the skirt which came undone and caught my ankles, pitching me onto the sandy ground. Seeing his chance, Arthur feinted toward me, and when Hillary made a grab for him, the gardener slashed the machete across his chest and shoulder. Hillary screamed, and Arthur moved in, seeking to trap him against the shed or the thicker shrubbery. Hillary tried to pick up the shovel but could not lift it, and he was forced backward, dodging the blade, which came closer with every swipe. I scrambled to my feet, using a wheelbarrow for support. There was a crunch of branches as Hillary stumbled back into the brush, and, grabbing both handles of the barrow, I swung it around and ran full tilt at Arthur. He saw me coming, but this time he had less room to maneuver. While Hillary slipped out of the mesh of leaves and branches, Arthur made a lunge at me. I ducked, but the barrow was longer than his reach. The big front wheel caught him under one knee, and he fell forward, the machete digging into the earth. I slammed my foot on his arm and grabbed the weapon, as Hillary staggered forward and aimed a kick to the back of his head. Arthur slid off the barrow, dazed.

"Are you badly hurt, Hillary?"

He moved his hand to show the blood seeping from his shoulder and from the red line traced across the front of his white shirt. "Nothing lethal. Never mind that now." He trotted painfully down the path toward the house, but before we reached the garden, we heard the crackle of a walkie-talkie.

"He'll call the goons on the gate," I said. "We can't go back to the car."

"The house, then."

"Party's over. Nobody there but the staff."

"Christ! We'll have to go through the bloody brush, then."

"There's a boat. Marcus was to leave the keys in it."

"He'll have moved it by now."

"Marcus won't be moving anything," I said, and cut across the back of the garden. The lights were still on by the water and a couple of small sleek boats were moored to the dock.

"Go see if the keys are in," Hillary said, "I'm moving a bit slowly."

I ran through the palms, across the drive, and down to the

dock, the machete still in my hand. The first boat had no keys, but the second, a smaller craft, had a leather case dangling from the ignition. I waved to Hillary, who came stumbling across the lawn, and scrambled back out of the boat to help him.

"I can make it. I can make it. Start the goddamned thing."

I turned the key and the motor roared. Hillary lurched into the seat, spattering blood across the immaculate white deck, and put the engine into gear. "Get that rope," he yelled.

I swung the machete once, and the speedboat leaped away from the dock and headed south, leaving behind a white wake and Arthur, whose figure appeared on the lawn as we sped down the waterway.

Chapter 13

"IT's LIKE DRIVING a car," Hillary shouted over the chill morning air that blasted by on either side, flapping my costume and stiffening the wide, blood-soaked sleeves of his shirt. A heavy mist had settled during the night, blurring the trees along the bank and dangling ghostly veils above the murky surface of the water. As we cut through these wet phantoms, the landscape rose in quick gray and green flashes, and Sebastian's magnificent house disappeared as if by a conjurer's trick.

I wrenched open the metal first aid kit. Inside were some bandages and a roll of gauze that looked utterly inadequate to staunch the blood flowing from Hillary's chest and shoulder. "We'd better get the bleeding stopped."

"The cut's not deep. Take the wheel and keep it straight. That's all you have to do."

"I think you'd better let me — "

"Just steer the damn thing. I'll do it myself."

I took over the boat. Hillary unbuttoned his shirt and got as far as laying a trail of gauze squares along the red line on his chest. Then he attempted to patch his shoulder and crumpled forward across the wheel.

"Watch it, Hillary!" There was no answer. "God! Wait a minute!" I shoved him off the wheel and pulled us back from a collision with the opposite shore. Then I tried to steer with one hand so I could prop him against the side of the craft. Hillary's eyelids moved a trifle, but he was still out. Deceived by the murky shadows and mist, I wrenched the wheel, put the boat sideways across the waterway, and had to straighten the erratic craft with a lurch. "How do you stop this thing?" Still no answer. I looked back. They must follow, but there were no lights, and the roar of our boat obliterated any other sound. "Hillary! Hillary!" I shook him. No response; he looked very white. I fumbled about the dashboard and found the lights. A beam shot through the mist, revealing a wider place in the waterway, and I cut back the speed. Beyond a clump of pines was a small cove. I steered cautiously into the shadows and shut off the lights. Then I turned the key. The engine coughed and died, setting us to slosh in our own wake. There was a flashlight next to the first aid kit, and I switched it on, pulled Hillary's shirt away from his shoulder, and had a look. The cut was deep there, and although the rest was little more than a scratch, he must have lost quite a bit of blood. I tried futilely to remember where the pressure points were, then wound the gauze round and round the shoulder, made a pad with the rest of the bandages, and pressed it directly on the wound.

"Come on, Hillary," I begged, but the only answer was a distant soft throbbing too indistinct to identify for certain, but probably Sebastian's other boat. I was raking frantically through the first aid kit for smelling salts, when Hillary suddenly raised his head.

"Where are we?"

"I don't know. Not very far away. You passed out trying to bandage your shoulder."

"I'm all right. I've done that before. Every time I get a blood test — whump." He sat up, quite alert. "Did you let the motor die? Christ! We may not get it started again."

"You said it was just like a car. Here, stop fussing and press on this. See if that will stop the blood."

His eyes fluttered, but he shook his head and stayed upright.

"Just hold it there." I ran a few strips of adhesive tape across the other bandages.

"Never mind that. Try to start the motor. Wait, let me see."

"All right. You do it."

"Hold the flashlight over here."

He turned the key and the boat coughed. On the third try it caught. "Not much gas in this thing."

"They've got to be right behind us. We'd better stop at the first dock we see, get to a house and call the police."

Hillary nodded as he relinquished the wheel. I steered the boat cautiously along the side of the cove and headed toward the dim shapes of some houses. "Better give it more gas," he said. I did and the boat took off, throwing us back against the seat. "Watch it!"

"It is *not* just like a car."

"Close enough for your driving." A moment later, he said, "Over there. Isn't that a dock with a couple of boats?"

I flicked on the lights. A line of posts ran out into the water and a small powerboat and a fair-sized sloop were tied up to a ramshackle dock.

"Cut the lights," Hillary warned.

"Do you see something?"

"I keep thinking I can hear another boat. Ease off on the speed. More! No! You're too far out. Wait, wait." Hillary grabbed the wheel and brought the boat around, scraping the side of the sailboat and connecting us sharply with the dock. "Turn it off!" I turned the switch, reached over the side and grabbed one of the pilings. I spotted a ladder a few feet farther down and edged the boat forward.

"Can you climb the ladder?"

"Shhh."

As soon as I stood still, I could hear the engine, and there was a light flickering behind the trees across the cove.

"Get down," Hillary said.

"Come on. They'll recognize their own boat."

Hillary winced as he stood up.

"Go first — it's only a couple of steps. You won't fall."

He grabbed the ladder with his left hand and gasped as he slouched forward. I caught him, but the boat drifted treacherously out. "Step up, Hillary!" He swung himself onto the ladder one step, two, while I stretched across the gunwale and embraced a slimy piling. From up the waterway, the approaching engine came on with a high-pitched whine. "All right?"

He stumbled onto the dock. "Yes. Watch, there's some missing boards."

"Get off of there. They'll pick you out with the lights."

I slung the machete onto the dock, then scrambled up the ladder, one of my wretched sleeves catching and shredding on the nails and the rough wood. I wrenched away with a jerk that ripped out the stitching and left a purple pendant hanging from the side of the ladder. I reached to retrieve it, but the bright lights of a powerboat flashed around the cove, and I flattened myself on the dock. The boat raced by, and, forgetting the sleeve, I grabbed Arthur's machete and ran after Hillary. We heard the roar of the departing engine drop, then ominously begin to rise again.

"They're circling back," he said.

"Probably checking every dock — that's why they took so long. Someone's remembered how low the gas tank was."

I raced through a band of fat pineapple palms to the nearest house. Their feathery tops had concealed a trio of boarded-up windows and a porch minus screens.

"Gone for the summer," I called. "We'll have to try the next one."

Hillary limped into the next yard, and I followed, tripping over assorted rocks and potted plants and getting sand spurs in my sandals. This house looked occupied, but when we rang the back door bell, there was no response.

"Broken, maybe," Hillary said.

Out in the cove, the powerboat cut its motor, sending us scurrying to the front. The main door was a big, modern, double-hung job with an intercom that rang a complicated chime. The bells echoed through the house, jangling all my nerve endings.

"Damn idle rich," Hillary said. "Why don't they stay home

and spend the summer in their air conditioning?" I noticed the blood on his fingers: the cut was still bleeding badly. In despair, I glanced across the road and spotted a mailbox on the opposite shoulder. "There must be another house behind those trees."

Hillary gestured for silence. "They're checking out the boat," he whispered, pointing toward the water. "I can see them through the trees."

"They'll search this place first." After a moment's hesitation, we committed ourselves to a winding drive that led to a two-story house set smack on the beach. Once again, I rang the front door bell. This one emitted a loud, functional buzz, but no lights appeared upstairs. I pushed the button again. No sleepy head leaned out the window. A third time.

"We'll get in around the back," Hillary said, and without waiting for a response, ducked behind a fragrant boxwood hedge to the rear of the property. The white sand was within reach of the house, and an opaque sea thundered over the rocks a few yards away. It was still night, but against the pale sand it was easy to find the door to the porch. "Use the machete," Hillary whispered.

I slit the screen, reached in, and released the catch. The house itself was entered through a sliding glass door, which fortunately had been left ajar. We shut it after us and made sure of the lock. Extending the width of the house was a large living room with a deep carpet, blocky contemporary furniture, gargantuan lamps, and too many windows. The whole rear wall was glass, filled with the gray-green sea and sky. Hillary pulled the curtains shut, then stationed himself by the front door. I searched for a phone, feeling my way in the aqueous predawn light over ashtrays and knickknacks and a horrid fuzzy toy. No phone.

"Try the kitchen."

The kitchen was at the end of a short, narrow hall. I ran my hands along the sides of the cabinets and searched a breakfast bar, before I nearly fell over a little table near the icebox. It held the phone. I dialed for the operator. The connection rang and rang.

"Any luck?" Hillary's whisper traveled clearly.

"It's ringing, but the operator doesn't answer."

"Dial direct."

"Any sign of them?"

"Not yet."

"Yes? Operator! We need police and an ambulance. The key road. An accident. Number?" My mind went blank. Of course they needed a number. The number. I pictured the mailbox against the black trees and the pale sand. "Thirty-two. Thirty-two Key Road."

"I see them," Hillary exclaimed.

"And hurry, please."

"Your name?"

"Peters. Anna Peters. No, I'm just using the phone here. Their name? For God's sake, my friend is bleeding to death, just get the damn ambulance." My voice rose in exasperation, and Hillary whispered a warning. I hung up on a fluster at the other end, returned to the living room, and parted the curtain on the rear windows just a fraction. How long for police and an ambulance? No traffic at this hour. How far were we from the connecting road to the mainland? I was trying to work out the distance we'd come by boat, when we heard a crunching sound around the corner of the house: someone was walking on the gravel. They had obviously split up to search the area.

Next to me, a stylized blue dancing girl supported a lamp with a large silk shade. On the table underneath children's snapshots were clustered, and there was a needlepoint pillow on the sofa, another accretion of sentiment to style. Beyond the glass, the Gulf rolled on its green belly and threatened, but inside all was conventional, even cozy. It was the Sebastian place all over again. There beauty was added to comfort and wealth to convention, but still it was hard to unite the guards and the flowers, the manicured yards and grandchildren's pictures and the man prowling on the gravel. The man who would see the cut screen, I thought, as I reached for the machete, but the footsteps faded. I peered around the curtain: only the sea. Had he noticed and gone back for the others? I tried to attract

Hillary's attention, but he was resting on a hassock with his back to me, watching the front window. I crossed the living room softly. "See anything?"

He pointed to a flashlight glimmering at the top of the drive. "He's suspicious," Hillary whispered.

"He didn't touch the screen door. What do you suppose he saw?"

"Blood," Hillary answered. His hand looked black in the dim light.

"Hold on." I went to the kitchen for a towel. I opened the drawers, putting my hands in carefully to avoid knives. Cutlery. Cooking implements. Towels. They felt clean. "See them yet?"

"He's still waiting by the road."

"Here." I discarded the blood-soaked compress and tied a dishtowel tightly around the wound.

"Easy," Hillary warned. "I don't want to pass out again."

"Put this around your neck. It'll make a sling. That way you won't be moving the wound all the time."

"Got it tied?"

"No. Stay still."

"They're coming."

Through the curtains, two flashlights bobbed. A third joined them at the top of the drive and pointed toward the house. I returned to the back window and soon heard the sound of steps on the gravel. Someone was rustling the bushes on the kitchen side of the house, too. I gripped the machete tighter. A man appeared by the porch where Hillary and I had entered. He fingered the torn screen, then opened the door. I drew back flat against the wall as his feet moved softly over the straw matting. He stopped, inches away from me, to test the lock on the sliding door. The handle clicked. He tried to force it, then left the porch around the kitchen side. A few seconds later, there was a rattling sound, as if someone were fiddling with a door, and Hillary leaped up behind me. "There'll be a door from the garage," he hissed. He banged through the hall to be sure there was no access to the house, but before he could reach the door there was a crash of cans and bottles and almost instantly the whole yard lit up. Spotlights concealed in the palms cut through the morning fog, and bounced off the white sand. The paths to the house sprouted a file of square yellow lights, the blue dancing girl held up a hundred-watt bulb; the recessed lighting above the couch came to life, the fluorescents over the kitchen stove cast their blue lights, and a big hunk of frosted glass in the hall revealed Hillary with boots, bolero, and bandages like a Mexican desperado on a bad day, and two very startled people in nightclothes. The woman, plump, her short gray hair in blue curlers, wore a pink nightgown with a low top and a ruffled bottom. The man, a shade taller, was thin and primly attired in check pajamas. A pair of horn-rimmed glasses sat on the bridge of his nose, and resting uncertainly against his neat little tummy was a .22 rifle.

"What are you waiting for, Sid? That man is in our living room!"

The rifle trembled slightly as he raised it. Outside, the sound of running feet: the goons were leaving. Suburbia had reasserted itself in what looked like a thoroughly dangerous manner.

"Shoot him, for God's sake, Sid!"

Hillary raised his hand in a placating gesture and pointed to his wounded arm. "As you can see, Madam — "

The woman yelled. "He's stolen our dish towels, Sid! I knew he was a robber."

"There's nothing to worry about," I said in a voice that was as loud and firm as I could manage. The old couple on the stair jumped, and the rifle made a shaky quarter-turn in my direction.

"Oh my God! It's like the Manson gang, Sid! Do you see how she's dressed?"

"I've called the police," I said, "and an ambulance for my friend." I pointed toward Hillary.

There were gasps. I was still holding the blood-smeared machete. Realizing my mistake, I set it carefully on a stool. "Blood," I explained. "It would be hard to clean off your rug."

"Yes," Hillary added quickly, "we've gotten some over here. It couldn't be helped. I'd try a little cold water right away on it. And perhaps another towel. Still bleeding." He held up his blood-smeared hand.

The rifle swung belligerently. "Just what the hell do you think you're doing, young man?" Sid adjusted his glasses and waited for the answer.

"Sitting down," Hillary said. "I get faint from loss of blood. Happens every time. I passed out once fishing when I cut my hand on a hook. And before I got married when I got my blood tested." He looked very pale and his eyelids twitched. "And I cut my leg as a boy. On a skate — out like a light." He smiled at the woman rather desperately and got his reward.

"Put down that fool gun, Sid. The boy's hurt."

"Now, Ad, be careful."

"Nonsense. Go get some bandages." She gathered up her nightgown daintily and bustled down the stairs. It did not take too much effort on Hillary's part to look pathetic. "Bring my scissors," she called. "Dirt. This'll infect. You should know better," she said to me.

"Under the circumstances," I began, but Hillary was willing to be bullied.

"Oh, yes, it's a mess," he agreed.

"This will need stitching. Here, leastways. My brother Wilbur — the one who owned a big farm out in Iowa — he cut himself just like this. Thrown off a sled into barbed wire."

Hillary grunted sympathetically.

"Today they'd have stitched and given tetanus shots, too. Not in those days."

"He mended on his own, I suppose."

"Had to. Did you say you called the police?"

"And an ambulance," I added.

Sid brought in the bandages, but he was not resigned to our presence. "There's a public phone up the road," he said.

"There were some problems with that."

"Three," Hillary said.

"We'll pay for your screen."

"I'm not sure you need both," the woman said. "The police do a very good first aid training here, you know. When Sid had his last attack — "

She began to relate this with some enthusiasm, but her narrative was interrupted by a blue revolving light that found its way through the pebbled glass by the front door and ran back and forth across the hall ceiling like a nervous mouse. Sid went out to greet the officer. There were snatches of animated conversation, until his wife called for the first aid kit.

"Yes, yes, dear. We haven't had so much excitement here since the hurricane."

The cop eased past Sid. He was a tall, lanky southerner with a mild, bony face and cautious eyes. When he saw me he raised his eyebrows, but when he spotted Hillary he was genuinely surprised. "You're John Hillary?"

"The same."

He shook his head with real regret. "You are sure having a run of bad luck, Mr. Hillary," he said.

Chapter 14

I ATTENDED the opening of the Sebastian Museum Sunday afternoon, walking into the gleaming marble building beside the art students, society matrons, politicians, contractors, and journalists, the heat-struck tourists, civic boosters, and free loaders. There was no reason not to go; I felt invulnerable. Everything had already happened; the excitement was over, the game finished, the cards dealt. I was dislocated from lack of sleep, but I was right about one thing: we'd already had our quota of bad luck, as pleasant Lieutenant Chadwell had recognized. That he knew Hillary was a bit of a help, but not much. Our story was preposterous, our appearance outlandish, our presence scandalous. No one was eager to upset a power of the county on the very day when he was gifting the public. Not for a reformed alcoholic who was hung up on murder in Guatemala. And not for a female detective, presently attired like a dancing girl after a rough party. Certainly not for her. Hillary got the stitches and shots, some plasma and antibiotics, and I got the needle from the police. There were questions and forms to fill out and a pushy detective with a boiled, red, high-domed head who wanted to know all about my business in Ibis. I referred him to Hillary's vandalized home, the burned-out shack near the Myakka River, and to my friend's quite impressive injuries, which even he and officer Chadwell could identify as gunshot and knife wounds. We discussed these and other details in the green-painted corridor off the emergency room.

A friendly nurse loaned me a hospital robe, and, shivering in the air conditioning, I paced back and forth and tried to explain why Vlad Sebastian's gardener had tried to dismember Hillary with a machete and why I was certain the "developer-philanthropist" was behind our near barbecue twenty-four hours earlier. We didn't make much progress. The detective took off for a consultation with higher powers, and I borrowed a dime from Lieutenant Chadwell to call cousin Luccio Romersi of the Miami police, whose number was tucked in Hillary's wallet. He accepted the call, listened to what I had to say, and announced that he and Theresa would be in Ibis by midmorning. I told him I'd meet them at the hospital and thankfully emerged from the phone booth's stale odor of smoke, disaster, and disinfectant. Lieutenant Chadwell rose from one of the molded plastic seats. He had orders to keep an eye on me, but I was destined for relief from his surveillance, because a nurse came through the swinging doors and summoned me. "Would you like to see Mr. Hillary now?"

"Is he going to be all right?"

"The blood loss was a concern — and infection if the wound had been neglected — but he's coming around. No signs of shock."

"I want to see Hillary," I said to Chadwell.

"I'll wait outside."

"I'm not the one who tried to do him in, you know."

"Sorry, but I have my orders."

I looked at my watch. It was just after 3 A.M. "If they're not changed by breakfast, I'm hiring a lawyer and suing the county for mental anguish and harassment."

Chadwell was sympathetic. "There'll be a warrant out for Arthur Jensen, the gardener," he whispered. "This is simply routine."

"And what about Vlad Sebastian? Don't tell me they're proceeding on that front, too?"

He shrugged. "That will take time. All the brass are going to his party today."

"They should have been there last night."

"Half of them were. The connections are only circumstantial so far, so — "

"So delay, I know. But we'll see about that." I turned to go, then stopped. "And I want to go back to my apartment and get changed. I have some work to do."

"What about that phone call? Who did you call?" He reached for his notebook.

"I notified Hillary's wife. I talked to her cousin, who's a detective in Miami. She's been visiting family. They'll both be here sometime late this morning."

Chadwell seemed impressed, but unenthusiastic, about the imminent arrival of a big city colleague.

"Miss Peters," the nurse interrupted in a weary voice, "do you wish to see Mr. Hillary or not? This is an emergency ward. We don't have a great deal of time." She pushed open the doors. In the corridor beyond, wheelchairs, beds, and rolling stretchers lined the walls. Some were occupied by gray-faced patients wrapped in white sheeting like Roman senators. Bottles of clear and grape-colored liquids were suspended above their heads and yellow bags dangled under the frames. Hillary was at the end in a big, square room divided into three bays by curtains hung from metal tubing. Next to him lay a young man with a broken leg, and, in the farthest enclosure, two interns examined a screaming child whose mother detailed its symptoms in a frightened monotone. Hillary's skin looked livid in the greenish lighting, but he was decently clean and bandaged, although missing a chunk of hair from the side of his head. They had given him a white hospital gown and his blood-soaked shirt lay in strips on the floor. I would have to add the costumes to the total cost of my working holiday in the sun.

"Feel better?"

"They've been strip-mining my chest," he said with a resentful glance at the intern. "I'd have been better to stick with that old gal on the key road. She had a gentle touch."

"You appealed to her maternal instincts."

"I have a way with women."

I sat down on the green metal chair by his bed. "I hope so," I said. "That's going to be put to the test later today. I called your wife's cousin. He and Terry should arrive before noon."

"Oh, Christ!" Hillary drew himself further upright, wincing as he put some strain on his shoulder. "Did you speak to Terry?" He loved her: there was no doubt. His face mixed joy and longing; aggravation and apprehension. He wanted her here and simultaneously he wished I had never called her. Under the present conditions, that was love.

"No, I got Luccio. I let him break the news to her. I wasn't sure just how you wanted our adventures edited."

"It's the house I'm thinking of. I hope to God she doesn't go there first."

"I warned Luccio about that."

Hillary nodded rapidly. "Do you have my coat?" he asked suddenly. "That bolero thing?"

"Yes and your wallet. I may have to borrow a few dollars. I lost mine."

"Take the film that was in the pocket. Don't let the police get their hands on it. They'll grab it for evidence or some crazy thing. Develop it and if the snapshot of Arthur is clear have Luccio telex the picture to Guatemala City. And he's to contact Señor Diego Morales. He'll be in the city at the Museum of Anthropology and History."

I rummaged through the ruin of the bolero and found a film cartridge. My camera, of course, had been lost along the way. "Will someone at the paper develop it?"

"Yes, or leave it to Luccio. He knows how to get things done."

"Incidentally, Arthur will be brought in, according to your friend, Lieutenant Chadwell."

Hillary dismissed this. "He'll be gone by this time. What do you think the delay was for? Allowing everyone to save face. Allowing Vlad Sebastian, Sun Coast money man, to put his house in order. Don't lose that film."

"You can trust me, Hillary. I'll take care of it."

"I keep forgetting you're the pro," he said drily. It was bugging him to have to stay in bed and to depend on my uncertain talents. Hillary was not fond of delegating anything, and he was anxious about his wife's arrival. That would be worth observing. In my view, Hillary could either make a play for Terry's sympathy and act the invalid or try to pass off the incident as a trifle and do his stiff-upper-lip routine. I guessed the former, because, insistent that he disliked emotional scenes, Hillary adored being fussed over. I knew him pretty well.

"Do you need anything?" I asked, standing up. "I'm going to persuade Chadwell to drive me over to my apartment."

"I want out of here."

"You'd better wait for your wife. I'm not taking you to my place, and your house is a wreck. Besides, the local inquisitor wants to talk to you, so be sure you stay off the Brammins."

"They can take care of themselves," he said sulkily. "I don't want to sit here all morning."

"Get some rest. Maybe Theresa and Luccio will escort you to the opening," I added, which was a trifle malicious.

"They can't be here much before eleven."

"Rest, Hillary. I'm taking most of your money, all right?"

"I'll report you to Lieutenant Chadwell," he said, then lowered his voice. "Here comes that brute with the hypodermic again."

It was time for me to leave. I turned in the striped robe, used such charm as I possessed on Chadwell, and hitched a ride to my apartment. By now, my gloomy landlord must have been indifferent to my mysterious comings and goings and to the regular arrival of squad cars. I changed, retrieved the last of my traveler's checks from the bottom of the suitcase, and slipped Hillary's film into the pocket of my slacks. Lieutenant Chadwell and I ate a somewhat strained breakfast along Route 41, then proceeded to headquarters, where I retold my entire story and signed a statement. At 9 A.M., I was free to go. They had brought back the rented car from the Sebastians — but not

Arthur. The car would do for now. I drove to town, making sure the police weren't following me, then phoned Old Brammin. He was surprised that I had called him at home.

"It doesn't matter now. The police are involved."

He still preferred not to have me at the house. That left the public beach, where I bought a container of coffee from the convenience store and sat on the empty white sand to wait for him. The air was cool, and the transparent water, dead calm. I wondered if Rod were sailing somewhere on that great green glass, and whether or not he intended to return.

"You're at work early for a Sunday," Old Brammin commented. He had on a navy windbreaker and the usual straw hat and covered his nervousness with a cheerful banter.

"I've been up all night."

"The Sebastians' party?"

"And its aftermath. Shall we walk?"

"If you prefer." We crossed the rocks and headed away from the store, the shelter, and the condominiums. Pelicans glided overhead like bombers in formation, and grackles, sparrows, and mockingbirds chirped in the grass covering the tops of the dunes.

"Something very serious has happened," I said.

He took it better than I'd expected. Probably he'd had little hope for Rod anyway, having seen disaster approaching for some time. "And Sebastian?"

"It depends on who talks. There's no doubt in my mind that he originated the scheme. Rod never had that kind of money, but unless the sculptures turn up on Sebastian's property — "

"I mean, who is he?"

"Still mysterious. He's a thug, though. Whether he's yours or not." I shrugged. "Does it matter? He's ruined your nephew, anyway."

Brammin gave me a pained look. "It was self-defense?"

"Rod had no choice. And I'm a witness, although he doesn't know that. I don't expect he'll be back."

"No." There was a pause. "I should never have meddled in this."

"Someone else would have. John Hillary was interested. Sooner or later, Sebastian would have found himself in a position where he'd rather not have a partner."

"The man is dying," Brammin said. "Later, Rod might have been safe."

"Might have been, but for both Rod and Sebastian — "

"What?"

"The adventure was part of the beauty of the thing. The danger was not part of the risk but part of the reward."

"That is simply an imaginative way of avoiding our responsibility," Brammin said severely. He seldom articulated his deeper knowledge of human motivation, and he took a low view of curiosity and of investigators. Despite real and kindly feelings for me, I knew he wished he had never called me, had never seen me again. And worse, to tell the truth, I felt the same way about him. That was a real grief. I realized that our friendship was not destined to survive on this ambiguous moral terrain, where he could retain his balance only by regarding me as suspect.

Theresa Hillary was prepared to take a similar view. I met her and her cousin next to a clump of sad palms in the blazing white hospital parking lot. Fortunately heat, lack of sleep, and my painful interview with Old Brammin had given me a certain detachment by the time Luccio's enormous blue Chevy pulled up and disgorged Romersis. The family type struck me as more appealing in its feminine incarnation. Theresa was quite splendid in her own way. She wore high heels and a severe two-piece navy dress, with her dark hair under a scarf and sun glasses over her angry eyes. In ten years, if she wasn't careful, she would go to fat. Now she was voluptuous and damn sturdy-looking. I had a momentary fear that she was going to haul off and slug me. But Luccio was in attendance, and he proved a more subtle influence. Like his cousin, he was short and stocky with black hair, broad shoulders, and wide hips. He had sat behind precinct desks and the wheels of squad cars for too long, and late suppers of beer and hastily eaten hamburgers had given him a rotund appearance, although he moved lightly and quickly on his feet. Unlike many of his calling, he was clean-shaven. His smooth, soft face gave him a young and innocent look, until he raised his sun glasses and showed fine Latin eyes that were as hard as two marbles.

"Miss Peters?" he inquired.

"Anna."

"How is John?" Theresa asked. "Where is he?"

"They had him in the emergency room, but probably they'll have moved him by now. Out the door, if he had his way. He's okay and wants to go home."

"Just like him. He'll have to stay, of course. Or we can take him back to Miami. Excuse me, I'm going to see my husband."

"I ought to tell you — " I began, but Theresa swept up the steps, and Luccio prevented me from following. "There'll be stuff for them to straighten out," he said. "Let's have something to eat. We didn't get any breakfast."

In the hospital coffee shop, I handed him the film and relayed Hillary's instructions. "No problem," he said. "That's what I came for. I figured John would need some help."

"I thought it was to lend your cousin moral support."

"Theresa can take care of herself. John gets into deep water. Am I right?" He looked at me with interest, sizing me up.

"That's why I'm still here. We're old friends. Both Harry and I have known him a long time." Emphasis on "Harry and I."

"Exactly what I told Theresa. My cousin is one of those women who overdramatizes life."

"Hillary was worried about her. That's why he encouraged her to go to Miami. I hope she understands that."

Luccio lifted his hands. They were plump but neatly made, tapering to slender fingertips. "Talk to her yourself," he said. "I'll deal with this." He tapped the film, then stood up and waved. "Theresa, over here. I'll be back in about an hour," he said when she reached the table.

"Where are you going? I must see the house. They're going to discharge John this afternoon, and he won't hear of going anywhere else."

"Anna will take you. There are pictures of the man who attacked John. They've got to be developed. I've got things to do."

Terry looked startled.

"So how is he?" her cousin demanded.

"He lost quite a bit of blood. He's the same as ever, though, insisting we go to the museum opening this afternoon."

"You didn't marry a saint," Luccio said. "What do you expect? Have some coffee, Theresa. You'll feel better."

"I'll feel better when the son of a bitch who tried to kill John is in jail."

"What do you think I'm here for? Can you take Theresa to Sarasota?" he asked me.

"I'll rent a car," she said quickly.

"Here? On a Sunday? You're not in the big city now."

"It's all right," I said to him. "Go ahead. I'd better see your neighbors, anyway, Theresa. The police will be around about their cottage. We owe them an explanation." I looked at her cautiously to see if Hillary had recounted that sad story.

"A total loss, right?" Opening her bag, she produced a pack of cigarettes.

"Right."

She slapped her hand angrily against the table. "How can two adults be so childish? You're not a good influence on him. I'd have thought a successful businesswoman would have been smarter than to get mixed up in such nonsense. And John! That man attracts degenerates, crooks, torpedoes of every stripe. It's Miami all over again. He has no sense," she said, the voice of maturity and reason. "And you ought to have stayed out of it. Of course, we know why."

"Do we? I thought *I* was paranoid."

"Don't try to bullshit me."

"All right." The waitress approached. "Why don't you have some breakfast?"

"You're not eating."

"I ate at six this morning with a charming police officer."

"I'll have toast and coffee, Miss. Black coffee."

I took a deep breath, mostly of her cigarette smoke, and plunged. I didn't want to disappoint two old friends on the same morning. "What I was about to say, and no baloney, is that your husband is crazy about you and quite right to be. You've saved his life. Any fool can see that. Even this one." That was a bit thick, but I must have been in the mood for self-abnegation.

Theresa looked as if this proposition appealed to her. Like most dynamic personalities, she was inclined to conceit.

"Hillary and I were close friends a long time ago," I continued. "Did you know that? Close friends."

"You lived together at one time."

"That's right. At one time. It didn't work out."

"His drinking?"

"That didn't help, but he was always a controlled drinker — heavy but controlled. He got worse later. Liquor wasn't the problem. The problem was that we are two of a kind — too much alike. We accentuate each other's bad habits. Things just didn't work out. In any direction. We need different types of people."

"Then how did you get involved in this mess?"

"I was down here on business. My business led to Vlad Sebastian." I explained about the day their home had been wrecked, about warning Hillary. "I could hardly not have called him, could I?"

"You should have gone to the police. I see what you mean. This sort of intrigue is what you and John love." She made a disgusted face. To say "you and John" was bitter to her.

"You'll find the police here very protective of Mr. Sebastian."

"There are always alternatives. You might both have been killed."

"But for your husband's presence of mind, we would have been. That worried him greatly — because of what you might have thought."

"What about your friend? Harry, is it?"

I was about to say, "Harry knows me too well," but was that true? If a day or a week after the fact, fishermen or hunters had stopped at the cottage, or a farm hand had taken the trouble to sift the rubble, or, officious, phoned the authorities, and our charred bones had been uncovered, what would he have thought? Wondered? Believed? Certainly that mutual pyre would have been more suggestive than a curry supper on Baby's hot plate. And who knows what elaborations grief produces. "There was a risk involved, but I felt a certain loyalty. Just as Hillary felt that his friends in Guatemala were owed something. You don't always think things through before you make a decision. Especially when you're in danger, imminent danger." Folly, in short, is self-perpetuating.

"That kind of impulsiveness will ruin him." Theresa declared, but she had calmed down. She had, I think, a feeling for truthfulness rather rare in jealous natures.

"It's your own fault," I said, switching to the offensive.

"What does that mean?" She had been holding her lighter and now she set it down with a sharp smack.

"You've enabled him to become brave. You've removed the excuse that kept him from doing anything worthwhile, that kept him weak. If you'd wanted him totally domesticated, you should have left him a problem drinker. As it is, you've assumed his routine worries, and now his peculiar abilities have free rein."

"You consider me bossy and domineering, don't you?" She was still fighting an impulse to tell me off in a really profane, satisfying way.

"I think you're exactly what suits him." At close quarters, we'd soon get on each other's nerves. We were diametrically opposed female species. She would find me evasive, cold, and whimsical. I would find her abrasive, melodramatic, and obvious. But the management of men forms a surprisingly strong bond between women. She gave a wide grin.

"Have some of this toast. You look as though you need food."

"Forty-eight hours of sleep and a large bourbon," I said, but I accepted her offer. Probably she was dieting, but the cold, limp, margarine-smeared toast was a genuine peace offering.

"How bad is the house?" she asked after a few minutes.

"It's totaled. No structural damage, but just about everything else is smashed. I'm really sorry."

"You have to keep these things in perspective," she said briskly. "Better the house than John — or someone else."

"We can drive over."

"As soon as I call Emmie. Disaster protocol — let the neighbors tell you first. What do you suppose their cottage was worth?" she asked as we rose from the table.

"Not much to sell, but a fancy bill to replace."

"We'll contact the lawyer about a civil suit. That's a promising area these days, did you know that? Sure. Damage suits against criminals. Our rape crisis center in Miami helped out in one. I'll have to discuss it with Max and Emmie." The possibility of a court fight seemed to please her.

I agreed this was an enticing prospect and endorsed, as I remember, several of her other notions. One was a lightning attack on the damaged house, which was stifling hot and smelled disgustingly of soured milk and rotting food. Emmie pitched in, and we labored like three house-mad women. At least they did. I was hung over with nerves and exhaustion and was eventually assigned the trifling task of reshelving the books and sweeping up the glass. We carried the gutted sofa pillows out to the garage to be refilled by the upholsterer. Emmie brought over an awl and sewed up the gashes in the chairs. By two, the place was bare and battered, but clean, the putrid odors replaced by detergent smell. Emmie opened three beers, and Theresa closed the windows and switched on the air conditioner. We sat talking with our shoes off and our feet up, and I vacillated between the luxury of total collapse and the Sebastian Museum opening. Then Luccio phoned to say that the pictures were on the way to Guatemala and Hillary was on his way home, and I decided on the opening. Truce, peace, and sisterhood or not, it seemed a good idea to clear out before he arrived. Theresa was cordial without urging me to stay. I couldn't blame her; she'd want to have a quick, private chat with Emmie and another with Hillary.

So, at precisely four o'clock, I walked past the smiling, newly uniformed guards into a cool, glass-roofed octagon beyond which the Impressionists, Post Impressionists, and fauves fractured and rebuilt light with angelic eyes and glorious palettes. How many geniuses had labored to produce this array, some of them on the verge of destitution, so that Sebastian could make one last, splendid display? There were murmurs of delight and congratulation. His taste was exquisite, perceptive; his habits of acquisition, beyond doubt, ruthless. There was a tendency that day to celebrate his cleverness at the expense of artists, but grouped together, row upon row, the sheer weight of his treasures favored Sebastian. I wondered what had motivated this restoration of art to the public and decided Cheri ought finally to be satisfied with her launching into society.

In one of the last rooms was a splendid Bonnard depicting a garden, vast, mysterious, and powerfully structured, its trees and branches forming a secret world. Many of Sebastian's finest pictures had that in common: they seemed to depict the entrance to another, richer existence. The artists of his fancy knew the escape routes, but my ruminations on this suggestive topic were almost immediately interrupted.

"Would you come with us, Miss Peters."

It was not really a request. The man at my shoulder was young and slight but self-important. A Marcus in training. Something about his older, huskier companion was familiar. I recognized him when he spoke: he had driven the old station wagon the night I'd gone to Rod Brammin's shop. "Mr. Sebastian wants to talk with you."

I surveyed the crowd. A blue-jacketed guard was nervously trying to keep people away from a priceless Cézanne. A man with graying hair spoke loudly about the integrity of the picture plane and complementary colors, while a hollow-eyed blonde sipped champagne and, adjusting her transparent black shawl, estimated his value. Behind me, an older couple squeezed past to examine the Bonnard, their eager excitement exaggerating heavy accents: apparently they had seen it forty years before under vastly different conditions. The murmur of these many voices reverberated off the marble with a sound like the surf. "Why not?" I said and started through the crowd. Sebastian's flunkies walked on either side of me. I was not the slightest bit worried. Emmie's beer had gone to my head.

"Mr. Sebastian's in here." The gallery wing was connected by a short corridor to a second octagon. This was a reference library, and off it, like the exhibition rooms in the larger building, were staff offices. The plate on one glass-fronted office read "Head Curator" and Vlad Sebastian sat behind the large desk. His young aide held open the door.

"Alone," I said.

Sebastian looked at me with his yellow lizard's eyes and nodded. "Wait outside," he said.

The door closed. Through the darkened glass I could see the crowd, inspecting, eating, drinking, admiring, gossiping. "What did you want to see me about?" I asked as I sat down.

"I am too feeble to greet my guests in such a crush," he rasped, lifting a spotted hand to gesture toward the party. "My daughter has taken quite an interest in you."

"She is a charming young woman."

"This museum was her idea."

"A very good one. You have amassed a brilliant collection, Mr. Sebastian. The museum lacks only the works you have in your own home to be rarely distinguished."

"The best are here."

"The paintings are wonderful, but the flavor of a collection depends on the personality expressed in the choices. By a certain indulgence of eccentricity."

A smile flickered across Sebastian's thin lips. He looked dreadful but energized, like an electrified corpse. He must have been heavily medicated for his illness, but I wondered if he were not using other things, too, amphetamines, perhaps. His eyes were dilated, and he kept sipping restlessly from a tall, pale drink. "You are right," he said in his metallic, amplified whisper. "A collector is like a critic with power, selecting, composing, arranging a certain environment, a particular effect. The collector makes a new world out of available materials."

"From the imaginations of others," I remarked.

"Their imaginations ran deep, yet most of these painters couldn't afford their own works. The collector has certain advantages." His eyes narrowed to slits. "Do you know," he said, abruptly changing the topic, "that certain Balkan tribes sent messengers to the dead?"

"Human sacrifice?"

"Yes, but not with the dead king or queen, before."

"Difficult to coordinate," I suggested.

"You are too flippant, Miss Peters. Your imagination is deficient."

"On the contrary: it's all too vivid. I was recently in precisely that position. Fortunately, I did not get close enough to the nether world to receive any signals."

Sebastian's habitual look of disgust deepened. "There's no competency anymore," he said, precisely as he might have complained about a careless mechanic. "In my day — " the smile flickered again, and he stopped. "They are ceasing to fear me." Sebastian's doctored voice was eerie, like listening to a robot or an oracle. Instead of feeling sorry for this horrid mutilation, I had to keep reminding myself that he was human. But no doubt I was prejudiced.

"Marcus, at least, was loyal," I said.

Sebastian studied me without answering. He appeared neither shocked nor surprised, but I think until that moment he had not realized that it was over, that he had truly cast off the protective garments he had worn for so long, that the viciousness was showing under "Sun coast developer-philanthropist." "Marcus is in Spain. He needed a holiday."

"Perhaps he will take your messages for you."

There was a silence. The thick glass subdued the sounds outside, the feet on the carpets, the high voices echoing off the smooth walls. Sebastian's eyes were dangerous, drugged, without fear. His acts were irrational. I had perhaps been wrong to consider myself invulnerable. There was nothing to stop him from opening one of the soundless drawers in the large, expensive desk, taking out a gun, and sending me into darkness.

"Such men are barely alive to start with," Sebastian said, his voice like tinsel disturbed by a breeze. "The power of beautiful objects is nothing to them. Only money. You spoke of the completion of my collection. You were correct. It needs something more. For a detective, you have a certain appreciation."

I did not feel the necessity of applauding his cleverness in finding me out.

"But," he continued, "you lack the imagination to see what is required. I did not find out right away. Only very recently, when it was almost too late, the chance of a lifetime presented itself."

The whistling in his damaged voice reminded me of the hiss of the sea, and I remembered swimming at night in the Gulf. I had looked back to the shore with its tiny lights and glimpsed a connection between oblivion and the stimulus of danger. Certain personalities are driven to utilize their potentiality, to complete the design. Why else was I here, when my job was over, when I longed to be home? Sebastian's obsessions took a more dangerous curve, the consummation of his nature had more exotic requirements, and therefore pressed closer to annihilation. He was something of a crank, as well as a connoisseur.

"The souls of superior men are nourished by art. Today, we underestimate the nourishment of art, but the ancients knew. Why do you think the Pharaohs, the high priests, the god-kings, the warriors smothered themselves in jewels and surrounded themselves with paintings and statues even in death? They fed themselves from the souls of others."

"And from their bodies," I said. "How many died for such tombs?"

"Everyone dies over trifles, Miss Peters," Sebastian said, touching his throat. "I am dying from the by-products of a territorially ambitious cell. Do you suppose it pities me? There is no reason for me to limit my desires when we are all being devoured. All of this moralistic cant sickens me." He shook his head and sank further back in his chair. "I will say good afternoon, now. I have met my messenger and heard the report. Even if you appreciate my collection, I would rather not see you again, because my impulse is to kill you, Miss Peters."

With this, he smiled an exhausted, hateful smile and touched a button on the desk. The outside door opened at this signal, and I got up, pushing back the chair with less than dignified haste. At the door, I made myself pause. "All those tons of rock are going to be hard to conceal," I said.

Vlad Sebastian gave a dismissive wave of his hand, and the door closed in my face.

Chapter 15

Two paragraphs appeared in the local Monday newspaper, topped by the headline, BRITISH JOURNALIST INJURED IN PARTY FRACAS. Hillary was described as a former Reuters correspondent and the creator of several television documentaries. Arthur Jensen was identified as a part-time employee at the Sebastian estate and the gardener for the Mangrove Villa apartment complex. A "spokesperson for the Sebastian family" had expressed shock, regret and mystification. That was possibly accurate. Cheri had sent an expensive bunch of flowers with an invitation for a tour of the museum to Hillary, since, restrained by a slight fever as well as by Luccio and Theresa, he had not been allowed to attend the opening. The accompanying note was sympathetic.

Approaching the pink mansion near sundown that evening, I wondered if Cheri suspected the magnitude of her trouble from this tiny, if alarming, story. Perhaps she did. She had a touch of her father's strangeness, as well as his fondness for the dramatic effect. When she opened the door, she was dressed to match the hour in a beautiful violet dress, so deep-hued as to look black. It suited her.

"John! Anna! Who are all these people? I didn't expect you to bring company with you."

There were quite a few of us, and except for Hillary, none could really count as company. There was the assistant chief of police for Sarasota, a state police officer, Luccio, our dependable Lieutenant Chadwell and his disagreeable captain; an intense, malarial gentleman from the Guatemalan police and Señor Diego Morales, Hillary's archeologist acquaintance, who had a large Mayan nose, a narrow skull, and a wide, stern mouth. Hillary made the introductions, and Cheri agreed to admit us. It was just as well. In Lieutenant Chadwell's shirt pocket was a search warrant.

"This is all unexpected," she repeated. "I hope there's a good reason for it, Mike." Mike McLaughlin was the assistant police chief, a big, shambling white-haired man who seemed acutely embarrassed.

"We really came to see your father," he said. "I think he's the one who can help us."

"About Arthur?" She gave a short laugh. "I don't think my dad's spoken to him more than once or twice. He certainly wasn't a man of any charm. The only reason any of us knew him was that he did the yard work at the Mangrove Apartments. Rod Brammin has an apartment there, and I met him through Rod."

"We had originally wanted to talk to Mr. Brammin, but his uncle tells me — "

"His sailboat's missing! It was due two days ago. The Coast Guard's been notified; they've been searching. This has been quite a week."

"We understand." There was an awkward moment. We all stood in the foyer, because Cheri had not invited us further. A murky pinkish light filled the long windows, signaling rain, and strong gusty winds disturbed the line of palms along the shore. "I think it would be advisable if we saw Mr. Sebastian. He's not at his office."

"I'm sure he can't help you about Arthur," Cheri said. "You're familiar with his condition. I don't let anyone disturb him unless it's absolutely necessary." She flashed her hostess smile.

"It's not only about Arthur."

"Perhaps you ought to come to the point."

"May we sit down?" Hillary interrupted. His return to the

restrictions of Theresa's custody did not appear to have oppressed him. On the contrary, he seemed almost cheerful. The rest of us wore long faces, especially the two gentlemen from Guatemala, who had had a long flight on short notice. "I'm a little shaky, still."

Cheri was all apologies. She took Hillary's good arm and led us to a small sitting room. I noticed he whispered something to her on the way: Hillary's loyalties had a certain complexity.

"It's difficult to appear on business," McLaughlin began, "when I've been your guest so many times, but I've no choice."

Cheri looked composed. Perhaps her former nervousness had simply been the strain of anticipation. With the arrival of long-submerged fate, she might come into her own.

"Arthur Jensen," McLaughlin continued, "has been identified by the Guatemalan police as one of several men wanted in connection with looting a Mayan site. He is also a suspect in the murder of two monument guards."

"In Guatemala?" Cheri exclaimed. "That's unbelievable. Haven't you any idea of his whereabouts?"

"Not at the moment. Señor Morales and Señor De La Cruz have flown here from Guatemala City hoping to apprehend Jensen, but also to locate and identify the stolen antiquities. They have reason to believe that certain of these sculptures were smuggled into the States on Rod Brammin's sailboat."

Cheri's laugh skittered across the silence like a stone on a pond. "And what would Rod do with these antiquities? He runs a shop for chic decorators. He wouldn't have room to store them or a clientele that could appreciate them."

McLaughlin's embarrassment deepened, his healthy sunburned face darkening a few more shades. Señor Morales spoke up. His voice was gentle, his English impeccable, and his face impassive. "Señorita, your observation is correct. Your friend, Señor Brammin, could not sell such things openly in his shop. In my estimation and in the opinion of Señor De La Cruz," he turned toward the police officer, who nodded his gray head, "these treasures were stolen on order. Necessarily for someone of a certain wealth." Morales' eyes flicked over the rich furnishings, the high ceilings, the gilt-framed paintings.

"My father is an art collector," Cheri said evenly, "not a receiver of stolen property."

"Your father's reputation is well known," Morales said. "I have read about his insistence on the provenances of his art works. But even reputable collectors have been tempted — or misled — concerning items they desired."

"You see, Cheri," McLaughlin added hastily, "there is almost no doubt that Rod brought in some Mayan sculptures. We have just come from his shop."

"Don't try to tell me you found stolen Guatemalan art there," Cheri said. "I've been in his shop regularly."

"We found a complete set of stone-working tools. They would be needed in fitting together the cut-up stelae and for repairing damage to the stones."

Baby had slipped up on that. She'd believed that any instruments were for cabinet work. That was understandable — she knew nothing about tools.

"That hardly proves anything."

"There are other details."

"Which you are not at liberty to tell me."

"We would rather discuss the matter with your father, Cheri. Is he at home?"

"No."

Outside the wind was becoming stronger. The lanyard slapped against the high flagpole and the shrubs near the house scratched against the windows like cats wanting in.

McLaughlin cleared his throat. "Do you know where he is?"

"No. He said he was tired after the opening party and that he would stay in town. He has an apartment near the museum." She gave McLaughlin the address. "I called this morning, but he wasn't home."

"Is there anywhere else he might have gone? A friend's home, a favorite hotel?"

Cheri shook her head. "That's extremely unlikely."

The state trooper rose and McLaughlin said, "We will check his apartment and the museum."

"I'm not sure that's necessary. I'm not worried about him. The car is gone. He's probably had Marcus drive him somewhere. I expect he'll be back later this evening."

"Which car?"

"The Rolls he always uses. The chauffeur took him to the opening but was sent home early. That's not unusual."

"And you're sure Marcus was with him?" I asked.

"I didn't see him, but he's not here, either. Where else could he be?"

Perhaps Rod Brammin was going to get lucky. "Yes, he's with your dad most of the time."

"Just the same," McLaughlin said, "your father is in delicate health. Isn't it unusual for him to remain away without informing you? You haven't heard from him for over twenty-four hours. And he must have seen the newspaper story about Jensen."

"Poor John!" Cheri said, reaching over to give his good arm a sympathetic pat. "How I wish it hadn't happened. And at our house!" Then she stared at the policeman. "What do you want?" she asked bluntly.

"We'd like to have a look around the estate. Rod Brammin had close financial connections with your father. We'd like to be sure that he hadn't involved your dad in his extracurricular business as well."

"I hope you're not asking to search the house."

"It's a formality," McLaughlin said. He was one of those awkward, but insistent, people who never seem to manage things smoothly. "But an important one under the circumstances. After all, one of your father's employees is under suspicion of murder as well as for assault with a deadly weapon. Had Mr. Hillary attended your party alone, Cheri, he would very probably have been killed. In view of the circumstances, we have tried to minimize the attention given the incident, but this is a serious case."

"You wouldn't try this if my father were here."

"Your father might have been able to provide the information we need. If we could locate him — "

"I hope you will do that and soon. Better yet, find Arthur Jensen, who is, after all, the man responsible."

"I assure you we are — "

"Never mind." Cheri stood up quickly. "Let's just get this over with. Anna, you've already seen the house, perhaps you'd prefer to wait here."

"I'll tag along if you don't mind."

She gave me a quick, hard look, but could not find the connection. I wasn't surprised: I was here because Old Brammin's nephew had too much money. The others were assembled for similarly peculiar reasons.

"What about you, Hillary?"

"Oh, I'll wait here — until you do the other buildings. I always love seeing your father's cars."

"Very well. This way. Feel free to check the closets," she said acidly. "I suppose these are small things?"

"Some are, but the sculptures Rod Brammin and Arthur Jensen are accused of taking are large," Señor Morales said. "A Mayan stela may weigh a ton or more. It depends on the size and on whether or not it was cut into pieces and 'thinned' for transport."

"Then I can assure you right now, there's nothing here," Cheri said, and she brightened perceptibly as she went into her guided tour, which, despite an appearance of spontaneity, was obviously rehearsed. None of the Sebastian outfit left things to chance.

Nothing at all. Up in Sebastian's private library, the parquet flooring was bare, with a Chinese rug under the desk, instead of the bloodstained broadloom. The glass of the shattered cabinet had been replaced. Only the lamp gave any clue, and then only to someone who knew where to look. I noticed that the sphinx's headdress was bent and flattened on one side. There was nothing else of interest. McLaughlin managed to look simultaneously relieved and embarrassed; the other locals were impressed; their Latin colleagues were philosophical. They had not expected to find everything at once. Downstairs, Hillary joined us, and we made our way through the garage, the sheds, and the boat house. It was dark by this time and threatening rain again at any minute. "You'll have to forgo the chapel," Cheri said. "I don't have the key."

The state trooper examined the solid, expensive lock, and she added, "Anna has been in it recently. Haven't you?"

"That's right. It's only a small room, with a madonna, a chair, and a tapestry — and scarcely space for those."

"I think this can wait," McLaughlin said quickly. "We would like your father to notify us as soon as he returns, Cheri. That would save us all a great deal of unpleasantness." He looked at the door again and shrugged.

During this exchange, Señor Morales had wandered a little way into the trees, where he stood pondering the shape of the tower.

"An unusual building," I remarked.

"Yes, a fascinating structure — full of architectural allusions."

"That was my impression, but, since you're an archeologist, I am sure you see more in it than I can."

"To me the treatment of the top is like the Caracol at Chichén-Itzá, although it's not symmetrical. Who designed it?"

"You will have to ask Cheri. I've forgotten the name. Some Florida artist."

"Señor Sebastian is a collector of rare talents."

"You would find him a unique individual."

"You know him personally, then, Señorita Peters?"

"I've met him twice. On the second occasion, he went out of his way to make an impression."

Señor Morales might have pursued this matter, but the rain started, the wind blowing wet gusts in every direction, and the group broke for the house. He hurried after Cheri, and I heard her say, "Spring. Arline Spring. She's something of a recluse, has a big place in Lake Worth. My father believes her to be very talented, although you don't often see her work."

"Well Señorita Sebastian, how many people have space or money for castle towers?" Morales asked as they entered the house. I remained outside under the terrace awning, watching the gray radiance of the storm until Hillary arrived, shaking the water off his hair and wiping the wetness from his sling. I'd scarcely had a chance to talk to him. "How are you doing?"

"Not badly, considering. You're looking pensive. Don't tell me the outcome of this visit surprised you."

"Not at all. I suppose the museum is next?"

He shook his head. "Apalachicola. I'm taking my cameraman with me. Marvelous idea, really. Terry sanctions anything that's to be recorded on film."

"The warehouse, you mean?"

"Sure. I'm following the investigation — 'On the Smugglers' Trail' — that sort of thing."

"Is this whole crowd accompanying you?"

"You weren't invited?" He made no attempt to sound surprised.

"Not yet."

"McLaughlin is prejudiced against private investigators. Particularly if they're pretty and female."

"Save it, Hillary. I doubt it's my ravishing person he's objecting to."

"Well, not entirely. He suspects you've been less than candid."

"That's his loss."

"I implied as much, but he seems to think you're withholding information from him."

"I hope you didn't make any insinuations about that."

"No, no. Dear girl! But there are times when I wish you had a more confiding nature."

"It's nothing that would help you."

"I had assumed as much," he said with a smile.

I could just make out his features in the light from the windows. I liked him a great deal in spite of the aggravation we gave each other. And we always had a lot of fun — he and Harry and I, too. American culture is rather weak and awkward about friendships, always attempting to subsume them either under family or sex. Ours was definitely in another, odder, category. "Are you really all right?"

"Yes and no," he replied. "This last week has made me think it's almost time we joined the grownups."

"I don't know about you, but I've been feeling distinctly old, lately."

"I don't mean that. I mean taking a — a more mature perspective."

"Look who's talking. You look like the Spirit of 'Seventy-Six, and you've just told me you're running off tomorrow to Apalachicola."

"With my cameraman. He's arriving on the night flight."

"I could hardly film my investigations. Even Assistant Chief McLaughlin wouldn't expect that."

"I was thinking along other lines."

"Oh?"

"You ought to marry our mutual friend."

"I believe you've already made that suggestion."

"Good advice can bear repeating. You're like me, you need a stabilizing influence."

"Harry's doing his best already in that department."

"Yes, and virtue is its own reward, but — "

"But I should reward Harry with my troubles on a permanent basis?"

Hillary laughed. "Keep it in mind."

There was a bustle behind us, and Luccio called from the house. "We're leaving now, but don't get that arm wet, Hillary. Come through the house, and we'll get an umbrella."

"Come on, invalid," I said. "You might as well get all the perks, because you'll be mended in a few days."

"A few weeks," Hillary corrected indignantly. "Ten days for the stitches. And no yard work for ages."

"We're driving back to Sarasota," Luccio explained, "but Lieutenant Chadwell will drop you in Ibis, Anna."

"Thanks. Have fun in Apalachicola," I said to Hillary.

"Remember what I suggested," he replied. "And don't do anything cinematic while I'm gone." In an undertone, he added, "CBS is interested."

"I'll save all the good stuff for you," I promised. This caused McLaughlin to assume a peeved, suspicious look.

"My advice to you, Miss Peters," the assistant chief said, "is to return to Washington. This is turning into a fairly sensitive investigation."

"Obviously, you don't feel you need me."

"I think our combined forces here can handle it." He buttoned the center button of his jacket and glanced around at his colleagues, Hillary included by male courtesy.

"Fine," I said. "I have things of my own to do."

Hillary winked. "Call us before you leave."

"I shall. Good-by, all. Good-by, Cheri."

The others shook hands, but she did not. "I have the oddest feeling that you're to blame for this," she said and left the room.

There was a tropical depression in the Gulf, and the gusty shower blew into a real storm during the night. The next morning, branches and palm fronds and hunks of Spanish moss littered the lawns, and great waves chewed at the beach. I got up early, had breakfast like someone taking a mature perspective, and went to the public library to consult the Lake Worth directory. Then I returned and started with the phone: Arline Spring of Lake Worth was out inspecting the storm damage, my informant said. My informant was the housekeeper, and by the end of the morning I felt I knew her well. Her employer, after inspecting the storm damage, spent time with her flowers. Then she worked in her studio. I finally got her as she was sitting down to a one o'clock lunch. The voice on the other end was remote and soft, but her memory was exact, and an artistic temperament was evident. "How large?"

"I'm not sure exactly, but as tall as a two-story house and big enough for a small room."

"Nonsense."

"I've been in it."

"I shall have to speak to Vladimir. That was unauthorized. It's like making a tree house in a Calder."

"Yes, I can see that — although it's very impressive. And you'd never know anything was in it, except for the door."

"Of course. All the venting would be on the upper part. Oh, it's possible. Undesirable, but possible. Now let me find the original plan."

She shuffled papers around her desk. "You say you're working for the family. Is that right?"

"In a manner of speaking."

"In what manner of speaking?"

"You know that Mr. Sebastian has been in poor health?"

She had known that, although it didn't weaken her resolution to pursue the matter of the tower. She hinted at a suit.

"Mr. Sebastian has been missing now for two and a half days. His daughter is, of course, anxious, and, for various business affairs, she needs to locate some of his papers. He apparently hid them about the estate."

"Ahhh." There was a silence as the Lady of the Towers considered this tidbit. Whatever her conclusion, she became more cooperative, because we got on quite well. For a recluse, Arline Spring was not short on worldly gossip, and by the time I hung up the phone, I had a lot of ideas, including a few about Vladimir Sebastian.

I stopped at a hardware store that afternoon on my way out of Ibis and bought a hammer and a stone chisel. Then I headed northwest up the road through the keys. A lot of debris lay along the beach and the road, and although the afternoon was almost as hot as usual the storm's aftermath was in the wind and the flat gray clouds. At the Sebastians', a gardener was busy raking the torn vegetation into tidy brownish piles. I asked whether or not Miss Sebastian was at home. "Try the house," he replied.

"Thanks." Fearing that Cheri might not condone the research I had in mind, however, I proceeded down the length of the building and along the garden wall. Rounding the corner, I heard voices, one of them hers.

"All right," she said, "you'd better bring the cart and have Mary give you some blankets unless she can find that special padding. The green stuff. Do you know what I mean?"

"Yes, I think there's some in the big cupboard, Miss Sebastian."

"Well see, but if you can't find it right away, bring a blanket."

The young man set off through the garden. I deposited the paper bag with my hammer and chisel behind one of the roots of the banyan tree and strolled over to the chapel. The metal door had been lifted from its hinges. Inside, a square battery light was sitting on the floor, and Cheri was standing on a chair unfastening the tapestry.

"Your father's not back yet?"

She turned quickly.

"Sorry to scare you. I thought you'd have heard me coming."

"No, I didn't. And he's not back."

"Shall I hold this end?"

"Please. The storm knocked out the power. Everything else is on, but the line into this building is down. There're so many lines out, it may be days. Old wooden sculptures can't stand sudden changes in temperature."

"They crack?"

"Yes. So I thought I'd take this as well and store them in one of the air-conditioned rooms in the house." She handed me the other end of the tapestry. "Careful, it's heavy."

"I've got it."

"Thanks. We'll fold it once again." She set the cloth carefully on the chair and carried both out the door. "It's stifling in there." She wiped her forehead. "What are you doing here?"

"I was on my way to the airport and thought I'd stop and see if your father had gotten home."

"Well, he isn't here."

The implication was that I needn't wait. "I also wanted to have another look at your tower. I found an article about the woman who does them. That Arline Spring. Very interesting. They're usually hollow, but without access. She doesn't approve of your father's alterations."

"Huh," Cheri said. "Not much she can do about it. I can't discuss her now. I want to get the statue moved."

"I'll give you a hand. Too bad about the door. You'll leave it off, I suppose, until McLaughlin has a look?"

Cheri didn't answer. "Lift it carefully," she said, grasping the torso. "It's valuable. Ready?"

The statue didn't budge. The madonna was plump, well draped, and solid black walnut, but she was too heavy for her bulk. "It's attached to the base."

"Damn." Cheri moved the light closer. "It can't be nailed on. You don't nail statues like this. No, there's nothing holding it. Try again."

We did, and this time the madonna moved a fraction, sideways. "Could it be screwed onto the base? I thought it moved."

Cheri grasped the madonna's shoulders and twisted them. Clockwise produced nothing, but when she pushed the other way, the statue pivoted smoothly, and there was a soft, scraping noise and a click as though a handle had been turned or a lock released. "There must be a door somewhere in the back wall," she said, startled by the sound, and as she ran her hands along the bricks, an irregular line appeared about six feet above the floor and shot down to the tiles. Along that line, a sweetish, putrid odor emerged that grew stronger as the mass of bricks pivoted on their hidden axis, revealing the opening of an inner chamber. Cheri gave a cry of surprise and horror. Grabbing the light, I pointed it through the doorway. The beam picked out an astonishing face, serene, dreamy, vaguely oriental, with full, red-stained cheeks and lips, a long, elegant nose, and hooded, almond-shaped eyes. The figure was surmounted by a tall headdress and ornately clothed in feathers and tapestry and skulls and grotesque ornaments. Indeed, so rich was the decoration that except for the pure lines of the head, the human form seemed merged in a lacy pattern of stone as complex as the leaves, branches, and mosses of the jungle. The figure held something in his arms, a bar encrusted with ornaments, symbols, serpents, the exact form blurred and lost. The man-god held this object to his breast, half-clutching it, half-offering it to the waxy, diminishing figure that lay before him on a long beige banquette. Vlad Sebastian was already decomposing; his rotten odor filled the tower and clung to the stela and to other hastily glimpsed treasures, glyphs, sculptures, and some pale, lovely pots on a low shelf. Cheri pushed past me and ran into the yard, screaming for help. In her haste, she knocked over the chair by the door, spilling the dark red tapestry onto the white sand where its heavy folds lay like congealed blood.

Chapter 16

THE NEXT TIME I saw the stela, the stench was gone, leaving only its echo in a faint, rotten sweetness. The electricians had fixed the power line and the ventilation system was drawing in clean sea air. The lights were on, too, and I could now examine the extraordinary detail of the sculpture: the enigmatic beauty of the face, the splendid feather headdress, the masks and grotesques elaborating the clothes and ornaments, and the hieroglyphics, half-mutilated along the side, that retold some strange and indecipherable tale. The whole baroque assemblage was a mixture of barbarism and sophistication, of the cleanest, purest lines and of almost insane elaboration, of delicacy and brutality. The serene figure wore a mane of plumes and a girdle of skulls. It was easy to comprehend the sculpture's attraction for a man like Vlad Sebastian, whose life had been built on a dense undergrowth of violence and deceit, overlaid by the brilliance of his possessions. For a man of his character, this sacred Mayan king must have seemed an ideal companion, lending a touch of sinister drama to his final embarkation.

But precisely what Sebastian had in mind the night he entered the chapel remained mysterious, as did the question of how he had gotten back home without being noticed. The coroner, of course, had an opinion on the first matter. Perhaps seeking to spare Cheri, he had ruled the death accidental, which was fair enough. Sebastian had died of suffocation when the chapel's ventilation system lost power during the storm, an accident he failed to escape because of the massive doses of morphine, pills, and alcohol that had served him for months as painkillers. His death, in any case, had been imminent. If the storm hadn't toppled the power lines, or if Marcus had survived, or if the collector had indulged in fewer pharmaceuticals than usual, he would, at best have had only a few months. Less. From the moment he knew Marcus' death had been discovered, the life he had lived for the past decades was doomed. I suspected he would not have cared if he had heard the air system switch off.

Cheri, innocent of these details, behaved as though her father's death had been an absurd accident. Their relationship had been peculiar. For all his material indulgence, Sebastian had been engaged in a power struggle with his daughter, one of the aspects of which was his secret collection. Cheri had made a mistake in pushing him into society, in urging the museum, in making public a life and personality that had thrived in anonymity. Begun at almost the same time, this collection was clearly the obverse of the Sebastian Museum and closer to his nature, and it was with a certain chagrin that I found I shared his fascination with the Mayan stela. There was something about the lacy patterns of the stone, the interwoven designs of feathers and snakes and geometric symbols that stimulated the imagination and encouraged it to wander. In spite of the artificiality of the elements, the sculpture suggested a natural thing, or an artifact long since overlaid with greedy vegetation or marine life. It made me think of the sea, of green water deep enough to hide a statue until it was encrusted with a lace of coral and barnacles, and mysterious like the smooth, heavy swells on the Gulf at night. Sebastian's hidden collection, his irrational efforts to seize and retain this remarkable idol, these hinted at the sea as well. What were his actions but the results of storm waves from the depths of personality? Weakened by age, illness, and drugs, Sebastian had no longer been able to restrain the tides of his nature, and his impulses had broken through the careful façade of business and philanthropy. Rod Brammin, I thought, was in a different position, the captive of less exotic impulses. It would be interesting to know if he still had time to get his life under control.

Señor Morales interrupted these odd meditations. "The air is still not good in here," he said.

"You should have been here the other day."

"A tragedy. Poor Señorita Sebastian. But these — " he gestured toward the stela and the stucco heads — "would have been unsurprised. For them, he provided the appropriate atmosphere."

Señor Morales' imagination was also meandering. "How's that?" I asked.

"The Mayas practiced human sacrifice. The Aztecs and the other Mexican tribes went to excess, but the Spaniards describe even the Mayan priests as stinking of blood. Naturally, the conquistadores had reasons for wanting to paint them as servants of the devil, but there's no doubt the practice was fairly common, along with other forms of bloodletting. Self-mutilation was believed pleasing to the gods."

"Vlad Sebastian drew the line at that. He was a barbarian, not an ascetic."

"So John Hillary tells me. It is unfortunate that we are not all born into the times that suit our personalities," Morales said philosophically, and returned to his work. He was cataloguing the contents of the room before the pieces were packed for shipment to Guatemala. The stela would go to the museum, because, having been cut apart and shaved down for transport, it would now be too delicate to stand outdoors in the jungle. Rod Brammin's excellent wooden mounting would carry it back to the museum. The carvings that had adorned the back, had, of course, been damaged beyond repair. Only a few glyphs and a serpent bird remained, which Morales had photographed and checked against detailed drawings done of the stela before its removal.

The archeologist made a few more notes and nodded. "This is definitely from the stela. The rest of the material will have to be evaluated when we get home. Much of it is not from our site."

"You can tell right away?"

"In many cases. The great cities have distinctive styles. That was one of the things which made our explorations so interesting. We could document the spread of influence from Copán, one of the major centers in Honduras. This piece — " he tapped a carved head — "is almost surely from Palenque in Mexico."

"I'll take your word for it."

"The differences seem subtle to nonspecialists, but for Mayanists the characteristics of the major styles are obvious." Señor Morales smiled like a man immersed in a particularly felicitous phase of his work. "These are all very beautiful examples in classic styles. However obtained, they will be magnificent additions to our museum." He pocketed his notes and said very formally, "I believe I should thank you, Señorita, for your efforts. Without your influence, I doubt Señorita Sebastian would have donated the collection."

That was true. Cheri had dropped her original idea of fighting the Guatemalan government's claim and had thrown in the rest of the pre-Columbian pieces, most of which had been legitimately acquired. Some were extremely fine, and Morales was pleased enough to suggest publicly, at least, that Vlad Sebastian might have been misled by his associates. Otherwise, he was content to leave the case shrouded in mystery, where, despite Hillary's projected documentary, it seemed fated to remain. "These are our cultural heritage," he continued. "Señorita Sebastian has been generous, and certainly she was not responsible for their removal."

"She may continue to be generous in the future, Señor Morales, but I'd be careful about that. She drives a hard bargain."

"I will remember your advice," he said. Beneath his impassive courtesy, I sensed a sharp operator. That was good because, with her millions behind her, Cheri Sebastian would have quite a bit of clout, and she was considering an involvement in pre-Columbian archeology. At least she had been, when I talked to her about the collection the previous day. I found her downstairs in the library answering condolence messages at a big ormolu desk. She was simply dressed in a black silk shirt and slacks and her thick, furry hair was drawn away from her face. She had obviously been under a strain, but black was flattering and power appeared to be a tonic. Being in complete command was going to agree with her.

"Even though I asked you to come, I almost refused to see you, Anna. Your visits seem to end badly."

"I hope this one will turn out better."

"It could hardly be worse."

There was a pause. "I suppose you've guessed why I invited you?"

I had a number of ideas, but I settled on a fairly unlikely one. "I've heard you're thinking of retaining the stela."

Wrong guess. And I'd hit a sore spot. "You do get around. Why should you have any interest in the disposal of my father's collection? Or have you picked up a new client?"

"No new client; in fact, no old client, either. Some personal advice for you: give them the stela and throw in the rest of the Mayan collection."

"Do you realize how much money you're talking about?"

"I can guess that you won't miss it. Not nearly as much as you'll miss the good press you might enjoy by doing the generous thing. The art doesn't appeal to you anyway, does it? You'll only sell the sculptures and have to pay tax on the profits."

"I'm glad you mentioned generosity," she said. "Are you in a generous mood?"

"I'm afraid the last couple of weeks have almost exhausted my better nature."

"I'm not asking much," she said. "I just want to know about Rod." As I started to speak, she waved her hand impatiently. "You were employed to spy on him — probably by that stuffy old uncle of his. I worked that out from things Rod told me. His uncle never approved of me."

"I was retained to protect Rod's interests," I protested with such dignity as I could muster: this case had not covered anyone with glory. "In my estimation, you were very much in his interest, but his financial dealings with your father constituted a more dubious category."

"Do you know what's happened to him? There's been no trace of the *Melody*. Nothing! The Coast Guard, the police — no one can tell me anything. If you know, tell me! I love him. I want to know."

I said nothing.

"Please, Anna."

I felt sorry for her, I really did, but I couldn't exactly trust her. "Let's go out for a walk," I said.

She looked surprised, but got up at once. "Where do you want to go?"

"Just outside somewhere. Down to the water is all right."

"You do know something, don't you?" she demanded, but I did not answer until we were halfway across Sebastian's fairway-sized lawn.

"I don't know where Rod is now, but I can assure you he was not lost at sea."

"I knew it! I knew it! He contacted you, didn't he? Why didn't he get in touch with me? Neither one of them trusted me." She dug her long lacquered nails into her palm in anguish.

"He didn't contact me. I happened to see him. I think he tried to meet you, but he was prevented. There was a quarrel between him and your father. Rod believed your dad was threatening him, so he took the *Melody* as his share and left."

"That's a lie."

"No, that's the truth. It's not the whole truth, but it's the major part."

"Someone paid you to say that."

"The only person with that kind of money was your father.

Even assuming I really am unscrupulous, death cancels those agreements."

"Did Rod come back here? Answer me, Anna! I can prove he did. I've figured it all out."

"Then why are you asking me?"

"He's dead, I'm certain."

"I can assure you he's alive."

"They changed the rug — Arthur and my father — the night of the party."

"What rug?"

"In Dad's private library. They ripped it up and threw it out. The butler told me."

"So? A man like your dad must have occasionally indulged in whims."

"And I've been inventorying Dad's coins. Quite a few are missing; what does that suggest?" she asked, glaring at me.

"That your father was the victim of a robbery."

"The police can't locate Arthur. That's easily explainable. He's the sort of man who could hide — who should hide," she added tartly. "But Marcus hasn't come back, either. The Rolls was at the apartment in town. A cab brought my father home. Without Marcus."

"That doesn't mean anything has happened to Rod."

"You asked about Marcus the other day."

"He's the man who could clear up a lot of questions — if he shows up."

"Will he show up, Anna?"

"It's unlikely."

Cheri reached into her pocket and drew out something wrapped in a white handkerchief. "Do you recognize this?" It was one of the elaborate medallions Marcus had affected. The last time I'd seen it, it had been lying in a pool of blood just below his shattered temple.

I nodded. "Where was it?"

"I found it under the dock. It had slipped through the boards and caught on a nail. That's blood, isn't it?"

"Might be. You could take the medallion to the police and have the stain analyzed."

"Would you recommend that?"

"It depends on what's important to you. It depends on how far you want to pursue this."

"It makes no difference to you?"

"I have nothing to be afraid of, Cheri."

"You were upstairs a long time the night of the party. You could have been in my father's wing."

"It's possible, but it's scarcely possible that I'm responsible for this." I pointed to the blood-stained medallion.

"I think that slimy s.o.b. hurt Rod. And you knew about it. You've kept quiet because you helped yourself to my father's collection."

"Then why did you ask me here? Why didn't you take the medallion and your story to the police?"

"Why will no one trust me?" she cried. "Why won't anyone ever tell me the truth?"

That was the painful part: the two men she'd loved had refused to confide in her. Cheri was going to be dangerous any way I handled the situation, and candor had certain psychological advantages. "There was a fight," I admitted. "Marcus was struck on the head. I saw it all."

"A fight with Rod?"

I nodded. "I'm not sure he realized Marcus was dead, but obviously he couldn't stay. He pocketed his share of their joint venture and left. He was in a difficult spot. He was afraid of what your father would do — intended to do: Marcus had been armed, after all."

"This was at the party?"

"Rod was wearing a red devil's mask and a gray cape, and carrying a leather sack."

Cheri's pale skin looked like wax. "I saw him leave," she said. "Oh, my God, it's true."

"Yes. Unfortunately."

"Then Dad and Arthur found Marcus."

"So I assume."

"Oh, Jesus! What do you suppose they did with him?"

I nodded toward the Gulf, and Cheri sat down suddenly on the grass. "Rod will never come back," she said. "Never, never." She pounded her thin hands against the grass, ignoring the tears running down her face.

I sat beside her and waited. When she was calmer, I said, "I'm glad you understand his situation."

"Situation! He could be charged with accidental homicide — even murder!" She gave me a sharp glance. "You'd be some sort of accessory."

"I don't intend to be implicated. I really can't afford that."

"It would hurt your business, wouldn't it?" Her voice was bitter.

"We all have to eat, Cheri."

"Rod could be tried for murder."

"Frankly, the difficulty for me isn't Rod, it's his 'stuffy uncle,' who happens to be my oldest friend."

Cheri seemed satisfied with that. After a moment, she asked, "What should we do? We must do something."

"No. I think we can trust Arthur and your dad to have taken care of Marcus. If Arthur's apprehended, of course, everything comes out in the wash. Otherwise, I suppose the assumption will be that Marcus and Arthur took off together before their part in transporting the artifacts became apparent. But this is up to you. I won't try to stop you from turning in that trinket Marcus wore or badger you to return the stela, but the sooner this whole business is allowed to quiet down, the better for Rod and for you, too."

"John Hillary's filming that TV program."

"Don't expect me to interfere with him, Cheri. Hillary was nearly killed and don't forget those two poor Guatemalan guards. I don't have a lot of sympathy for Rod or your father or Marcus. But I don't want Rod's uncle hurt, and I didn't like to deceive you unnecessarily."

"If that's true, you're the only one," she said tartly and stood up, wiping her eyes and her runny nose on the back of her hand like a child. Cheri folded the ends of the handkerchief around the medallion and knotted it tightly. Then she crossed through the narrow band of palms to the road and the shore, where she ran far out onto the rust-colored rocks and hurled the bundle into the waves.

That same day, she'd summoned Señor Morales for a long discussion, resulting in his presence with tape measure and clipboard in Sebastian's "chapel." He was set for a semi-triumphal return with the loot. Hillary was preparing to fly south with him to film the installation of the recovered pieces, and Cheri, if I read her right, was set to make another move into the upper reaches of Society. Hillary had favored me with only bits and pieces, but Theresa had been more forthcoming. It appeared Cheri was planning to fund several seasons of work at Morales' latest site. No doubt in the coming months we could anticipate articles about the "new breed of responsible collector" or whatever journalists decided to term her, and, in a few years, papers and scientific conferences produced on Sebastian largesse. There was a certain opportunism in her character, but she might have done worse. I half-hoped she'd graduate to social *grande dame* or party-giver *extraordinaire* or whatever it was she aspired to. She was ready to make a start anyway, and so was I. My bags were packed. I had already said good-by to Hillary and Theresa. I shook hands with Señor Morales, took a last look at Vlad Sebastian's magnificent garden, and drove down the key road. At the junction, I hesitated; I had several hours before my flight to D.C., and I turned into the southbound lane back to Ibis.

Henry Brammin's cottage was two blocks from the beach, a low, white building with a gray tiled roof, surrounded by a great many handsome trees.

"Come in," he said. "I thought you'd already gone home."

"Later today. I have an evening flight."

"Why don't we sit through here on the porch? It's nice this time of day."

"You have a lovely place."

"Thank you. I'd forgotten you hadn't seen it. All that cloak and dagger foolishness. The Sebastian girl's in the paper again. Did you see this?" He held out the evening paper, folded to the article.

"I knew about it."

"Damn generous. She may turn out all right. She has a certain style. Course she'll have her nose in everything they do."

"I would imagine."

Old Brammin's face went serious. "Nothing more about Rod?"

"Nothing."

He looked out at the trees, then sat down heavily in one of the wicker chairs. "I'm ashamed to admit I don't know which would be worse: his not coming back or his coming back."

"I don't expect he's returning. I'd guess he made his decision before the party. He wanted to get away."

My friend sighed. "It's his dad I think about. They were much alike. Course you didn't meet Rod under the most favorable circumstances, but it seems such a waste."

"Yes, he was very pleasant."

"That was his dad. Always put himself out."

"We could have handled the smuggling charge, too," I said, "since he wasn't implicated in the violence in Guatemala."

"If he hadn't tried to settle with Sebastian and Marcus! I blame myself for that. Money. Everything with Rod came down to money. Or the lack of it."

"Marcus' death may not come to light," I said, and described how Cheri had thrown away the medallion.

My old friend was not happy. "That's making you an accessory," he said angrily. "I didn't ask you to do that. I didn't want you to lie to the police, either. Now you've prevented us both from telling the whole story."

That was it, of course. Everything that touched on Rod drew him onto dubious ground. "I know, I did it on impulse. It seemed the right thing at the time, and the story is quite safe with Cheri. All she wanted was to know, to be included. The men had shut her out. I can't blame her."

"A modern young woman," he said drily, but he was developing, it seemed, a soft spot for her, and he realized that a full confession would drag her into the mess as well.

"Anyway, I believe we can count on Arthur to keep ahead of the police. Without him — "

"There's no case. Yes, having concealed the body, I don't suppose he'll volunteer any information. Do nothing seems to be the motto. Never interfere: I'm old enough to have learned that by now."

"You're younger than you think."

"Huh."

"And you know, if you'd kept out of it, chances are Rod would never have survived in Apalachicola. As it was, he was on his guard. Remember that."

Brammin nodded, but it was a bad moment. I opened the envelope Hillary had given me and took out several large, beautiful photographs of the stela. Only the artist had managed to dominate his impulses: he had transformed the currents of the soul into something strange, yet stable. "I thought you might like to see the cause of all the trouble."

"So this is it? The — what did you call it?"

"The stela. Yes, what's left of it. The back had been removed to reduce the weight. It was originally much thicker. There were carvings on the back once, too."

Brammin reached for his reading glasses and put them on. For several minutes he peered at the sculpture. "Who is this guy?"

"A priest-king. A sacred man, according to the archeologists."

"Cornered the market and had more spearmen than the next fellow?"

"Probably."

To my surprise, he studied the photographs carefully before

putting them down to stare out at the cloudless sky. After a few minutes he turned to me with a bemused smile. "I'm trying to decide if this would have appealed to Sebbie R."

"How are you betting?"

"Purely on intuition, yes."

There would be a sort of dramatic rightness if my friend were correct, but life is rarely so neat. "Do you want me to keep pursuing the matter?" I asked reluctantly.

He shook his head. "No, it's a temptation, but no."

"I understand." How powerful our desire to complete what we begin, to tie off the ends, to finish the picture. Brammin, Sebastian, and I had something in common, a kindred impulse, but one touched with futility. Our efforts came to nothing, and it seemed to me that there were no net gains.

"Any further probing," my old friend continued, "could only upset Miss Sebastian. I misjudged her. She's behaved rather well."

"I'm glad you agree about that."

"Not exactly aboveboard, but I'm old-fashioned when it comes to young women. A little indulgence never hurt them." He got up and went to a cabinet in the living room. "A drink before you go, Anna?"

"Please."

He returned with two glasses of very good Scotch, which we drank slowly in between reminiscences. It seemed unlikely that we would meet again, and, conscious of that, we talked long and pleasantly. Our attitudes, outlook, ways of doing things had all diverged, as our reactions to Rod and his affairs had revealed. The case had put a period to friendship, if not to affection. This was an ending.

At four, I finally rose to go. "It's been good to see you," I said.

"And you, my dear. You have my thanks," he said, shaking my hand. "What are you planning for the future?"

"I've been advised to take a mature perspective."

"What does that entail?"

"I'm considering marriage."

"Marriage certainly requires a mature perspective," the old man agreed, "and a considerable amount of luck."

"After this case, I feel I'm due."

"I hope so, my dear," he said as he waved good-by. "I certainly hope so."

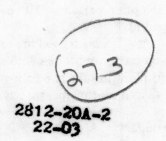

2812-20A-2
22-03